Beneath the Silent Heavens

"FOR EVERYTHING THAT LIVES IS HOLY."

~ *WILLIAM BLAKE*

BENEATH THE SILENT HEAVENS

A Fantasy

BRIAN CHRISTOPHER MOORE

Angelico Press

First published in the USA
by Angelico Press 2019
Copyright © Brian Christopher Moore 2019

For information, address:
Angelico Press, Ltd.
169 Monitor St.
Brooklyn, NY 11222
www.angelicopress.com

ppr 978-1-62138-474-8
cloth 978-1-62138-475-5
ebook 978-1-62138-476-2

Cover:
"Noah and the Fire of the Sacrifice,"
by Adi Holzer, 1975
(Wikimedia Commons, modified)

Book and cover design
by Michael Schrauzer

CHAPTER ONE

The Boy Who Talked to Animals

"SO, I SAID TO ROY, 'WHY DON'T YOU try Farmer Brown's place? There's plenty of peafowl there.' But you know Roy: all he had was excuses. Goes on and on about Farmer Brown's dog. That mutt's all bark, anyone can see that, and then there's a nag of a horse he's afraid of. A horse, I tell you! Whoever heard of such a cowardly fox?"

"At least your fox is around," said a sad eyed vixen, the corners of her mouth curling into a dreary frown.

"Ha! Around, Henrietta? A millstone around my neck, I don't know why I put up with himself. Why, only yesterday — Henrietta, are you listening to me? I'd thank you kindly to pay attention."

"Oh, I'm sorry, Daphne. It's just, well, I'd swear . . . "

"Don't swear, Henrietta. I hate it when Roy stubs his paw. The language that fox uses."

"Daphne, shut up!"

And Daphne Fox was so stunned by this unexpected vigor in her sister that she nearly forgot about Roy.

"That boy covered in ringlets of black hair and holding a bowl of grapes, the serious one staring at us with eyes like blue sapphires."

"All the bald faces look alike, Henrietta. What about him?"

"I do believe he is listening to us."

"So what if he is? I don't care who knows about Roy. I wish it would get back to that no good waste of fur. Did I tell you how Roy is scared of his own shadow? The other day over at . . ." Even Daphne Fox could see she wasn't being listened to. She wasn't a demanding vixen. She did not require her sister to actually listen, not much anyway, but she did have to pretend. "What a goose you are, Henrietta. Everyone knows men can't understand the language of animals."

"This one does."

"Oh, pshaw. You always were the silliest vixen, Henrietta. I can't believe we came from the same den. Look, I'll prove it to you. Go up there and ask him a question."

Henrietta Fox ran to the wall of the garden. She daintily sat and peered up into the pink face of the human child. "I don't suppose you'd like to share a few grapes with a lady?" she asked in a low voice. Her heart was beating wildly and she could barely find courage to break a whisper.

"I'd be honored," said the boy, and he tossed a grape down towards Henrietta, who caught it perfectly in her mouth. "You're a very pretty fox," he said, "but I do believe that Daphne is a terrible scold. It's no wonder Roy is a wastrel."

"She's not that bad," admitted Henrietta, who stood and sashayed so as to best show off her plume of a tail, which was undeniably one of her finer points. "She really loves Roy, you know. She pretends she doesn't care, but just you watch if anyone else dares to criticize her fox."

"It's like that, is it?"

"Just so."

"Would you like another grape?"

"Yes, please."

The boy tossed her another, which the vixen primly caught and swallowed in a single delicate action. "Yummy." Henrietta glanced up shyly at the human. A strange sensation she could hardly explain had come over her. She felt a sort of surge of joy and couldn't help smiling. "What's your name, if you don't mind my asking? The Two Legs usually don't understand us, you see."

"Yes, I've noticed. Somehow I think we are supposed to." A woman's voice could be heard calling the boy from his perch on the wall. "Noe. Noe, stop playing games and come here."

"That's my mum," said the boy, and he tossed one last grape to the vixen before disappearing from her view.

~~~~~~~~~~

One day, there was a thumping, thumping, thumping in the earth, a soft drumming trudge. Noe heard it while at the house of his grandfather, Methuselah. The boy hurried to the tallest room, crept out upon the balcony and peered into the distance. He could see the tops of trees swaying, the thick and verdant foliage trembling, hear a line of heavy footfall, but no cause revealed itself to his searching eyes. Below him, on a lower deck, Noe spied Methuselah standing, putting aside for the moment the watering can with which he had been satisfying the thirst of his pet violets.

"Grandfather," he called, "is it the Ancient of Days?"

"It may be," answered Methuselah. "It has been many years since any have heard Him, but I do not think it is the way of the Mystery to announce itself in thunder. Go to the watch-tower and look out."

Then Noe ran down the stairs and out to the tower of

his grandfather's house. He climbed swiftly and without fear, heaving himself onto the floor of the observation deck. From this height, he could look down upon the trees and discern moving amidst them a trail of giant creatures unlike anything he had ever seen. They were thick, paunchy beasts with leathery skin the color of storm sky. Ivory tusks ploughed the air before them, their enormous wide ears and long, impossible snouts flapping as they marched. Most surprising, men sat upon them, dark-skinned and turbaned; some saddled in small tents.

When Noe had taken in the approaching army — he could think of no other reason for such a procession, he raced down the tower, nearly falling in his haste.

"It is men," he declared excitedly to Methuselah, who waited at the base of the tower. "Men who ride upon beasts as big as houses. Close the gates, grandfather, for surely they have come to make war."

"Steady. Steady, Noe. We will not close the gates. They would not withstand the siege of such creatures, if they are what you say they are. Let us see what happens."

"But Grandfather!"

"My boy, we are given a great gift. We are left defenseless and perhaps beyond the cunning of shrewdness. Let us be children and trust the Source that guides all things."

And so they waited, Noe and his Grandfather before the gates of Methuselah's house. The shaking of the trees became louder and the procession of mammoths came nearer until the riders halted their fantastic train. A grave prince, dressed in silk, emerged from the caravan, stepping down from a high perch. Solemnly, he made his way to Methuselah.

"I am Iradon, a trader from afar," he announced. "I seek Methuselah, son of Enoch."

"You have found him," answered the old man. "My grandson, Noe," he added, with a gesture at the wide-eyed boy. "Peace. Won't you come in for tea?"

~~~~~~~~~~

An agreement for trade was struck between Methuselah and Iradon. The prince would build apartments and warehouses in the land. There would be amity between their peoples. The kiss of peace was given. Methuselah sacrificed to the divine power that governs the cosmos and caused a great feast to be given, so that many sheep and oxen were slain. There was venison and pheasant, great ladles of barley soup, fish stew, and fresh provision from the larder sea. Scallops and clams, lobster, oyster, and shrimp. There were eggs deviled, poached, and cajoled into omelettes. Neither was an abundance of vegetables and fruit neglected. Cabbages and squash, yams candied in sugar, and all manner of legume were consumed. Mushrooms sautéed in butter, carrots roasted with the beef; melons, strawberries, blueberries served in a silver boat of milk white cream — it was a great feast.

Now Noe's father, Lamech, sat at the high table, but the boy could not be found. Noe hated ceremony and preferred the play and roughhouse of his peers, batting balls, racing, wrestling, and performing feats of skill. Noe could have been the king of country lads, except that he preferred solitude too much for the boys to think of him as anything other than an occasional and capricious hero. So it was that Noe was juggling in the outer court, amazing his fellows, for he was nimble and daring.

As he was tumbling and catching, almost forgetting where he was, a procession of richly dressed maidens came upon the boy. At the forefront of the young women was a girl striking in appearance. Her hair was lustrous, raven black, her eyes wild, possessing a pretense of scorn, yet somehow open and innocent. Never had Noe seen such beauty. His world of boyish pranks, of sporting with the beasts, of solitary enterprise had hardly given thought to a fair face. He was struck dumb by the lovely girl before him, literally shocked that the world could contain such enchantment. The pins Noe had been juggling rolled and scattered to the far corners of the room, one miscreant dawdling in obeisance at the foot of the maiden.

He stood, imbecilic and gaping, whilst the crowd of maidens fluttered about the girl as minor satellites around the sun. After a prolonged silence, the girl laughed and turned to her friends. "I see they make them stupid in this land," she joked. The entourage laughed agreeably, though they did not blame the boy and thought more kindly of him than not. Noe did not know this, however. Blood rushed to his face, but before he could act, the girl was gone, disappeared with her court of admirers into grander precincts.

Awkwardly, Noe searched for a fleeting glimpse of the beauty, while his country comrades laughed at his befuddlement. They were greatly amused.

It would not, perhaps, have been difficult to discover her, yet Noe could not reason or act with his ordinary boldness. He was suddenly shy. He asked some of the older youths he knew — casually and imitating with a light-hearted tone what he imagined would be the carefree attitude of a practiced lover — if any had seen an attractive girl, somewhat beautiful, dark hair, swimming eyes, oh, you know, a dashed pretty girl. A half dozen names were offered. There were girls aplenty — why bother with just one?

He spent the rest of the feast in a restive haze, tried tossing bottles into a fountain, ended up retreating to the kennels and talking to the dogs, which had plenty of advice on bitches.

~~~~~~~~~~~~

For weeks he sulked, distracted and confused. His mum noticed and made his favorite foods. When this did not work, she spoke to Lamech, who suggested the boy investigate the new stables and the horse track Iradon had built. Noe was always restored by contact with the beasts, and he especially loved horses.

It was good land in the valley that Methuselah had sold to Iradon, and the Prince of Auramoosh had built well, using local labor, but also artisans from his own country. The outer buildings were painted a gleaming white and gilded with twining, curving patterns of extraordinary complexity and beauty. Covered walkways were adorned with streamers of azure and scarlet. A pavilion bearing banners and crest stood on a hillock from which one could view the many structures of the edifice and the smooth, elongated oval track that astonished Noe, for there had been no such idea in the land before.

Wondering, the boy descended to the level of the track. A number of diminutive riders sat high on the shoulders of their mounts, bobbing up and down with the gallop of their horses like corks in a bucket of disturbed water. Noe leant upon the post of a fence and forgot time. When the riders finished their runs, they slowed their horses, came side-by-side and talked amongst themselves. There was a familiar, jocular way about them, a tired happiness. Not long ago, Noe had known such happiness in swift games in the forest, in listening to Grandfather speak of strange, mysterious things, in a dozen ready activities gifted him by the world, but now he felt always wounded and incomplete. Loneliness shook him.

He was about to turn for home, pleased with the horses and mildly placated. Then there was the brief speech of men and the unmistakable cadences of respect that come when the power of rule enters among its servants. Noe expected to see Auramoosh, but instead, his eyes took in a sight that made his heart leap — the princess of the feast. Confusion came over him. He felt pulled in opposite directions: suddenly shy and desiring to hide; at the same time, wishing to be seen and acknowledged. In the end, he remained frozen at the fence.

The girl rode upon a slender horse, its head fine and tapered. When she took her mount into a gallop, it moved like wind in the desert. Noe marveled at the speed of the horse, its silky gait, and the pride and courage of its rider. He longed to try the risk of chasing the light air himself. He watched them transfixed, as if in a dream. Then the girl slowed her ride into a canter, pacing the stallion until it walked in slow steps, the bellows of its chest heaving from the violence of the run.

Up close, Noe could see again the beauty of the girl, her dark eyes haughty, her fine nose set above lips slightly parted into a barely visible smile.

"Who is she?" he asked, without knowing that he had asked.

"That is Priyanka, the daughter of Iradon," answered the Prince of Auramoosh.

Noe started. "Excellency, I did not notice you."

"My daughter has that habit."

Noe could think of nothing to say, but Iradon expected no words and moved on in his silent, formal way to speak with a merchant of spices and fine cloth who formed the center of a quorum, men of business waiting under the eaves of an outbuilding for a chance to advance their fortunes.

Ten feet away, a little cinnamon skinned stable boy was japing at Noe.

"Why are you smiling like that?"

"Because she is a devil. Don't fall in love. She is too proud."

"Maybe I am prouder still," said Noe.

"You admire her, so you are not more proud."

"Rather clever for a stablehand. I'm Noe."

"I am Ravi," said the boy, "but my friends call me Pook."

~~~~~~~~~~

The next time Noe came to the stables, he carried with him a hedgehog nestled in his jacket, a present for the princess. She was not there, however, and Noe felt foolish for assuming she would be. He glanced haphazardly into the stalls and wondered if there was any point to waiting.

"Hallo!" cried a familiar voice. It was Ravi.

"Peace," answered Noe, coloring. "I just came by to look at the horses."

"Well, then, this is the place," said the stable boy, ignoring the squirming motion apparently disfiguring the tranquility of Noe's coat. "Lots of horses here. We got walking horses, pacers, swift desert horses, even a draft horse or two. Prince Iradon means to sell those. Then, there's the hunter."

The way Ravi paused promised a tale, if Noe could find the right words to purchase it.

"Something funny about the hunter?"

"Oh, not funny," said Ravi, allowing his eyes to hover over Noe's jacket. "It might even be serious, but you shouldn't like to hear about that. Priyanka can hardly speak of it. She's not riding today because of her sadness."

"I suppose it's none of my affair," said Noe. He turned

his back to Ravi and spoke softly to the hedgehog, soothing it with sweet words. He saw then a group of men, one the foreman in charge of the stables. They stood chatting in front of a stall, peering in with expressions of dubiety and chagrin at a tall, dark horse, its noble head staring back at the men in grim challenge.

"That's the hunter," informed Ravi. "It's a magnificent beast but throws everyone. Iradon is running out of patience with him."

"Is he going to be sold?"

The face of the stable boy darkened. "Iradon is angry with him. He thinks he cannot be sold but must be punished."

Noe looked sternly at Ravi. "I think I understand you, Ravi. And the princess? Naturally, she is upset about this?"

"She loves Hadar, but the prince will not allow her to try and ride him."

Noe was quiet, his thoughts easily guessed. "Listen, Ravi…," he began.

"Pook," said the boy, entering into Noe's hopes with friendly favor.

"Pook," said Noe. "I've got a little friend with me. He's here in my jacket. Would you like to take care of him?"

The stablehand clapped his hands at the sight of the hedgehog. "I knew we should get along the moment I saw you," he exclaimed warmly. "I am sure the horse can be saved, but we'll have to find a time when the men are away."

~~~~~~

It was some days later that Noe arrived early at the stables of Iradon. Priyanka was already there, at one with the breath of morning. Warily, she gazed upon Noe.

"If you're looking for a job in the stables, you'll have to talk to Jimmy. He's the headman and does all the hiring."

Noe stopped a few feet from her and smiled. He wondered if she recognized him… "I thought you might put a word in for me," he said in a mild, merry voice.

"What should I tell Jimmy? That you juggle badly and lose your voice in crowds?"

"I do not juggle badly," said Noe.

"I'm not the one you have to impress," answered Priyanka, her expression a little softer and more subdued.

Noe shrugged. "Still, as long as I'm here. I'm very good with horses."

"Yes? Your father keeps them?"

"My uncle Hamish has a donkey named Irma. She wears a straw hat and pulls a wagon."

"Such a powerful creature as all that! And you've driven the wagon for your uncle?"

"Oh, not so much as that. Aunt Zelda thinks I am a rash and reckless boy and forbids Hamish to let me near the beast. But I am prepared to prove to you just now my prowess with the horse. I can muck a stall, brush a coat, put any beast you like through its paces."

"Who would you ride?"

Noe walked at once over to the stall where Hadar was kept. The hunter was more than sixteen hands high, pitch black. Lightning seemed to flash across his satiny coat.

"My father has forbidden it." The spirit in Priyanka rose in her. She spoke with anger, but sadness was in her eyes.

Noe answered her with light playfulness. "What? The Prince of Auramoosh explicitly commands that Noe should not ride this horse?"

"You don't understand. They say he's a brute, the adorable thing. No one is to ride him; yet if he is not tamed, father will put him down!" Now Priyanka looked at him with softness, her mask of proud fury diffused into warm appeal.

Noe's heart raced. He turned to the stallion, met its eyes, and whispered into its ears as he had done for some nights secretly in the company of Ravi. The horse whinnied softly and nodded its head.

"Hadar agrees to allow me to ride him," announced Noe.

"Oh, but you mustn't!" Priyanka suddenly believed the boy would try in order to impress her, though she dared not hope that somehow the stallion could be saved. She feared that Noe would be hurt and the horse destroyed.

"I assure you, it's quite alright."

"Look," she said desperately, "I think you're very brave. It's fantastic of you, really, but truly you can't. Papa's best riders have tried."

Noe ignored these protests and swung the gate of the stall open. He began patting Hadar's neck and flanks, speaking in a quiet, conversational tone, as if he expected the horse to understand him. The steed took a step and struck the ground with its powerful right foreleg. Then it bolted forward so quickly that Priyanka shrank back and fell. When next she looked up — she could not tell how it happened — Noe was settled bareback on the mighty horse.

Hadar trotted smoothly about the paddock, and then obediently moved into the ring. Noe leaned down and spoke new words to his mount, whereupon the stallion broke into an elegant canter.

"Honestly, that was a good one. You almost had me believing you," called Noe, grinning at Priyanka.

The stallion moved past her with measured strength. To her surprise, the boy sat a good seat. Evidently, he was a natural. "Yes, wasn't it?" she said — and her face flushed.

~~~~~~~~~~

Imagine her surprise when Priyanka discovered that the young man who had come to her stables for a job turned out to be the grandson of the renowned Methuselah, the son of Lamech, a great man on his own account. They began to exchange courtesies and to speak in little jokes. She told Noe of her youth in Auramoosh, of her mother, who had died in childbirth, and her younger brother, who resided in her homeland, instructed by a great tutor in the ways of wisdom so that he might one day rule. Noe discovered that the maiden friends of Priyanka were less proud than he thought. They welcomed his favor upon the princess and laughed at the revelation that he was the scion of a great house.

~~~~~~~~~~

Anjanette and Mitenka were in the larch forest hunting for mushrooms. The sun's rays poured a slanted, mottled light across their path, the greens and browns sprinkled by light emerging from a darker verdure.

"We have enough, Anya," cried Mitenka. The little girl was tired and she was wearing a new frock she had so far diligently kept clean in spite of the wood sprites and Anjanette's insistence on crawling through tangles of wood and brush. Anjanette peered into the wicker basket where "the prisoners" as she called them trembled at her every step. "Not yet," said Anjanette. "I know one more place."

"That's what you said last time!" protested poor Mitenka, running after her pitiless friend.

They followed a winding off-shoot from the usual trail, the trees bunching so that four or five trunks rose up from a single rooted place. They looked like whispery, bony hands shooting from the earth. The girls suddenly halted at a rocky piece of granite.

"Shh! Listen!" commanded Anjanette.

"I don't hear anything," answered Mitenka after a short while. She made to resume the search, wishing to end it all the quicker, but Anjanette grabbed her arm.

"There it is again. Don't you hear it?"

Off to their right . . . a rustling, undeniable. Visions of bandits or beasts filled the heads of the little misses. They could not run; it was too late. A tall man appeared from the hiddenness of an obscure path, his hair and beard a brilliant, shocking red. He was aged, but still spry — a green old man, with sap and sinew yet to live. Laughing, he turned to a companion.

"Well, now! What have we here?" Seeing the girls frightened, the ruddy man chortled to himself. "So that's how it is," he said. "They think we are beasts, Methuselah, come to carry them away." Then the traveler made horns of his hands, holding them by his temples and advancing towards the girls with a funny grunting noise meant to imitate a boar.

"It's Matty!" hallooed Anjanette, running towards Methuselah.

"And Jeshura! Don't forget Jeshura!" added the red-haired man, laughing heartily.

Collectively, the new formed party made its way to a common end — Lamech's house, where a small feast was planned. The stars were propitious. Lamech's wise men told him so. Besides, it was an anniversary of his nuptials. Guests came from the city and the countryside, several leading men of the area with their wives and children. A troupe of actors arrived to add their sport to the merriment. Doran, a student and friend of the family, brought with him Herrod, a man of letters. A few priests and wanderers showed up, their bellies were adept at finding largesse when it was offered. Many of the simple folk came with gifts of bread and wine, with little treats that carried with them a meaning obscure to outsiders: the red cord worn about the waist to fend off evil, the penny cookies made in the shape of wings. Peasants were always welcome. How should one relate all who were there and all that they did? It is too much to tell; besides, these things are much alike.

There were some young gentlemen, stylish and rather taciturn. Two came together, yet seemed to talk neither to one another, nor to anyone else. They seemed to take to heart the ready prescription held out for children: that they should be seen and not heard. Noe, caught up in first love, watched these two ambassadors from the city. He thought he might learn a thing or two. One of these youths stood in the drawing room, his head inclined slightly with practiced nonchalance. His pallid brow, his purple cravat, the fox skin gloves, one did not need to be told he wrote verse, though, truth be told, he was a poet more in the performance of his social duties. Feeling deeply left him few reserves for composition. Noe had not encountered such sophistication before. Daunted, he made acquaintance with the poet's somewhat older friend. This urbane fellow was also elegantly dressed. He, too, stood off to one side, though with a wry smile of bemusement lacking the tangible angst of his comrade. One could hardly tell if it was a cough or a laugh that he presented to Noe, though he was evidently happily inclined towards the son of his host. He looked upon the obvious attachment between Noe and the foreign beauty with the tolerant condescension of someone long familiar with the caprice of love. Why, it had been at least eighteen months since he himself had momentarily lapsed into indiscretion, discovered himself pulled along by the wanton frenzy of amatory illusion.

"You do not seem to be enjoying yourself," remarked Aunt Zelda, an impertinence that provoked a tremor of a smile in the dandy.

"Not at all. I am perfectly serene," answered the gentleman, an explanation that Noe's aunt could not decipher. Thinking it might be the polite conversation she no longer knew, Aunt Zelda bowed her head in the old manner and sought the company of her sister whom she at least understood.

"She meant no unfriendliness," answered Noe, feeling something for his kin. "It is a strange sort of sociability that comes from the city to the country only to jibe at country folk."

"Oh, it doesn't matter if you are in the city or the sticks," admitted the youth. "People are generally a bore anywhere. Surely you've discovered that much already." The townie allowed himself a glance at Priyanka. "Though naturally, when one finds enchantment in a singular soul, the tendency is to gentle one's thoughts of everyone."

Noe frowned. "I believe you are what my uncle calls a misanthrope."

"If by that you mean philosopher, I will agree with you. Why, listen to them. All this jabber about their livestock and their health. Then it will be time for the women to put in: babies and fashion. In the city it is the same, except less livestock and more money and gossip about affairs."

Later, Doran brought forth his special contraption. He'd only come so as to surprise everyone. The thing had been

agitating him all the time so that he hardly heard any conversation and had made embarrassed smiles to try and cover up
that he hadn't been listening. It was a camera. They were new
then — the big box, the silver plates. It took a long time to get an
exposure, so that the subject had to stay very still for an exceed-
ing duration. The children were particularly bored. They could
not understand the point of it; had never seen a photograph.
The servants, but everyone else, too, thought they were being
preserved for posterity, so they all looked particularly solemn.
True, as well: one couldn't smile for ten minutes at a sitting.

Lady Abatha was most keen for the experiment. "You must
come and make a portrait of my dog," she said, pressing the
young student's hand.

Then there was a tribe of gypsies, showed up for the gaiety. They juggled and told fortunes and sang and drank. An
ancient fellow, his beard dirty and unkempt, played upon his
fiddle odd, wistful tunes. Best of all, they danced. It was a
bit of a melee. A wild beauty caught all the eyes. She tilted
her head back and smiled with a proud, open freedom. The
girl spun and kicked her legs. The poet and his jaded friend
themselves took notice. Toward evening, the gathering broke
up into smaller groups. Iradon bid his neighbors adieu. Priyanka stayed behind with Noe, though she was distracted. Her
ancient wet nurse, Siri, was sick.

Balak was a distinguished man of the stage. He had a sharp
voice and wore a paisley waistcoat. The old actor turned to see
if he had the attention of the ladies, then winked, told a risqué
joke, only it was so crusty with age no one was shocked by it
anymore. All the same, Aunt Zelda began to talk about the
weather. Where was Uncle Hamish? He was there but said
nothing. He was content to watch and smile on every one with

a tolerant eye. It was his way of negating Zelda's censorious ire. Someone began to talk about the stars and omens. A mischievous actress recounted a dream she had in which a parrot kept beating her at cards. The silly dream caused Priyanka to think of one of her own. She would not have shared it. For some reason she felt shy in that company. Yet as Priyanka began speaking her memory almost without thought, she was obliged to make her contribution to the general divertissement.

~~~~~~~~~

"I dreamed I was at my Grandfather's summer cottage, only it was impossibly tall, reaching high into the clouds. I was a child of three or four and there was Grandfather, with his red suspenders and his long, white beard. My nurses were present, too, and cook, and a young woman I did not recognize. She had long black hair and gamine eyes, was radiant as the day with a new child thriving in her womb. She smiled as if listening to a soft, amusing song that only she could hear. It was my room, I knew, but suddenly I could not find myself. I had been at grandfather's feet playing with a kitten, but now I was nowhere to be seen. It was odd that no one should mind. Everyone was in a happy mood. Grandfather was the center of attention and he was sitting in his funny way that was a bit formal and stiff, yet secretly full of play and mischief. He was indeed sometimes very stern, but no one believed it, least of all himself. He would be very formal for weeks on end, until he could no longer stand it. Then Grandfather would wink at the household and dispense candies and silver coins, as if life were a long, strange joke. In my dream, Grandfather clapped his hands on his knees like a peasant and looked outside my window. We were so high that the tops of trees, leafy branches, were just outside. Everyone was looking now and there at last I discovered what had become of me, Priyanka. She was outside, wrapped in a harness that was attached to seven or eight oblong balloons. I was floating, far above the ground, and everyone was laughing."

"I knew that I was supposed to fly up towards the sun, but, instead, I began to plummet. The balloons were not helping and I fell swiftly towards the ground, which became flat and barren as I neared it. I felt a mild dismay, but was not terrified; or, rather, my terror was kept in check by a feeling of humiliation. Why was it that the balloons would not hold me, that I was falling to the earth and not floating into the clouds and sun? I felt vaguely responsible and embarrassed, but before my consternation had time to grow, I hit the ground with a thud. She, Priyanka, me, I mean, expected to feel a great deal of pain. Most likely I should be killed, but as is the way in dreams, I somehow survived. I lay motionless. Though I could not move, I was otherwise unharmed and breathing comfortably."

"I looked down at Priyanka as if I were a hawk soaring high in the air. She was a tiny bundle and now she was in the center of a perfect circle of small animals that closed in upon her in a synchronous, choreographed dance of slow approach. Rabbits and deer, impossibly small ponies, and the fierce badger peered upon her with eyes of concern. Then she heard her grandfather whispering to her, though he was still far above in the lofty trees. I remember it clearly as a crisp whisper and not at all a shout: 'Fear not, dear one. The Deliverer will come.' I felt my heart leap at the news of the Deliverer. I was greatly interested in meeting this person; but just then, unfortunately, I awoke from my dream. I was in a farmhouse, miles and miles from tall trees and the only eyes that were watching me were those of my maid's, imploring me to rise and be done with sleep."

Priyanka closed her eyes and was quiet a long moment before taking a sip from her tea. "The funny thing, you understand, is that I have no such grandfather. I have never been to a summer cottage. It was all a dream, but I believed it so. Yet the face of Grandfather is always so real, so insistent. I make him sound like an old, familiar dear, but it is really a fierce face, like an old warrior, and his eyes are searching. They look at you as if through a mirror of water."

When everyone remained silent, I'm afraid out of desperation Priyanka told a small lie. Looking at Jeshura, she proclaimed that the grandfather had appeared quite a bit like that red-haired devil. This pleased the old man greatly, and it was not, perhaps, so great a lie.

"Come to me, Granddaughter," laughed Jeshura, spreading his arms wide.

Noe and Priyanka lay upon the roof looking at the stars. From the adjacent corner of the building, they could see the golden light of the lamps and hear the voices of those who refused sleep so that conversation might not yet end. The elders stayed up late into the night. There was more discussion of the foibles of the body — the worry of gout, the fear of pneumonia, a half dozen ailments interspersed with recollection of the dead. Lamech told again the story of his friend, Uri, who was famous for belching, and everyone laughed again, as if the tale were new. Noe's mother pulled out a swaddling cloth that had held her child in his cradling time. She said then that Methuselah had spoken to her husband, declared the boy would be a sign of hope to the world. At this, Priyanka turned on her side and peered into the eyes of Noe. He colored briefly, then touched her lips lightly with his own to keep back her question. Jeshura and Methuselah, who had been silent, smoking their pipes and half-dreaming of their youth, made little grunting sounds. Then Jeshura cleared his throat and sang in a lilting voice a soothing melody. It was a lyric that recalled the lost peace of Eden.

Everyone was silent after this. The stars, themselves, seemed to muse in gentleness upon forgotten joys. The creak of a chair scraping against the floor could be heard, then the soft padding of feet — Noe's mother hurrying to secure one last round of tea and biscuits, the servants having long since been dismissed to their beds.

"It's a wonder to me," said Professor Herrod, "that in these enlightened days anyone can seriously entertain such fairy tales."

"Be silent, George. It's not the time for it," rebuked Balak.

"No, no. Let him speak," said Methuselah. "Let us hear what intelligent men are saying behind ivy walls today."

"I beg your pardon," continued Herrod. "It isn't just my profession, you know. Every shop girl knows it. Ask the courier boy when next you come into town."

"We do not come into town," declared Jeshura with a triumphant thump of his cane.

The professor shrugged. You could hear the shake of his head in his voice. "Be that as it may, and I don't wish to take from you your stories, mind you. Keep them. Just do not confuse them with knowledge. Men and women today have learned the value of experiment. Nature can be questioned. We can discover what is real and what is some humbug of the imagination. Science, gentleman, will not be kept back by quaint myths best left behind in the nursery."

"The nursery, is it?" grumbled Jeshura, too angry for lengthy speech.

"Ah, the tea," announced Doran. The men retreated into an uneasy quiet.

"Your butter cookies are particularly fine this evening, Senta," said Lamech. Noe's mother laughed, and Noe imagined her still childish, guileless smile, the corners of her eyes taking on fine, spidery wrinkles as her mobile face flushed with unaffected pleasure. A few soft jokes were half-heartedly expended. A memory or two, fragile as the wings of a long-dead moth, were floated upon the silken evening air. A lamp was put out, then Lamech's baritone voice pronounced "Time for bed."

Still, Methuselah and Jeshura remained behind, accompanied by Noe, Priyanka, and the young man, Doran, who kept the small fire going.

"I'm sorry about Herrod. The professor is too used to reigning over an abundance of attentive and worshipful students."

"An idol of the ignorant," grumbled Jeshura.

Doran neither agreed, nor disagreed, but remained silent. He took a poker and played in a desultory fashion with the remnant wood in the hearth.

"You do not think so?"

"He is a very learned man, Methuselah. It can't be wrong to be rational, after all."

"Ah, but is he reasonable? That is the question."

"I don't see how he isn't. You can't dispute mathematics. You can't dispute evidence."

"Seems to me there's a lot of silliness spread about under cover of reason and two plus two equals four," complained Jeshura.

"Well, we understand much more about nature, for instance," asserted Doran, running his fingers nervously through his mop of thick, unruly hair. "There's no need to posit some anthropomorphic maker, you know."

"There is no experiment to test origins," said Methuselah calmly.

"We can get very close, infinitesimally close."

"What you discern, Doran, is a construct built of man's limitations. The nature you quantify is not the nature of the Ancient of Days. It is nature wrought in man's laborious image. Of course, you may take that tiny part for the whole and call that being reasonable."

"Okay, okay," laughed the youth. "I am not Herrod's acolyte. I just argue for seeking the truth. Last summer, for instance, some friends went with me on a hiking trip. We were looking for this supposed Eden of yours."

"Blasphemy. Danger *and* blasphemy," warned Jeshura.

"Not at all, old father. Why should it be? We took along the best, most recent maps according to archaeology. Do you know what we found?"

"I can guess," came Methuselah's laconic response.

"Nothing like the story. A sort of barren valley with a sluggish little stream. We saw no garden, no angel with flaming sword. Why, you could go look yourself."

"Maps! You are a presumptuous puppy. As if the Mystery cannot shield from profane eyes what is not meet to be seen."

"Enough, Jeshura. We could argue all night. As it is, we shall sleep late into the afternoon. Doran, I ask only that you question the professors as thoroughly as you question the wisdom of your people."

"Selah."

"Selah."

"Selah."

~~~~~~~~~~~

"I have heard of this Eden," whispered Priyanka, when darkness had closed the lid of the last window. "My father's man sought the place. He, too, discovered no lush palace of trees and singing birds. It was just as the young man said."

"The scholars look in the wrong place. My family has known for years the location of Eden. No man since Enoch has sought it."

"And what did Enoch say?"

"He sent no word, Priyanka," said Noe gravely. "He disappeared and was not."

"They say there is in Eden a tree whose fruit shall heal all ills."

"Put far from your mind what you are thinking," said Noe.

"I do not ask for myself. Why should Siri be sick when she could be well? Why does your Ancient of Days look on while men suffer? How can he be good and let men die in agony?"

Noe was quiet. He knew the words of the sages, but those words did not satisfy him. There was a rattling down below that caused him to start and Priyanka to clutch at his shoulder. The gypsy girl who had danced so exuberantly escaped through a window of a servant's quarters, the silver moon reflected in her glistening hair. "Life is short. Life is short," the old fiddler man had cried.

"I can take you," he said in a raspy, choking voice. "We'll have to leave early, at first light." In his heart, Noe did not reckon with an angel of any sort. They would find a non-descript valley with a sluggish stream, only the girl would be satisfied that he had tried. Yet, he'd rather not go. He'd rather not know, so that one could continue to dream.

The path they took was not so long, but why tell of it? It will not be discovered. The experts who point here and there are doubtless learned, but they miss the essential; for the place is a sacred geography, hidden from the profane. It is the sort of place that reveals itself only to the one who can attend properly, and perhaps there is no one who can do so anymore. If you will come closer, yes, listen, strange as it may seem, everything is like that. The poet, William Blake wrote, "everything that lives is holy." But enough of this, if you think it is blather, you are probably the sort who cannot stand stories with talking animals so I won't worry about you. Your angel will have to find another way . . .

Noe found her waiting, dressed in some lovely thing entirely unsuited for the journey. She didn't know where they were going, after all. Noe had brought some robes, ancient furs. They were locked away in a cedar chest, but Noe knew where the key was hidden. Had he known their provenance, he might have balked at using such pelts. They were the clothes of exile, the prime bloody coverings for the First Ones.

They set out then surreptitiously. At the beginning, there was a mild, pleasant sense of escape and bright adventure; it was more like a lark than anything that might bring danger or censure. The two passed by familiar fields and the edges of woods. It was that time of morning when the moon is still visible even as the sun softly warms the sky. Priyanka laughed a bit for no particular reason. It was romantic to be going off in search of lost mysteries. Then Noe turned, took her to a steep path that led into mountains. It began with gentle hills and he took pleasure in holding her hand, leading her with authority. When the mountains began in earnest, they needed both their hands to stumble along, clutch to rock. There were places that one could peer down a long way. Noe glanced hard at her then. Did she want to go back? They'd made an effort; it wasn't a joke anymore. She looked at him, too. What did he want? Did he think she was a soft thing that could not be trusted in a pinch? Neither could answer well. They kept going out of a sort of momentum, though each was vaguely embarrassed and this meant that when they at last came to easier terrain, they were irritable and short with one another.

They marched in icy, uncomfortable silence through fields of wild rye. Below them, like the spine of a great beast, they could see a low stone fence that followed a curved path into the distant horizon. Before long, they found themselves following an ancient highway, its paving stones so large it seemed they must have been laid by giants. The road itself was desolate, so that their steps seemed to echo with an importunate strength. No wayfarer came to trouble them. Indeed, one could easily believe that centuries had left their path untrod. Though their brief anger had thawed, they remained largely mute. A feeling of hoary immensity stilled their tongues.

After an hour's walking, a breeze picked up. Gaps in the highway filled with tall grass until the path broke down into a smattering of rocks and vegetation.

"There is a lake to the left," declared Noe. A jump of relief and light-heartedness had returned to his voice. Priyanka grabbed his hand and swung it joyfully. They turned down a rolling hill covered in clover. It was a short way to the lake, wine dark beneath a golden sunburst. A dock of weathered wood and an ancient coracle bore testament to occasional human habitation.

"It is somewhere at the end of the lake. No one can find it. Not even Methuselah," remarked Noe.

They took off their heavy cloaks of fur then for the day had grown warm. "Come here, my dear," said the boy and she was touched by the courtesy in his command. Carefully, he took from his bosom a delicate lacework, a gossamer veil sprinkled with silver embroidery. "You must cover your beauty," he said gravely, placing the cloth softly upon her head. Noe entered the coracle, held it fast while Priyanka stepped with her dainty foot. As he rowed, Noe's arms glimmering with the first youthful hints of brawn, Priyanka began to sing a lullaby. Her voice carried such sad tenderness, Noe wondered at her. Afterwards, she smiled at him shyly.

There were trees enough — birches, willows, pines, and maples — without a hint of one bearing special properties. A meadow adorned in bluebells, pink azaleas, and salvia greeted the wanderers, beauties enough to please them. It was no desultory landscape, yet nothing like the garden imagined in the old tales. For an hour they searched in every direction until they were persuaded of the futility of the quest. When they had ceased looking, they stopped to admire a vista of speckled orange wild flowers, a pond green as emerald glass with white lilies wading upon its slow, syrupy surface. In the distance, summer lightning flashed from the heights of the mountains, seemed to nestle in the limbs of silver birch and linden tree. Was that a pair of deep, almond shaped eyes, warm and limpid like golden tea? Did it move with the silver sheets that dashed from one place to another, quick as thought? For a moment, the lightning sparkled like cool kisses, like the caress of a soft breeze fragrant with the scent of citrus and spices. It felt as if they were held in the embrace of a watchful, loving gaze. The sentinel of Eden was said to be no simple guardian, its terror the sublimity of pure love. Neither said a word: it was too frangible, too elusive a sensation. Almost immediately, it was gone, disappeared so completely that one could wonder if it was a trick of fancy; they had wished so much for contact with idyllic, transfigured time.

It was late afternoon before they were safely home. Everyone was offended at their absence. Not quite believing in their mission, neither had bothered to leave even a brief note. Then there were storm clouds and wrath. It was nearly a fortnight before it was safe for them to meet. My, did the maids whisper and scurry about with passed notes. It was "dear Miriam," "dear Betty," "dear Abishag."

~~~~~~~~~~

Time passes, though it is an ancient and banal observation that, for those in love, time has a particularly fluid effect. Lovers inhabit a world separate, free from the obligations and cares of weary men. The world smiles, forever golden; the groans and misery of earth appear but ghostly distraction. Every task apart is sustained with desire and joy in impending meeting. What is romance if it is not suffering and waiting for the time to be together, say everything, say nothing? Hours of courtship seem as the slightest tick of the clock. The music of being sings in elemental celebration. Knowledge is no static thing. The other is discovered in drama, known, anticipated, yet full of surprise. So, imperceptibly, for Noe and Priyanka romance stretched into winter. Ponds froze and rivers filled with sculptures of misshapen ice torn from the mountainsides. In the mountains, perhaps some distant travelers stepped amiss. Far from this, far from tears, Noe met with Pook to cut a hole and dangle bait for fish beneath the ice. Priyanka would call upon him to drive a sleigh festooned with bells. In the evenings, they would meet at hall, drink warm cocoa, and tell rambling, silly tales whose point was only to stare into each other's eyes. Never had Noe considered life so sweet. His life before the princess seemed but a prelude to life. He did not know that he had been living trapped, when there was life and expansion in the soul of another.

Priyanka elevated him in the eyes of folk he scarcely knew. No longer was he the eccentric son of Lamech, living with his head in the clouds. The beloved of a princess was surely destined for greatness. Merchants began to point at him as a man to be reckoned upon and made jokes about his luck. Half seriously, the young men kidded Noe, whom they had only ever thought of as the strange child who spent his time chasing after wild birds and holding conversations with farm animals. What unexpected shrewdness in catching the fancy of the girl before anyone else had a chance to capture the regard of the house of Auramoosh.

Everything was fine and full of hope. The world, covered in blankets of white snow, seemed to slumber content in innocence.

Erik Otter sped from his hiding place and pounced upon Reggie Ferret, the two rolling in rambunctious frolic.

"Oh, I got you! I got you good," rejoiced Erik when they had come to a breathless halt to their games.

The ferret was unwilling to admit his friend's triumph, but, as he had been thoroughly surprised, was reduced to a mere mumble in response. Erik's brother, Olaf, presently joined them, shaking his head at their youthful play. He was the eldest and naturally serious. Reggie's agony was further heightened by the sneaky, gamboling hijinks of the Weasel brothers, Frank and Louis, who came tramping through the gulley in search of fun.

"What's fun?"

"Who's fun?"

"It's here."

"We're here."

Frank and Louis were twins. They would often go on in antiphonal glory for minutes on end, declaring themselves the veriest life of the party. Fortunately, Erik was considerate enough of Reggie's feelings not to trumpet his successful ambush to them.

"So," said Frank.

"So," said Louis.

Erik stared at the weasels. His mother had warned him not to associate with a bad lot and weasels were known rabble rousers, though usually not wicked.

"Feel like fishing?" suggested the otter with a sinking feeling, for fishing was too tame.

"Fish?" said Frank.

"Fish?" said Louis. "Why fishing is fine, if you like that sort of thing."

"What did you have in mind?" asked Reggie Ferret with a false bravado — he wanted to impress Olaf and regain standing with Erik.

"There's a rumor," said Frank.

"No, a secret," said Louis.

"A rumor."

"A secret!"

Then the weasels nipped at each other's necks and pulled at tails and entered into a scrum which lasted several minutes, after which they resumed with sedate aplomb.

"There's a secret rumor," said Louis.

"I don't think a rumor can be secret, can it?" Olaf hoped the dubious note in his voice would not provoke a larger fracas.

"That is an interesting question," observed Frank Weasel. "My great-uncle Bob was an entomologist."

"You mean an etymologist," corrected Louis. "An entomologist studies bugs."

"Bugs are very like words."

"How so?"

"They each have six legs," asserted Frank in a pugnacious tone.

Louis almost answered him, knowing that a further fight would ensue, and that probably the prospect of the new game would be lost. Yet he did not. Appeased, his brother gazed amiably on young Erik Otter and his pal, Reggie. "But to return to our question, Uncle Bob undoubtedly could have told you, distinguishing meaning first in order to unite, if possible, but he was eaten by a red-tail hawk and poof! So, the question cannot be answered by authority, but we could —." The weasel paused and lowered his voice, sinking his head down so that his listeners had to huddle near him to hear. "We could investigate, see if it is true. Rumors having a certain untrustworthiness about them."

"Hearsay is practically worthless," added Louis. Their father was a lawyer.

"But what is it that you want us to investigate?" asked Erik, feeling hopelessly muddled. The sinking feeling was growing stronger in his heart.

"Why . . . didn't we tell you?"

"It's a rumorous secret."

"The most stupendous nonsense."

"Delicious nonsense."

"It can't be true."

"Unless it is."

~~~~~~~~~~~

Noe discovered that, even in his own house, he was looked at differently. He would sometimes catch his mother gazing at him with a bittersweet smile unconsciously crossing her face. And Lamech, too, now considered his son. He'd begin numerous conversations that were abruptly begun and inconclusively ended. One evening, near dusk, he told a story about the time he met Eve.

"When I saw her, she was an old woman.

But still beautiful, the way a few old women can be.

Not beautiful like an ingénue or a woman in command of her poised skin, her full, beckoning breasts, lithe limbs.

Her beauty was in her eyes and in the way she carried herself and spoke.

There was something bold in her without vulgarity, which is hard to pull off in an old body. Too often it is desperate or irritable or a grotesque mimicry of the most banal and faddish play of the young.

She said what she thought. She punctured sacred cows. I liked being looked at by her. There was, I admit it, a certain wild and impish arousal. Unspoken, mind you. Not unmannerly. She smiled with just that gleam of recognition, as if she realized she was still sending out the perfume of desire."

"'What can I do?' she seemed to say, then laughed and started talking about what I had asked.

'It wasn't exactly clear in the official records,' she said.

There was Eden, where the beasts of beauty and kindness lived. Inside of Eden there was the walled circle, the garden of life. Outside of Eden there was Nod, a place of darkness and nightmare.

'But all that was long ago. So long ago,' she said, as she trailed a hand through her long gray hair, still streaked with a shock of dark luster here and there.

'I may not be able to say anything much at all, that's the truth, yet I shall try because, well, to be frank, because one must fight against the heaviness that sinks the body, that says there wasn't much point in it, the years that ran by pretty quick just like everyone said they would. Or lightness. Some say that is lightness.'"

"They say," said one of the weasels, Erik and Reggie had lost track of who was who, "they say there is something in the Woods."

"Oh, what rot," exclaimed Reggie. "There's trees and birds and squirrels and all manner of folk. Something in the Woods, indeed."

"Not like that," said a weasel. "Some *thing*."

"Something," said his brother, "that has frightened everything off. The birds and squirrels have all moved off. No doubt, the trees would, too, except that they are incommoded."

"Incommoded?"

"It means they lack a commode," said Frank.

"It means they can't move," said Louis. "So, shall we?"

"Shall we?"

"Shall we what?" said Erik, feeling great dismay and wanting very much to find his mother. She would make scones and tea and the whole house would smell of cream and butter.

"Why, go look for the Something!" said Frank and Louis in unison.

"I'm in!" said Reggie bravely.

"How 'bout you?" said a weasel, indicating Olaf.

The moods of Olaf were inscrutable. He was a sensible beast and preferred to be left alone, but on this day, he only shrugged, a noncommittal gesture that brought fear to his younger brother.

"Is it far?"

"Not far."

"At least, not very far."

Erik felt a lonely shadow begin to descend through his chest to his stomach and his bowels. He wanted to say "No, I'm going home," but his tongue cleaved to the top of his mouth. He was struck mute, felt tears welling in his eyes, until he heard himself, far away from his heart, thickly assenting to the quest.

"She said the official story was pared down. When she said that, there was irony in her glance. Did they really think the God was petty and jealous? Did they think the man of dust and his glory were so stupidly gullible? Did they think it was all about an arbitrary prohibition, some rule to discover if they were obedient little children? Then she paused, as if she would have liked to explain something, but when she spoke again she spoke of what it meant to be a mother. 'And when I smiled, the first time he smiled back, I knew that we had found one another. He was real then, he had come to his name. My love had welcomed him to the land.' *She was speaking of Cain.* Abel had always been a gentle child. He did not understand his brother's passions. There was a hurt in Cain from the beginning no one could heal."

She loves him. Lamech had puzzled over it ever since. It was the bad son she loved.

———————

"Hehe."

"Hehe."

The twitter of badly concealed giggles followed them for the better part of a mile. Erik ignored them, Olaf studied the ground with the alertness of an Indian guide, whilst Frank and Louis pretended to be afraid of the goblins that were supposedly pursuing them. Reggie said nothing. He was already regretting his brave display. His feet were cold. The beautiful white snow was heartless and his bones shivered.

"The goblin is a known carnival," said Frank.

"You mean carnivore," said Louis. "They especially likes to eat ignorant weasels who get their words confused."

"Says who?" asked Frank.

"Says you," claimed Louis.

"I did not," said Frank.

"If I ever wanted to know what I would look like stupid," said Louis.

Another mindless brawl was likely to occur, but this time

Olaf's patience was worn thin and concern quivered in his every nerve. "Hedwig, Sigurd, come out," barked the otter.

Two young pups came laughing from behind a snow drift. "We're hunters," said Hedwig, the baby.

"Hedwig's a hunter. I'm a goblin," corrected Sigurd.

"What do you think Mother is doing right now, you idiot whelps? She'll be a mess." The otter yelled at his younger siblings; but, in truth, he was grateful for their presence. They offered an excuse to turn back. "We'll have to go home," said Olaf, turning to the weasels.

"It is getting cold," admitted Frank.

"I think I see something," said Erik.

~~~~~~~~~~

Lamech was never good at keeping the thread. In the end, he gave up and came to an exposition he had practiced several times. He was not sure if he wanted Noe to take it to heart, but he was soon perhaps to enter the world of men. He should know what he was about.

"In fairy tales, it is often best to be the seventh son. It is surely best to begin the pauper, the forgotten child, the lost — for in the nature of things, the high fall and the low are given happiness, the tale fading before the wheel can turn again. In such tales, there is frequently a test. One shall be presented with three boxes, for instance. One box shall be of gold, another silver, while the third is plain wood. Here, the rule of inversion also holds, for the wisdom of the fairy tale is that appearance is misleading and that true merit is disguised. It is the unwise who select the gaudy metals and their fate is never good.

However true, and there is usually a great deal in folk wisdom that one should not ignore, the translation to quotidian existence is hardly without its dangers. I supped on such tales as a young man and determined to choose the wooden box, forgetting that in our world, such a construction is frequently the prelude to a tomb. The anguish of the test is relatively brief in the tales. Quickly, the casket is opened to reveal the golden ring that leads to marriage with the princess, the kingdom and happily ever after.

Not so, in the life of the world. Accountants and lawyers and doctors flourish in the world outside of dreams."

~~~~~~~~~~

Rolvag Otter was in a state. Never had her pups stayed away so long. She had called them and searched for them. The father had searched with a neighbor badger. A few birds of the air had offered to help, but none could find the children. The otter fought back tears. Thoughts that ravaged in nightmares had come to her in waking hours. What could she do? The youngest, the sweet youngest, were nowhere in sight. They did not respond to her pleas, to her soft and plaintive cries.

Henrietta Fox, however, insisted that she knew a boy. That is what the Two Legs called their male progeny before they had come to maturity and begun to father litters. This boy, named Noe, would help them. She was sure of it.

And so, on a frozen and gray day in November, a party of entreaty was sent. The vixen, along with a raccoon and the distraught otter, picked their way carefully through the snow, avoiding contact where they could. A few alley cats poked their heads out, stared at them with round eyes, and a stray dog, mangy and uncouth, barked at them, calling them hicks and strangers and a few other things less kind, chasing them a short but scary path down the backyards of a row of dilapidated townhouses. Once they had passed out of the canine's territory, however, he left them in peace and generally the beasts were unremarked and left alone.

Soon, they came to fields and tree lined avenues that led them to larger estates surrounded by pastures and patches of woodland. Rolvag simpered and bit upon her lip for dread much of the way. Henrietta did her best to boost the spirits of the otter. The raccoon, on the other hand, turned out to be an unfortunate choice. He had stopped numerous times in the city at various places where the Two Legs stored a mash of material called "garbage." "Such treasures," he would tut-tut at the waste and exclaim his imminent entry into the ranks of the wealthy. Still, the misery of the otter had eventually prevailed upon him so that the raccoon did not desert the suppliants, though not without a few larcenous backwards glances. They found the boy, Noe, in spite of the cold, spooning with a female of his kind in the open view of a gazebo.

Noe took his hound, Bashir, and went out in search of the pups of Rolvag Otter. New snow had fallen, covering the tracks of her children. Bashir could find nothing definite, though now and again he would sniff the ground excitedly and look wildly into the air. They followed a path along the gulley, but the trace petered out in the forest near Darkwing Canyon. After hours in the cold, they were forced to return home. Bashir felt personally responsible and hung his head in disgrace.

"Come now, Bashir, you are the best tracker. The scent was none the best and led us nowhere."

"There is something strange at work, master."

"Yes. I sense it, too."

The hound shook his head auspiciously. "Very strange."

~~~~~~~~~~

It was not long before word came to them. Frank had come limping home, more than half dead. The weasel was barely recognizable. His skull had been mashed and one eye lost. Breath came in laborious bursts, blood filling the mouth of the beast. "It was Something," he said, looking fervidly at them with his one eye, overwhelmed with perplexity and fear. Some of the younger beasts began to whimper and whine. A badger growled and peered grimly about. The wretched beast could not explain the evil that had appeared. From his rasping and wandering account, the animals gathered that the weasel had come with his brother, Louis, Reggie Ferret and the pups of Rolvag Otter upon a monstrous, unknown creature. At first, it had seemed harmless, indeed, comic. They were impressed by its great, hulking head of flesh, rounded and translucent like the balloon of a jellyfish, studded with spots resembling a pair of morose, timid eyes. The weasel's party had approached it and spoken greeting and the unknown creature had seemed to hum a juvenile, mawkish lullaby.

Closer still, they came, curious and feeling less and less threatened. Then, when they were no more than ten feet away, the monster turned, revealing a different face: deep set, scowling eyes the color of marsh gas, a strangely formed pair of mandibles, opening horizontally and reeking a malodorous stench. Two tiny tusks jutted from the heavy muzzle. The youngest of the otters had panicked and run screaming from the beast. What happened next was unclear, though evidently terrible. The weasel groaned in an agony beyond physical pain. Shortly, he died.

Noe arrived with Bashir too late to hear the tale. A party of boar and lion and wolves had collected, set to pursue the enemy in the forest. The boy and the hound joined them. Noe carried a staff of ironwood, a bag of sharp rocks, and a sling. Swiftly, rich in wrath and foreboding, the beasts trudged through heavy snow. No one spoke. Silent in their thoughts, they came to the place of destruction.

The moon was high on the horizon. The snow glistened. Quiet. Innocent. The snow. No monster could be seen, though an ominous totem had been left for them to find — the pups of Rolvag Otter, strung up and skinned, their skulls shining in the night air. Bashir galloped over the ground, searching for scent or sign. Then he began to bay for sorrow. A chorus of howling, roaring sorrow incensed the air. Rolvag will die of it, thought Noe. He was right, but there was no more violence that winter.

By spring, it seemed a nightmarish, spectral memory. So quickly do the living forget violence. It's better that way. How else could one possibly live?

~~~~~~~~~

But early summer, without warning, the hideous thing returned. The animals of the forest retreated ever further from the areas where the monster had struck. Tales of horror seemed to reach every beast. Burrowing creatures dug deeper, birds took flight, deer ran in panic. There was often no sense to their actions, naked fear subverting instinct so that they sometimes ran right into the path of the monster. Oglath, they called it, which in the tongue of beasts means, "The Evil."

None seemed safe. In grassland, in marshes, at the edges of desert, in valleys and plains, rumors of torture, of odious cruelty were spread among the beasts. It was not just that beasts were killed. Nature was not sentimental. Beasts that lived on flesh required the death of prey. Something perverse was involved in the acts of Oglath. The corpses of his victims would be found displayed in gruesome rituals that demeaned the victim. The hide would be defecated upon, the head sometimes posed in a grotesque and ridiculous manner.

None knew what to do. In desperation, they entered into the haunts of men. The Two Legs were mercurial and known killers, yet they were not usually shameless like Oglath. Not usually. There remained the odd child who hung cats and set traps for squirrels and the like, so that they could do evil. Men could be like that. Oglath, in this sense, was like a huge, bellicose pitiless child.

~~~~~~~~

Priyanka reclined upon a low couch strewn with pillows. She had already begun to think of him as her man, to plan a future. She had not yet told him, of course, or her father. A woman could not rush these things. Noe loved her. She was sure of that. Lately, however, the boy was hardly with her, distracted by some heavy weight she sensed was nothing easily laughed away. It was because of this that evasion had entered his speech. Her intuition went further, said that great danger afflicted him, that he stayed from her to keep her safe.

"Noe, come to me," she sighed, but he did not come. The afternoon began to deepen into the gloaming. Her maid stopped to ask if she would like to walk in the garden. "No, she did not, but would the maid please to bring her a candle?"

The maid laughed. It was that "please to bring her" that outsiders never guessed in her lady. She lit a lamp and crept stealthily back, peering in concern upon Priyanka. *She's not happy. No, not unhappy, but troubled.*

The princess turned, smiling abstractedly, a little embarrassed by her maid's discernment. "That's good, my Katya."

"Is there anything else, dear?"

"No, nothing. I am a little tired is all."

When the maid had left, Priyanka placed the lamp on a high shelf and pulled out a finely wrought chest of cherry wood she never shared with anyone. It held her cherished things. There was a small drawer which contained a pair of jade earrings, a pearl ring, the tiny sculpture of a playful kitten, and a necklace that had once belonged to her mother. She had fine linens and a dress of brocaded maroon velvet she would never wear until the keeper of her own domain. The box had a false bottom. In the secret place, she kept the veil her mother had worn at her own wedding.

Noe, her sweet, brave boy. She would have held him by her warm, dark eyes, if only he would come to her. She did not understand his God. In Auramoosh, they had many deities, but Noe's supplications were made to One alone. It seemed to her austere, though not without a severity that slightly thrilled her. Quietly, she spoke in uncertain words to the power of Mystery, the one called Ancient of Days.

"Protect him. Keep him safe for me," she begged.

~~~~~~~~~~

Noe had an idea. He did not know his enemy, could only guess. Oglath was relentless yet did not seem to ponder strategy. It was an evil so confident of victory and so dismissive of its prey that planning was apparently unnecessary. So, Noe planned. He spoke to Nestor, the leader of swift deer, and to Ardian, the bold ram, made parley with Garulf, the ursine king. Then one day, Oglath was spotted and Nestor called upon his courageous bucks. The deer ran before Oglath, taunting him with speed. Oglath did not know it was a relay. Swifter and swifter, the deer seemed to run. On ahead, safe from the monster's vision, a new runner would take the place of the flagging buck. The spent deer would stagger into hiding, the fresh prey ever beyond the reach of the ghastly hunter.

Oglath, however, betrayed no impatience. The Evil seemed oblivious of frustration, remained secure that it would sate itself in perverse satisfactions. Subtly, the deer were running past the vast plains of low grass, speeding through the fields of Aglore that must end in a closed canyon. Its giant form striding with arrogant steps, the deer faltered. The last runner seemed to grow rapidly weary; it quaked, looking about in confusion. Then it was that Nestor himself stepped forth, guided his brother deer into a secluded hideout, a screen of trees. Then Nestor showed himself, beckoning The Evil to resume the chase.

At the end of the canyon was a series of caves, some of which connected through a network of thin corridors. Nestor panted, his last energy squandered. Oglath approached, chuckled at its hapless victim, even at a distance its breath stank of rot and death. Then, with a final burst, Nestor jumped. The buck seemed to discover new life, leapt into the mouth of a cave, turned a merry eye on his dreadful pursuer. Yet Oglath was not dismayed. Climbing with incredible pace, the monster gained on Nestor, so that the deer must scramble into the anfractuous interior of the cave.

Oglath followed, bolting into the cave. The monster hungered now with urgency, wished to crush the body of the deer, to tear it into pieces. Then Noe added his surprise. The entrance to the cave was sealed with falling stones. Ardian and Garulf played their part. Nestor had escaped through a narrow passage. Other animals then filled the gaps with ready stones. For some minutes there was silence. At length, a roar came from within the stony prison, so long and low and presaging terror that the beasts fled back from the trap. But the monster did not emerge.

And Noe did a good thing that day, though no one believed that Oglath might be kept forever in his cell.

~~~~~~~~~~

"Tell me, Grandfather, about the war with the giants."

"Why must you hear the old tales, my son?"

"There is Evil in the forest. It shames the beasts and I do not know how to defeat it."

Methuselah stared into the eyes of his grandson. He debated within himself. The boy was already a favorite. To speak to him of the old ways was a joy, but also a misgiving: for the world had turned against the ancient lore. Already, to speak in public about the Throne of Adam was to invite embarrassed silence. Matrons of taste would quickly change the subject. Yet Methuselah thrilled to sing of his own father, Enoch, enemy of the nephilim. It was Enoch who had turned back the giants. In later days, men would say the nephilim were merely the sons of Cain. And maybe they were only that. Let them have their stories. The old man hid his heart.

"The days are changing, Noe. Perhaps it is best that we change with them."

"They say that to slay a giant, one needed courage and weapons forged in angel fire. They say men no longer recall the secrets of the sword and spear and that we have forgotten much else besides."

"*They* is your father and me," laughed Methuselah.

"If I had a weapon, from the seraphim, perhaps I could defeat this monster that is humiliating the beasts."

The old man sighed and shook his head. "They have long since disappeared. The men who could wield them have gone." How many times had Noe pressed him about the end of Enoch? Even Methuselah became silent on the subject.

"Not one, Grandfather? Not even a dagger?"

Methuselah said nothing, but closed his eyes, lifting his arms in supplication. Then he raised himself from his chair by the fire and began to walk towards the barn. Noe followed him, too rich in feeling and anticipation to sunder silence. In muteness they climbed a small hill behind the barn and crossed a meadow punctuated by a screen of rowan and beech trees. They labored to weave their way through a thicket of trees overgrown with vines. Noe's eyes made out, barely visible within the luxuriant growth, the shell of a battered shed already much reclaimed by the earth.

"What is this, Grandfather?"

"A place my father showed me. Before he . . . before. He said if the need arose, I was to look here."

Noe struggled to unhinge a door rusted shut for years. He wished heartily for a small axe. With their bare fists, Methuselah and Noe beat down the rotten wood, tearing an opening for themselves. The interior of the ruin led downward into the roots of the earth.

"We'll need to go back for a lantern."

"If what we seek is not utterly lost, the light shall find us."

"What do you mean, Grandfather?"

"Walk into the darkness, Noe. Walk and trust. Pray to the Mystery for guidance."

Noe took a few unsteady steps into a pitch of night. He

nearly stumbled before his feet found a gentle downward path which ended in a small, hollow chamber. Noe stood, astonished. A lance, silvered and pearlescent, lay shining on a bed of stone. It glowed with unreflected light.

"How is this possible, Grandfather?"

Methuselah stood behind Noe. For a moment, he was himself a boy, the voice of Enoch ringing in his ears. "Truthteller," he cried, "the spear of Micha-el, angel of the unicorn. Take it into your hands, my son. Pray for good destiny."

~~~~~~~~~~

"Oglath is coming! Oglath is coming!"

Noe looked up from a sweet letter. He peered into the branches of a crape myrtle. A black bird ruffled its feathers and crooked its neck towards him. "Oglath," it said.

"Where?"

The crow hopped to the grate of Noe's window. "The falcons saw him from afar," it said. "The monster raged in the canyon."

Noe smiled. The Evil had not liked its last reception.

"Where now?"

"Oglath is coming."

"Yes, I know. Where can he be met?"

The crow shuffled its feet. It had delivered its message. The Throne of Adam must determine the plan. Noe surmised that The Evil was cutting a path in a straight line from the canyon to the plain of men. In that case, it would have to cross the forests of Shandar and the valley through which the river some called the Pishon and others the Nimbar ran. If Oglath could be set upon in the pass between the valley and the flatlands, they might gain an advantage. But Noe knew not the power of his enemy.

"Tell the beasts I will join them on the pass through the hills named The Old Ones," he ordered. "We will meet The Evil before it sets foot on the plains of Havilah. And tell Garulf the Grizzly to wait for me in Aglore."

~~~~~~~~~~~

To the gathering at Aglore, the beasts sent many of their number. With Garulf came a sleuth of bears more than seven dozen strong. Of the badgers, there was a great cete, warriors used to single combat, and many youth ready to test their strength. The lions in their pride and a leap of leopards answered the summons. The sky was darkened by a cast of hawks; an unkindness of ravens bespoke impending battle. From Auramoosh, a small herd of elephant and a streak of tigers came. Yet were there many deer and gangs of elk; prancers and hunters put aside their immemorial conflict. And the small folk would not be forgot. A romp of otters, a business of ferrets, a leash of fox came to lend support. Even from the domiciles of men, oxen came to oppose Oglath, and, from the mountains, a shrewdness of apes. Not intending to fight, but to watch and make joy, whatever happened, a cackle of hyena gamboled at the edges.

When the great company had assembled, the blood in Noe ran high. He felt his heart full. The courage and trust of the beasts humbled the boy. He knew then that to be a true king was not to be served, but to serve. He remembered the old amities, the story of the Adam who named them all. The secret of that intimate knowledge had been forgotten. Naming had somehow become a mere convention, a tool for utility. Only some of the poets and artists said this was wrong, but few had time for them. A trace of the gifted splendor lived in Noe. It was because of this that the beasts had heeded the call. Some other mystery teased the spirit of Noe. Life itself was concentrated here. Life with all its many variations and types — and yet, even in its appearance, something hidden and enigmatic.

For a moment, the boy was beset with shyness. They had come in great collects; they had come to honor the Throne of Adam and to resist The Evil. Noe's tongue cleaved to the top of his mouth. He was dryness and dust. What now should he say? Then there was a bowing little fox before him with such a mix of muddle and graceful intention he could not help but smile. It was Roy Fox. "My friends," he said, "I know not what destiny is written for us, but it is a meet thing to come together to resist darkness. This day, let us honor our fathers and mothers and give a good accounting of ourselves so that our kith and kin will rejoice to tell our tale."

Then there was such a roar of affirmation that even the Oglath must surely shudder in its steps.

~~~~~~~

First there was silence, then the buzzing. The sky grew dark with locusts and stinging flies. Long minutes of pestilence and pain and dismay; and then came Oglath, slow, almost comical, seemingly unconcerned about them, yet heavy with vicious intent. The beasts had come in waves at the dread thing. At first, Noe directed them, sending the flying creatures and the thundering herds. He tried to ride down Oglath with force of numbers. It was no good. Incredible missiles, like dark, splintering thorns were spewed from the gullet of the great antagonist. Noe looked on aghast as the deadly shrapnel flew forth rapidly, mowing down entire rows of brave animals.

Then the good creatures had become delirious with grief. All stratagem left them. They could not hold back. With wild fury they threw themselves in despair at the enemy or ran to the four winds. The battle, such as it was, threatened to devolve into a bloody rout. Taking courage, Noe praised the honor of the giant grizzly, Garulf. The boy hoisted himself upon the behemoth — Garulf was twice the size of a normal bear. Then Garulf charged with vigor, turned his great, fierce head, his eyes burning with wrath at The Evil. Eagles swooped down upon Oglath, sought to claw and strike at the monstrous visage. Yet the monster heeded them not. A gray fog, full of the buzzing sound of insects, hung about the head of Oglath. The foul mist seemed to kill every flying thing that came close. Noe prayed that he might get near enough to score his opponent. The mighty bear gathered strength, and Noe lowered Truthteller, its sharp point thirsty to strike.

Oglath allowed his new, most interesting foe to approach within twenty feet, before casually reaching into a pouch of deerskin. The monster issued a high-pitched gurgle, hurled a jagged rock with the force of a shot bolt, slew Garulf as if he were a babe in cradle. Tumbling into a heap, the Grizzly died in the midst of his rage, did not even know the mortal blow. Noe was forced to leap from his mount to avoid being crushed, his ancient weapon spilling to the ground. A mournful, whimpering lament went up from the beasts.

The field cleared between Oglath and Noe. The broken bodies of boar and stout badger, of puma and black bear lay strewn about the fiend. The terrible jaws of Oglath dripped in blood. It raised its fists to the sky, spread its arms, and made imprecations on all life and the Source of life, though in a tongue unknown to man and beast. Then it turned and steadied its mournful, lifeless eyes upon Noe. So this was the champion that had marshaled the beasts. A kind of sordid, sneering laugh was emitted from its foul mouth, the odor of rotting carrion drifting towards the youth. "Peeuwh, peeewn, puny!" The contemptuous word came groaning from the lips of Oglath.

Oglath stood and did not charge. It waited. Always, its pallid gaze would drain vigor from the foe. Its enemy, the boy-man, did not blanch, but horror was upon his face and Oglath rejoiced. This horror was the deep desire, the delight of the monster, the inevitable precursor to victory. Noe gripped his lance tight against his side and prepared for desperate battle. The fall of Garulf meant he had no hope of gaining force to pierce the monster. Retreat would have been wise, but Noe doubted the animals would recover from defeat. Oglath must perish and perish now.

"From what vile place you come I know not," he said in challenge to the fiend. "You set yourself against all life. You bear the swagger of death and in your pride dismiss all hope. Yet there is hope, even for the hopeless, and you will taste death this day!"

Oglath did not respond to Noe's brave words, except to take a slow, steady step towards the youth, who was unsteady carrying the long lance. Noe backed away, keeping distance. The Evil pushed forward and Noe tripped, Truthteller spilling from his grasp. Oglath rejoiced, slapped his thigh like a peasant. He would make short work of such a hero. The monster emitted a gurgling snicker, a sound so foul it seemed to contaminate all who heard it. The terror of the beasts turned to sick sorrow. The living hung their heads, awaited doom.

And then there was a scream, high and terrible. The monster gazed with mordant eyes after the cry. Noe scrambled to his feet, lifted the lance which suddenly had become light as goose down. He, too, looked to the source of the scream. *Priyanka!*

The girl had taken Hadar. The noble horse held his ground at the edge of the fields of Aglore. Noe raced to his beloved. Some noxious thorn of the monster lay embedded in her shoulder. She tried to smile bravely, but her face was ashen. The pain was too much for her. Priyanka collapsed in a dead faint. Softly, he collected her, kissed her cheek, and placed her in a bed of heather.

Oglath had stopped his march, stood derisive in the center of the field.

"It is you and I, Hadar," Noe spoke plainly to the horse. "We must pierce him, yet he has killed many. He murdered the grizzly. He slayed boar and stampeding buffalo. What strange thorns spewed forth from his filthy gullet!" Then Noe knelt by her. She was like one in a deep sleep. Still, she lived. He had no time to fear for her, to imagine a world without her.

Mounted upon the stallion, Noe braced Truthteller under his arm and prepared to charge.

"You and I. You and I. Run with courage and do not turn."

"Whhaaat? With Whhaat?"

The voice of Oglath met Noe, seemed to enter his mind as a whisper contemptuous and rough like sandpaper. Noe trembled and felt the light weight of Truthteller disappear entirely. The lance had vanished. He sat Hadar, holding to his side nothing at all.

Again, the foul gurgling assurance of the defeat of everything fair and kind. A snide, vulgar, glithering gloom. Oglath. Images gathered in Noe's mind, grotesque details of decaying flesh, a torpid, night-dark water glistening with the silvered bodies of dead fish, belly up and congregating in the thousands upon the mortal sea. Human faces distorted by anguish and dread. Children lay starving at the dry breasts of their mothers.

Men hobbled with amputated limbs. Imbecilic laughter, full of malice. Everything gentle and beautiful and complex mocked and uncomprehended. Crude simplicities taken for profundity. Wealth worshipped. The acquisition of income treated as wisdom. The rich buffoon unctuously attended, his shrewd pursuit of interest envied, his words parroted for sagacity. Cruelty was mistaken for strength. Bathetic weakness itched for causes. The pampered and privileged imagined themselves victims. The leper, the outcast, the drug-addicted, scorned as worthy of contempt. A dozen images followed by a dozen more; and at the end of it all, death. Death for the lion as well as the worm. Death, which brought everything to nothing. Noe felt himself begin to shut down. The passion of his heart trickled into little more than numbness and vague nausea. All this in a trick of seconds.

He had no weapon. He could think of nothing to do. Hope fled. Nothing would happen. Nothing ever did. All destiny ended where the Once became inexorably the Never. He knew only that Priyanka lay unconscious and unprotected from The Evil. Then his love gathered, a tiny flame against the cold immense darkness. A glare of defiance slowly entered his eye. Before he could say any word, Hadar charged.

The stallion raced boldly at the enemy. Poisonous thorns shot out at Hadar, but the horse veered neither left, nor right. Suddenly, Noe felt the heft of Micha-el's weapon. The Evil dream had meant him to feel abandoned and defenseless. Noe braced for impact, hoping his horse would not fall beneath him. There was the slightest tremor of resistance, and then the feeling of pushing through with tremendous velocity. Truthteller had reached its mark. The lance rove through Oglath. The monster was impaled.

Hadar's chest heaved with the effort, but not a scratch was upon him. The missiles had fallen tame and useless. In amazement, Noe jumped down to the ground. The gruesome body of Oglath instantly decayed. No monstrous carcass met his eyes. In its place, a litter of disparate things: rancid corpses of lobster, monkey skulls, oozing innards from a whale, the shells of coconuts, and copies of the Metropolis Times. Noe patted Hadar. Mournful, yet rejoicing, the beasts hopped and ran beside the hero. Dressed in the glory of victory, they led him back to Priyanka.

CHAPTER TWO

Rhumirrah

MANY GENERATIONS AFTER THE defeat of Oglath, after the name of Noe had passed into legend, a daughter was born into the family of Bali Bengal. Her name was Rhumirrah. She was like most tigers, fierce, playful, and slightly arrogant, but unlike them in one respect: she was impossibly curious about the Two Legs. And Bali saw this imprudence, his whiskers smelled danger, he dispensed fatherly advice.

"Mirra, do not venture beyond the jungle. Do not look to the dwellings of men, for their hearts are not one."

But Rhumirrah was ready for this expected proverb. She answered ancient wisdom with another old tale. "Papa, do you not recall the old stories? Remember the man called Noe who fought for us in the woods?"

Bali growled and stamped his paw, but Nyssa, his wife gave him "the look" — she knew her daughter — and he tried again to speak softly of his fear. "Mirra, do not venture beyond the jungle. Do not look to the dwellings of men, for their ways are dark and soaked in blood."

Yet again Rhumirrah made reply to the expected proverb. She answered her father with honeyed words. "Papa, is not the tiger a fearsome cat? Are we not cunning, our claws not red?"

Then Bali rose up and glowered at his daughter. "Mirra, do

not venture beyond the jungle. Do not look to the dwellings of men, for the stench of death perfumes their every thought. I forbid you to seek the Two Legs."

And Rhumirrah bowed her head and said nothing, but in her heart determined she would try another way to assuage desire. As everyone knows, to forbid something is only to make it more delectable.

Rhumirrah went walking. She did not go in the direction that would take her near the province of men, but moved with silent grace towards another frontier where the mountains of the forest began to rise into icy heights so severe that rarely did one see the hart or the wild goat. The tiger looked up into the sparse trees, searching. Then she bounded to the foot of an ancient oak where a jackdaw was perched. She did her best to present a friendly visage, though gentle was hard to pull off.

"Ahem," she said. "I beg your pardon, but I happened to notice that nice broach you have with you."

"Oh, this?" said the jackdaw. "This is not a broach. It is my family coat-of-arms. Been in the family for decades, centuries, lots and lots of seasons."

"I see," said Rhumirrah, wondering how to proceed. It was very strange for a jackdaw to have an ivory cameo for a coat-of-arms, but not so strange to find a blackbird full of vanity. "I suppose your family is quite famous," purred the tiger.

"Caw, caw," replied the crow, which is to say, "indeed, indeed," and the blackbird puffed out its chest and decided that perhaps the big cat did not have designs on the loot.

"A family such as yours must have venerable ancestors and bravery in this very day."

"Caw, caw," said the jackdaw.

"But I don't suppose…," Rhumirrah allowed her voice to become a little wistful and a bit, just the tiniest bit dismissive, "I don't imagine that a family so important and well established has any need to fly off in all directions. There wouldn't be any daring explorers among you."

At this, the jackdaw nearly lost her perch, the broach danced precariously in its nest. "Why, we are the most stupendous explorers!" exclaimed the bird, her feathers truly ruffled.

"Of course, of course, I see that now," said Rhumirrah in a soothing voice.

"Caw," answered the jackdaw, though her feelings were still uneasy.

"Have you done much exploring, yourself?"

"I have flown everywhere. Everywhere," boasted the blackbird. "There is no place I do not know."

"My! I did not realize that at all." And here is how clever Rhumirrah was. She did not jump to have her questions answered but was silent. She settled herself beneath the oak tree and began to bathe with a dainty and deliberate quiet. Before long, the jackdaw had hopped down to her shoulder. It had a tiny colored bit of paper in its mouth which turned out to be a fragment of a postcard advertising the delights of Shimbolah, which at that time was quite a bit like our Paris, which is to say, a Shimbolah waiter thinks himself better placed and more cultivated than a king elsewhere.

"I brought this back as a souvenir," declared the bird.

Rhumirrah admired the shiny paper, asking the sorts of things one asks, the price of hotels and the quality of the food, whether there was much to look at and if the tourists were treated well or with contempt.

"Oh, I would not know about the last," sniffed the jack-daw. "My family comes from the region and I, myself, often summer there."

"Really? I did not know."

"You are a very young tiger," observed the jackdaw with a touch of pity.

"Then I suppose you know all about the Two Legs? I mean, the men," said Rhumirrah in such a sweet and bashful tone. It was altogether winning.

"Men? Men!" shouted the jackdaw shrilly, and then she began to laugh. "Men are a myth, dearie," she said quite warmly. "They simply don't exist."

This was something Rhumirrah had not expected. She was astounded and for some time did not know what to say or how to proceed.

"You know much more than I do," she admitted softly, when at last the tigress had recovered her wits. "Yet I am certain I have often heard of men. How is it the whole jungle speaks of them?"

"Ignorance. Ignorance," pronounced the jackdaw. "Why, even my cousin, Clarence, the most silly grackle one ever did meet, goes on and on about the Two Legs."

"What does he say?" asked Rhumirrah, wishing the black-bird would reveal where Clarence could be found.

"The most utter nonsense! But what can you do with a grackle? They're practically only good for pies!" The wrath of the jackdaw was particularly extreme, because she suspected Clarence of thievery. A nice piece of blue enamel, a ceramic tile she had discovered near the home of an artisan, had mys-teriously gone missing shortly after her cousin had visited. (By-the-bye, a week later she found it hidden in another stash yet did not find it necessary to apprise Clarence. For some days, though, the frequency of imprecation against grackles suddenly dropped from her chatter.)

"There really must be *something*," insisted the tiger, "to explain the humans. When I was a cub, I once thought I saw one following a trail in the forest."

"It was an ape," answered the jackdaw with the assurance of one whose judgment has ripened to maturity.

"Oh, but an ape has a very different walk — and I am sure, a very different manner."

"Not so different," said the jackdaw. "You are a little young to know these things," she admitted, embroidering her words with the intimacy of disclosure. "A Man is certainly a kind of ape. Advanced in some ways, but an ape, nonetheless. Scientists identify them as 'the pants wearing ape.'"

"Why do they wear pants?" asked Rhumirrah.

"My, my," sighed the jackdaw. "Didn't your mother tell you anything?"

~~~~~~~~~

Rhumirrah was very surprised about the pants. She thought the jackdaw must have gotten confused somehow. And she was not yet satisfied with the monkey explanation. She thought she would speak to her neighbor, Harold. Harold was a rather crotchety orangutan, but decent if you approached him nicely and without too much hurry. He at least ought to know the truth of the simian theory.

"Harold, darling," she called up to him. The orangutan was in his loft, snoozing. He emerged from under his blankets, distinctly cross in appearance, but the tiger knew he would actually be pleased. He had a small crush on her, which made him feel ridiculous, since he was somewhat stout and middle-aged. Yet, when she spoke to him, he would sometimes forget that he was old and even when he remembered he allowed himself the pleasure of her company and would bring out dusty volumes of poetry or play records that were popular in his youth.

"What, what, she lives?" quipped Harold, surreptitiously trying to peek into a mirror and smoothing down his hair.

"How are you, Harold?" she purred. Oh, there was nothing like the flower of youth. The orangutan smiled, still looking disheveled. He tripped slightly over a flower pot because out of vanity he was not wearing his glasses.

"Your obedient servant," he said.

"Dear Harold," she began. "I'm afraid I'm going to be very tiresome."

Harold fairly shook with delight. She had been speaking a good half minute before he could remember what she was saying. He'd been transfixed by the "Dear Harold," so Rhum-irrah had to repeat herself.

"It's like this, Harold. I'm very interested in the Two Legs and papa positively forbids me to look for them. It's most annoying."

"Hmm. Hmm," said Harold.

"Well," said the tiger, "is that all you've got to say? I really thought you'd have something more than a hmm."

"Ah, how fetching a red-haired girl is," that's what Harold was thinking and wondered if he could provoke her to be a little bit genuinely miffed, because her beauty just dazzled when she was angry. In the end, however, his courage failed. "I've got a book here, somewhere, that tells all about them," he said.

"Oh, do you, do you? Why, you are positively bad, Harold. Why didn't you say before, me going on and on about the Two Legs and all this time — it doesn't have pictures, does it?"

———————————

Smith's Anatomy for Artists was not lacking in illustration and it did seem to put the lie to the jackdaw's theory of pants, all of which confirmed the tiger's prejudice, but there was something unsatisfying in the blocky poses of the humans. Why did they want to stand like that anyway? They seemed a most unusual creature. While there was, perhaps, a distant resemblance to apes, tending more closely to approximate the chimpanzee, Rhumirrah could not expunge the feeling that the Two Legs were a different sort of being. What, she could not say, but the fascination remained.

"Not apes," was Harold's considered opinion. "But if you really want to know, you'll have to ask Orianna."

The tiger felt a tiny thrill of anticipation. "And who is Orianna?"

"She is the wise, old owl who lives in the Salamander Tree," yawned Harold. It was time for his nap.

Now this is the kind of thing one hears about in fairy stories, which to our ear equates to "the sort of tale you tell to put children to sleep." You may therefore be inclined to think that Harold was lying about the Salamander tree, that there is no such thing. This is what Rhumirrah thought, because she'd never heard of a Salamander Tree in all her long years (which is to say, for practically two entire calendars). She said this to the orangutan, though at the same time wanting very much to see it. Harold recollected at her words that youth is terribly impatient and forgave her everything, as he knew he should, no matter if she took from him every stick and candle, let alone a few winks of sleep.

"Somewhere in this jungle you will find a lake at the bottom of a waterfall," said Harold. "If you look carefully, you will see, beneath the surface of the water, a sort of door. Or perhaps not. Sometimes you can see it and sometimes you cannot."

"When can you, exactly?" said Rhumirrah, feeling that Harold was spinning because he didn't want to disappoint her, but also feeling that he was having a bit of fun at her expense and would laugh when she came back all soaking wet.

"Oh, I cannot remember." The orangutan yawned again. "All this arcana is only whispered about." Then Harold began to doze, so that Rhumirrah was forced to pinch him. The orangutan gave no yelp or even an indication that he was aware he had fallen asleep, but continued his speech in a husky weariness. "The tree changes colors depending on its mood. Centuries ago, it disappeared from the ordinary realm of the forest. I hardly recall that there is a portal to the Salamander Tree."

"Why did it vanish?"

"Because men came and cut wood from the tree to make flutes and mandolins, instruments that would alter their pigment to match the music — and as there was only one Salamander tree and mankind finds it difficult to moderate his appetites, it would have disappeared entirely and been counted a mere legend, had measure not been taken to preserve it."

"But why couldn't the Salamander Tree simply reproduce itself?" asked Rhumirrah, naively and a little put out that such a wonderful tree had been taken from the world.

"Ah, but then it would no longer be unique," answered Harold, his own voice rather sad.

Rhumirrah knew of only one lake by a waterfall, a rather modest waterfall at that. The lake was nestled between the rounded shoulders of a series of low hills. In the mornings, one could hear the eerie call of the loon echoing across the waters. Making her way towards the falls, the tiger sauntered through a thicket of brush and a nice green meadow painted with cowslip and daisies. Rhumirrah tried not to pause at these. She was ashamed of her weakness for flowers. In the hills, she passed a brown bear who inquired where she was going.

"To the lake," she said, laughing softly because she felt foolish.

"I was just there," grumbled the bear (bears almost always grumble). "There is a most superior heron hanging about. Stealing the best fish."

"Goodness!" exclaimed the tiger.

"A tragedy!" said the bear.

"I'm terribly sorry."

"Oh, you're just saying that," groused the bear in a melancholy voice.

"No, indeed. I think herons are just awful."

The bear was surprised to find the tiger such a sensible creature. He had heard that they were boastful and savage. "I have some honey and berries, if you'd care to dine," grumbled the bear.

"Thank you very much, but I really must be going," answered Rhumirrah as kindly as she could. She was afraid the bear would be insulted, but he approved of her even more. The tiger did not know that rejected generosity is precisely a bear's favorite kind. A bright sort of girl, he thought, watching her figure retreat into the marshy land that surrounded the lake.

"Tell that heron he's a regular poacher. Tell him brown bear says so."

~~~~~~~~~~

The heron was wading in the lake, nattily attired in gray plumage, his steps stately and careful.

"There's a brown bear who thinks you're quite a bounder," said Rhumirrah in a cheerful tone.

"Ah, but bears say those sorts of things," answered the heron, turning a gladsome eye upon the newcomer.

"I dare say," agreed the tiger pleasantly.

"They call me Captain," said the heron.

"I'm Mirrah, but for some reason my friends call me the Brat."

"I'm sure it's in good fun."

"Mostly."

The heron darted his long bill into the water, spearing a silvery fish which flopped haplessly about in its death throes. Rhumirrah politely looked away while the Captain devoured his meal.

"Well, Mirrah, or if you'd prefer…?"

"I don't see why, really, they insist on Brat. I suppose I'm whining. Do you think that's it or don't you?"

"What I like about the sea," said the heron, "is the miles and miles of rolling water. It's quite beautiful from the air. And no one to tell you anything or criticize."

"It must be marvelous to fly."

"Quite the best," conceded the Captain.

"Captain, I have a funny question to ask you."

"That's all right, my dear." The Captain was naturally gallant.

"Have you ever seen a door in the lake? I know it sounds silly, but my pal, Harold Orangutan, says there is one. Sometimes, that is. Harold isn't very clear, I'm afraid."

"And does he call you Brat?"

"No, actually, but you see . . . " Rhumirrah practically blushed and turned her eyes down. "I think he rather likes me, so he wouldn't, would he?"

"No gentleman would," said Captain, "but I should point out that teasing is often a sign of amatory affection."

"Really, is it that terrible?"

"Oh, yes."

~~~~~~~~~~

The Captain knew nothing of any doors in the lake, though he knew a great deal about fish and flying and the fine points of etiquette. He spent five minutes explaining the proper way to tie a Windsor knot and another ten on the best way of putting a foreign ambassador at ease. (Not, apparently, bringing in a local choir to sing some popular native tunes, but simply to be kind, yet frank, and free with the food.) After the heron left, Rhumirrah stared for minutes at the edge of the lake. She peered diligently into the waters, which were fairly limpid at the edges, but dark and murky in the depths. The tiger walked all along the near shore and considered whether she ought to try and swim out into the waters. It was a large lake and quite too far to wade across. After some minutes, she became bored. There was patently no door in the lake. Harold had sent her on a wild goose chase. "I am a perfect fool," she said to herself. "I shall say to Harold, 'Am I a goose?'"

"I can show you the portal," intervened a whispery, silky voice.

"Thank you very much," answered Rhumirrah, looking about bewildered, for there was no one in sight.

"The portal is-s-s in the water," said the voice.

"I know, but where are you?"

"Here," answered the voice in a long, breathy whisper.

"I'm afraid I cannot see you in the least."

"The portal is-s-s in the water."

"Yes, I know!" said Rhumirrah, thumping her tail. It was a most exasperating voice. Then a small ripple broke the placid plane of the lake. A long snake slithered out onto the muddy shore and set a lidless eye upon the tiger.

"Are you very sure you want to s-ss-see the portal?"

"I think so. I am trying to find the Salamander Tree, you see."

"Sss . . . sss," said the snake, which was as close to a laugh as the snake could manage.

"Isn't there a Salamander Tree?" asked the tiger, feeling increasingly foolish.

"There is-s-s a portal," said the snake.

"How do you know about it?"

The snake did not answer her. It, too, knew the art of silences. After a while, it curled itself up into a coil and stuck out its tongue at her. Rhumirrah was about to be quite pert. Indeed, she was going to give the snake a piece of her tigerish mind, the sort of thing that made her friends call her the Brat. Yet, in the space between thought and act, the serpent began talking. "A great fish, ssso old it doesn't even remember itss name, slumbers-s-s at the bottom of this-s-s lake," whispered the snake.

"I wonder it hasn't been eaten," pondered Rhumirrah aloud, thinking of the bear and the heron.

"This -s-s fish, who has no name, was here *before* the lake."
The snake stared at her in a way most menacing. "It comes-s-s
from the abyss-s-s."

"How enchanting. I love a good abyss," remarked the tiger,
not willing to give the reptile any satisfaction, though her blood
ran chill.

"When you sssee the fish, the portal will be there," concluded the snake. Then it slithered sulkily into a dark hole
from whence Rhumirrah could hear it laughing. "Ssss. Ssss.
Salamander Tree. Ssss."

Rhumirrah waited nearly an hour by the shallows of the
lake. Nothing seemed to happen, though, of course, a lot was
happening; but as she was waiting for a mysterious fish to
appear and it decidedly did not, the tiger felt life disappointing
and lacking in incident.

"A fish with no name, indeed!" she said in disgust. All the
way home, she muttered to herself, "Yogurt! Yogurt! Yogurt!"
A well-bred tiger, though a warrior, avoids the most distasteful
language. The brown bear saw her brooding and reflected again
on how fine a girl she was, though evidently flighty and too
full of high spirits.

~~~~~~~~~

"Well, Brat, how was your day?" asked Osborne Ostrich.

"Most unsatisfactory."

"I'm sorry to hear it."

"Are you? Are you really?"

"You are quite the girl," said Osborne. The next day, he
could be heard telling all their mutual acquaintances of Mirrah's
recent penchant for melodrama. Ostriches are terrible for gossip.

"It's just that I can't get any clear idea about the Two Legs."

"And why should you? What good did they ever do anyone?"

"There's the story of Noe. He helped us."

"Well, Noe — if you believe that sort of thing. I mean, it's a story for children, isn't it?" And the bird peered with his large black marble eyes so acutely into the tiger's face that she became embarrassed.

"Honestly, Osborne, I can't say. I just have the feeling there is something important about the humans, if you see what I mean."

"Afraid I don't." The ostrich stretched its neck and gawked over Rhumirrah's shoulder. A fruit bat was sleepily descending towards them. "Look, here comes that bore, Glumwit. If I have to hear one more time about the horrors of rheumatism of the wings or how her aunts stole her plumb, I'll seriously have to think about leaving the country."

"Oh, mumble pie. I suppose it's too late to run?"

The bird did not immediately answer but dug a powerful claw into the sand. "If Glumwit asks, tell her I'm not here." With that, Osborne swiftly stuck his head in the sand. One has to remember that an ostrich's brain is smaller than its eye, which is more excuse than most people have, I'm afraid.

~~~~~~~~~

"Evening, Brat," said Glumwit.

"It *is* getting late." Mirrah gazed longingly towards home.

"Oh, is it? I should have known. My wings always hurt when it's late."

"I thought it was rain."

"Yes, rain, too. I don't know why these things happen to me."

"What things, Glumwit?"

"Well, lateness and rain. All sorts of things. I have the most tremendously difficult life."

Mirrah thought she might be very crabby. A day of disappointment and then Glumwit on top of it all. The tiger growled softly to herself and pawed the air in a menacing fashion.

"Is that Osborne?" asked the bat, nervously.

"Yes, it is. And if you don't mind, darling, I promised to be home for supper and I am rather late, you see. Osborne, however, was just telling me how pleased he would be if you would refresh his memory on how your aunts stole your plumb."

"Oh! Oh! Such an awful story. Are you sure you can't stay and hear it?"

Rhumirrah stretched and excused herself with crocodile tears, which is to say, with none at all, for crocodiles do not weep. Ah, it was a puzzle why her friends called her Brat.

In the morning, she felt considerably better. So much better that Rhumirrah chided herself for her behavior the day before. (As all the best scholars recognize, a tiger rarely indulges in self-chastisement except when in high spirits.) "I was, indeed, a trifle grumpy," she thought to herself. Soon, however, she was rehearsing the names of her ancestors, which is the tiger equivalent of brushing one's teeth in the morning. She was pleased to record the number of warriors in her family and was considering a nice antelope hunt when she became aware that her lovely paws had been padding along, all the time of her reverie, and that she was standing at the edge of the lake. "Oh," she said, "what's this?"

At first, she noticed only her reflection, which was, without bias, rather remarkably attractive. "My, that's really not bad," she said. But then, she noticed the water beneath the reflection. She saw, almost smiling up at her, but it was a most unnerving smile, a squinty, heavy carp the color of a worn copper penny. The fish did not acknowledge her but made a sound rather like a foghorn.

"Well, a bit too much noise for a fish your size, don't you think or don't you?"

The fish did not deign to respond but began to open and close its mouth, feeding on tiny bits of detritus too small even for Rhumirrah's eyes.

"Not much for conversation, are you? It doesn't matter. I don't suppose you know anything about a door in the lake, do you?"

As Rhumirrah was speaking these words, however, an odd sensation overcame her. She felt that she was getting smaller and smaller. Either that, or the fish was getting larger. She heard again the sound of a foghorn, and this time it did not seem comic. Everything became muddled. She felt herself falling into the water. She was tiny, tiny — and there was the fish, opening its, by now, giant maw. And then she was surrounded by darkness.

"How rude, really," is what the tiger thought, but as she had never been eaten by a fish before, she wasn't quite sure about the etiquette. "I'll have to ask Captain about this," she said.

~~~~~~~~~

She expected the ground beneath her to be slippery and soft, but it was solid. Peering up and about, she felt herself to be under the vaulted ceiling of a cave. She detected, though it made no sense, of course, a glimmer of light in the distance. The further she walked, the more the light grew in power, until she discovered herself emerging from a cave into a delightful expanse of grassland covered in glorious, fantastic flowers:

reckless, impossible shades of orchid; roses with white petals and magenta centers; tall, perpendicular skyscrapers of flowers draped in flags of gold and deep blue — petals, redolent of vanilla and sandalwood and a dozen other rich and intoxicating aromas. The tiger dipped her muzzle into flower after flower, until her head swam with dreams destined to excite the soul of a Dutchman named Van Gogh. She rolled over and over in happiness and then napped, though, in truth, she woke up with a bit of a hangover.

Treading somewhat unevenly, she followed no path other than the liking of her heart. She crossed meadows and green hills, followed a stream of impossibly clear water, drank its pure, cool sweetness, danced on a terrace of steppes girdled in pastures dotted with willow and poplar trees. A chill breeze kicked up and she breathed in the bracing air. The tiger felt cleansed all over and softly purred to herself. Across the fields she loped, kneading her paws like a kitten and thinking hardly at all. At the end of the pasture, she came to woods that seemed to be bathed in an almost palpable tranquility. The tiger could hardly discern a path through the trees, discovering in their maze a nearly infinite web of plant life, luxuriant, sleepy, enticing one to drop off into endless rest. Scolding herself, Rhumirrah roared, though her voice barely carried through the thick foliage. She leapt from one patch of fairly level ground to another, beginning to fear that she had entered a trap. At the dawn of real fear, however, the trees began to thin. Her feet touched down upon a small rise of lush, sweet grass. At the top of a hill, a thick-boled tree with branches waving out like the arms of a many spoked-umbrella stood alone under a canopy of light. What is more, the leaves were first golden, then red, then lavender, and green. A thrill raced through the tiger.

"Orianna, Orianna," she cried, thinking it must be the Salamander Tree.

A brief sound of ruffling feathers was followed by the appearance of a plump, white owl which peered down at her with eyes like merry lanterns. "Whoo, whoo?" it cried.

~~~~~~~~~~~~

"I'm sorry to trouble you," said Rhumirrah. Ordinarily, at the beginning of an important meeting, a tiger recites its genealogy, at least to five or six generations back, but Rhumirrah was always bad about formal rituals. "I don't suppose you are Orianna? I've come to ask you a question."

"Oh, no bother," declared Orianna. "It is always most delightful to discover one of my children." The owl cooed softly with complacent, maternal pleasure.

Rhumirrah was too polite to make an issue of owls and their offspring, though she had never before encountered one with such an ambitious claim. "I was hoping you could tell me about the Two Legs. What are they, exactly? Are they regular beasts or not? You see what I mean, don't you or don't you?" Now that she had begun, Rhumirrah felt foolish, quickly followed by anger, because a tiger hates to feel ridiculous.

Orianna flew down to a closer branch. She appeared to look at Rhumirrah with warm, merciful eyes. "Are you sure you wouldn't rather have a nice, succulent mouse? Scrumptious!"

"Thank you for the offer," she said, "but, as I'm here, I'd feel rather silly not to ask what I came to ask about. What would Harold say, I mean?"

"Whooo?"

"Harold. He's an orang. Prefers autumn, sad songs; hates mornings. That kind of fellow."

"Harold, of course," answered the owl. She nested silently on the branch, seeming to forget entirely that Rhumirrah was there. "I might not get anything, you know," added Orianna, just as the baffled tiger was about to speak. "The Two Legs are a little misty, dear. I'm not quite certain they are really mine, you see?"

Rhumirrah was quite prepared to intervene by this time with sincere protest. It was because she did not see that she had gotten herself swallowed by a sinister looking fish and gone all this way to find her. But just then a fit overcame the owl. The owl screeched and shook to the tips of her very feathers. Then Orianna cried and began to shout in a mantic tongue, chanting in a despairing rage. "Doom is coming! Doom! The skies are full of wrath."

Rhumirrah crouched down, cautiously looked about. The pleasant sky remained calm and lambent with a soft, nurturing light.

"There will be an unlocking of the gates. The dark waters will crash upon the land. The seas under the earth will break their bounds. Tears will wash the earth and the Heavens will be silent!" These last words came out in a hushed, mournful song more dreadful than a shout. Rhumirrah gaped in terror at Orianna. She did not understand. The owl blinked and hooted. She looked kindly upon the tiger, as if nothing had happened.

"Now about that mouse…," she said.

~~~~~~~~~

"Why, that is dreadful! Dreadful, the things you say!"

"But I don't say them. It's you! I heard you sing just now of catastrophe, the doom of life."

"Are you certain, dear? You mightn't be mistaken?"

"Oh, no. Look, look at the Salamander Tree." The leaves of the tree were black as ebony.

"That's not good," said Orianna. "The last time that happened . . . well, I shouldn't like to say." The owl paced along a branch, considering to herself. At length, she made a suggestion. "Why don't you stay with me? Much the best. It's quite safe here."

"But my family and friends. It won't be safe for them — or won't it?"

The owl sadly shook her head. "I shouldn't think so, dear, if it's to be as awful as you say."

"Then I'll go get them. Bring them back here."

Again, Orianna shook her head. "It is not in my power to control destiny, child. To you alone, who find yourself here, I offer sanctuary. Once you leave this land, I do not think you will discover it again."

"Well, then I must go warn them," was Rhumirrah's instant answer.

"They won't listen, dear."

The tiger snarled her determination. "I will *make* them," she said.

"That's just it. You can't. They aren't able to tell the difference between a prophet and a lunatic."

"How *do* you tell?"

Orianna assumed the expression of a mild, slightly exasperated governess. "The prophet turns out to be right, of course."

That's helpful, thought the tiger. Fat lot of good that does, when it's always after the fact. She would have thrown a fit, too, but for the pounding in her head. It was becoming quite sick making. All the colors of the Salamander Tree seemed to fall off in streams of whirling leaves. With a thud, her face hit the soft underground beneath the tree. She felt a spotting of water droplets. "Wait. Wait. I haven't had time yet," she mumbled, her mind fading into darkness. When next she opened her eyes, she found herself at the edge of the lake, her right paw trailing in the water. There was no sign of the ancient fish or of anyone at all.

~~~~~~~~~~

Harold, one had to admit, was not a creature constituted to welcome adventures. He could not hide from Rhumirrah the sinking of delight as she conveyed to him the singular occurrences of the morning. He was inclined to think that she had misunderstood the import of Orianna's words and when the tiger took umbrage, stamped her pretty paw, and insisted on danger, he lapsed back into a puddle of himself, assuming a pose of deep concentration.

"I suppose," he said, "we're in for a soaking."

"Harold, it is much worse than that, I am quite certain! You truly must believe me!"

If Harold did not believe her, there was no one who would be convinced. And he wanted to believe, if only to please her, but he just couldn't, you see? He could not imagine anything much beyond a good soaking. In the end, the dear girl became a bit tiresome. He didn't really have the energy to keep up with youthful enthusiasms. When she mentioned trying to get help, looking for Noe, well, perhaps it would do her good, give her a thing to do. She'd find it dullness soon enough, move on to some new interest. So, he told Rhumirrah about the pandas and the library. If anyone knew where to find Noe, they would.

Before leaving, she stopped by to speak with Bali and Nyssa. She meant to be circumspect, to say little, but had lost her temper, blurted everything. Bali was dismissive, told her she had dreamed it, that it was piffle, and even if it were true — and here, her father assumed the most condescending tone of rational objectivity, if it were true, see how magnanimous he was in granting her improbable premise? — there was nothing a Two Legs could do about it, even a storybook figure like Noe.

Nyssa had said nothing. There was no brooking Bali when he was in a pontificating mood. With tears in her eyes, she asked her daughter to be home for supper, to do nothing rash. Then she whispered, "Be careful, my love."

The tiger glanced first one way, then the next. Everywhere she looked, there were rows and rows of bamboo. She had never been one for books. Rhumirrah hadn't the least idea how to research a subject and the very idea of being in a library was both shaming and yawn inducing. The tigers were beasts made for action and for song. Occasionally, there *was* a learned tiger, true, but always one very old and living to such great age had a certain disrepute in it. Prowling about aimlessly, Rhumirrah toppled a loose pile of bamboo, disturbing the quietude of the place with the clatter of slender wood. One of the panda librarians arched an eye at her. The giant panda, Chu Shu, was nibbling on a large shoot of bamboo which happened to contain the first volume of *The Rise and Fall of the Gibbon Empire*. "Calm yourself," admonished the panda. "The truth does not come to the beast in a hurry."

"But the need is great," insisted the tiger. "I must discover where to find the man called Noe."

At this, Chu Shu stopped her munching and stared in astonishment at Rhumirrah. "You believe in Noe?" she asked in an incredulous tone.

"Don't you?"

The panda merely blinked and said nothing.

Rhumirrah swished her tail. She was not in the mood for cryptic librarians. "Naturally, one doesn't look for what one doesn't believe in."

"Yes." The panda put down her history and reached for a jar of berry water. It was very surprising to find a tiger that was interested in anything besides fighting. "So finding and believing sometimes go together," she observed. "Believing doesn't always mean finding, of course." The panda stopped and looked meaningfully at her, but the tiger could not detect the import. The big black patches about the eyes of the librarian absorbed all intent, keeping her emotions hidden from Rhumirrah.

"You think he's a myth, then?" sighed the tiger.

"We did not say."

Rhumirrah wished to pronounce her dislike of creatures who spoke of themselves in the royal plural; but, as she had not yet decided if the panda could help her, she held her tongue.

"Bring to me the shortest shoot in the third stack there," commanded the panda.

The tiger gingerly took the sprig in her mouth and carried it to Chu Shu. She began to dislike Noe for causing her to suffer such humiliation.

"No, this tells how one is to make goulash. It must be somewhere else." The panda leaned back and scanned the entire inventory of her library. "It is most unusual," she noted, "for any beast to spend time thinking of the Throne of Adam."

Rhumirrah's ears pricked at that. "The Throne of Adam?" Yes, she had heard of it. Once from an anteater drunk on fermented beetles and once when a flying squirrel misjudged a distance and knocked itself silly against a mahogany tree. Slowly, it had regained consciousness, babbling of having heard the voice of the Throne of Adam.

"It has something to do with the Two Legs, yes? But I, we, there's trouble coming. There isn't time for this thing called Adam. The owl, Orianna, told me. There's to be darkness and water, water, drowning the earth. Can't you see that I must find Noe?"

Again, the panda arched a brow at the tiger. She did not trust her visitor, nor did she entirely trust speech of Orianna. Still, there was sincerity in the barbaric cat. She meant what she said, at any rate, and had gotten some worry on her brain. "Toss me that little shoot there," she said, indicating a tiny tome sitting on top of a text devoted to the poetry of Agyar the Ape.

"There. There." Chewing delicately and deliberately, Chu Shu sipped and pondered, consuming the bamboo like a slow, melting candy. Then, with unexpected speed, she bounded to the entrance of the library, led the tiger out to the edge of a wide precipice overlooking the land of barren steppes.

"Ah, the ancients say Noe is across the desert. It is a long way." She spoke then with mildness to the tiger. The feline was a brave girl. She would have to be. The panda did not envy such a journey. It was so much easier to travel in the mind. "After the deadlands, you will come to new mountains and forest, then the tents of men. Somewhere in that far country is the abode of Noe."

~~~~~~~~~

Hour followed hour. The slate gray stone continued on with wilting monotony. Chu Shu could not tell her how many days and nights the journey would take. The last fair water she had seen was three nights past now. Rhumirrah was forced to search for caves with muddy pools, a plant that might be chewed for a drop of moisture. At first, she'd tried to pass the time by holding imaginary conversations, though it soon took all her concentration just to keep moving. Rhumirrah began to doubt herself. Her father's skepticism seemed eminently reasonable. What was she doing, really? What did she hope for? Could Noe hold back the skies?

Besides, one was never as eloquent when the time came. "Yogurt," she thought, because on the fifth or sixth imaginary try, she'd made an absolutely smashing impression on the legendary hero. The nice thing about being tired, she discovered, was that it left little energy for anxious introspection. As the pale light of dusk began to overtake the new moon, a convenient crevice in the granite presented a hidden, if rough bed. Silently she stretched and prepared to sleep through the daylit hours.

"What's new, pussycat?"

"Huhh? I'm sleeping. Call back later."

"I once heard of a tornado. It up and picked a rhino clear out of the savannah, took that ol' rhino across the ocean and deposited it in the middle of the Mississippi."

Rhumirrah cautiously allowed one eye to peek open.

"There you are! I declare," came a gravelly, joyous voice from the direction of a shelf of sunlit rock. Rhumirrah's golden-brown eyes saw a slight movement, a lizard flickering its tongue. The reptile inclined its head a fraction towards the tiger.

"I am Rhumirrah, daughter of Bali out of Nyssa. It will be a bad day for you if I decide not to like you," she growled.

"Hehe. Feisty. I like that. I'm thinking you're a long ways from home," drawled the lizard.

"Don't think too hard."

"You are trouble all over, sister. Bet you've got a string of heartsick boys a block long in the jungle. Married yet?"

The tiger opened both eyes now and glared at the interrupter of sleep. "I am Rhumirrah, daughter of Bali out of Nyssa," she began again.

"Sister Tiger, I heard you the first time. I'm just curious. We don't get many warm-bloods out here on account of the lovely climate. Must be something special to bring you all the ways out into the badlands, hehe."

Mirrah rolled, then yawned, stood tall. It was the afternoon. The golden disc of the sun hung oppressively over the horizon. "I am trying to cross to the forests on the eastern side. How far does this dreary business go?"

"Far enough to crazy. Why don't you go home, sister? This ain't no place for you."

"I cannot turn back! I must find help before the rains come."

The lizard flickered its tongue. "Rain! What rain? When's it comin'?"

"Near. And when it does, this whole land will be covered in seas."

Ever so slowly, the lizard edged away from Rhumirrah.

"If you're really going to cross the desert, it's best to follow the caravans. You'll see them. They mark the routes to the water holes. Only don't get too close. The men — they think a tiger's paw, powdered and mixed into an unguent, will make them powerful and attractive to their she-folk."

"Thanks," she said softly, drifting back to sleep.

"Only it's best you go home."

"Yes," she answered, no longer listening.

"Poor cat," thought the lizard. "Sun-blazed."

Eventually, the somber stone country gave way to a coppery land of dry, rounded curves. The footing became less hard, sandier. The jungle, clawed a bit, was full of sand, but not so copious and naked. It was difficult to get traction, hot in the day, cold at night. She held back for fear of discovery by the mysterious beast, caravan. It was unmistakable when one saw it. Many legged, with tents, the groaning of camels, and jabber. The Two Legs covered themselves from head to foot in linen. When they found water, they threw back their head scarves and soaked their faces, so that little streams of moisture would dribble down their beards.

Up close — as close as she dared — Rhumirrah felt the unhappiness of disappointment. She was not quite sure that the Parisian jackdaw had not been right. "Perhaps they are apes," she thought. "Greedy, industrious apes that wear pants." Still, the tiger was unwilling to close her thought. There might be other types of men. The men of the caravan might behave differently in other circumstances. Certainly, she remained convinced that Noe, if only she could find him, would be different. Her desire to be done with the desert eventually caused her to travel by day as well as night. She slept at odd intervals where opportunity seemed to present a respite of shade, though sometimes she found herself lying prostrate on the burning sands.

Tired and groggy, she had come too near the latest caravan, had spooked horses and summoned alertness in the corporate beast. She had been compelled to retreat and then keep such a distance that no longer could she count on finding water. Rhumirrah knew that she must soon come to the end of the desert or fail in her quest. As her thoughts grew less hopeful, her courage wavered and the anguish of her body became more acute. Her tail drooped in misery. She longed for company. Even Glumwit talking of her purloined plumb would have gratified her. As if in answer to her wish, a soaring bird with a bald head and wrinkled neck hovered, then flew low beside her. A vulture, it spoke in ingratiating tones. Like the lizard, it asked her where she was going. Frankly, Rhumirrah was not sure she had not invented her feathered interlocutor. She babbled rather volubly and incoherently of her mission.

The bird did not show a hint of scandal. The vulture stared at her with gentle, sleepy eyes. She felt creeping over her such a deep desire for sleep that she yawned outright. Listening to the lilting voice of the scavenger, the tiger seemed to sense for the first time the allure of the nothing. The desert was a symphony dedicated to bleached bones, to treeless expanse, to the big sky touching the barren earth. Next to the nothing, the richness of the jungle appeared an ugly soup of thirsting, striving, violent things. It was only death that was simple, only nothing that was pure.

"I know a short-cut," whispered the vulture.

"A short-cut to where?"

"To where you want to go."

A vacancy of voice and eye met her. The vulture would have disappeared if it could have, spoken only as a distant cry on the wind.

"Where do I want to go?"

"Where there is peace, peace," whispered the creature of unclean air.

This, of course, was a mistake. Tigers do not, generally, like peace, except when napping. Rhumirrah shook her head, peered askance at the bird. She saw, hiding behind the mask of tranquility—yes, indeed, a ravenous malice. So, the nothing was hungry, too.

"I will stay my course," she said, ignoring the oily protests of the proffered guide. For some minutes, the vulture went on whispering enticement, but as Rhumirrah paid him no heed, he flew off raging. His last words to her were of a dismal nature, promising slow extinction, pain, and corruption of the flesh.

~~~~~~~~~~

Her memory could never afterwards discover the precise moment the alteration of landscape determined her rescue. She had been walking in a rhythmic trance, hardly seeing what was before her when a giddy lightness entered her body. She sniffed the air. There was an odor of peppermint, some other resins that could only come from tall green trees, knobby shrubs with succulent berries and grasses that sparkled with morning dew. The good earth began to harden and solidify beneath her footpads. The tiny images of verdant foliage grew larger and larger until she found herself traversing the first outcroppings of authentic woodlands. Rhumirrah came to a stream and filled her belly, slept by the water's side, soothed by the tintinnabulation of its crystalline song.

Refreshed, she awoke and surveyed the arrow of her path, discerning a serpentine track through a rise of mountains. In a valley, she came upon a flock of wild sheep. An aged, blind ram was easily separated from the flock. With her first substantial meal in days, she journeyed with new vigor. Throughout a varied topography, novel sights arose to entertain her. On the plains, she was amazed by the seemingly choreographed speed of a herd of mustang. In forests she was met by inquisitive beasts of a more gregarious nature who had not seen a tiger before. To these, she did not speak any prophecy, but asked only news of the Two Legs. Coming nearer to men, her steps became more efficient and accurate. The number of humans was unknown to the beasts, but it was thought to be a great many. At the frontier, where the land began to be dotted with strange structures of brick and planed wood, the tiger met with beasts that lived in accord with men. Milk cows and hens, dogs and barn cats. Many were frightened by her appearance, some curious — the cats, in particular.

Rhumirrah tried to appear as mild as she might, asked if any creature had word of the man named Noe. None could answer her and the tiger felt a stirring of trepidation. She even began to feel that some creatures were laughing at her behind her back. Rhumirrah steeled herself by recollecting the vision of Orianna, yet could not utterly keep her mind from engaging ruminations of disaster and ignominy. At length, she entered into a country of low heath and rounded hills. A pack of hyenas caught her attention, a tittering, snickering roil of barks and excited jumping. The hyenas were half sitting and half rolling upon the hill, so full of laughter they could barely contain themselves.

"Why, that beats all," said one.

"I see'd it, an' I still don't believe it," said another.

"The Two Legs do put on a show," exclaimed a third.

Rhumirrah followed the path of their eyes. She saw a plain filled with the dwellings of men. Rising above the plain was a series of low hills ending in a stony ridge. The beasts were evidently drawn to a hulking immensity of wood and pitch, so large that at first Rhumirrah thought it part of the mountain. Yet she had never known a mountain to burn as this one did. A small riot of Two Legs, clustered about like flies on rotten fruit, stood gyrating and gesticulating below the fire. She then saw that it was some kind of craft that the fire burned, a boat as big as a forest. Against the flames, a small troop of men battled. The opposed parties of Two Legs, one jeering, the other dancing about, helter skelter, swinging buckets of water and wet blankets, made for a perplexing and, from a distance, ridiculous picture.

"Excuse me," said Rhumirrah. "I'm very sorry to interrupt, but could someone tell me how to find the Two Legs they call Noe?"

At her request, the hyenas lost what little composure they had managed to maintain and collapsed into a fit of prolonged and unrepentant guffaws.

CHAPTER THREE

Waiting

THE FIRST TIME HE NOTICED HER, the girl with the green hair, his wife was complaining about something or other. He wasn't really listening. He'd drifted into that comfortable haze where one can nod and make reasonable noises. Then a vagrant dog was chased out of the butcher's shop accompanied by laughter at the chagrin of the proprietor. The scamp had managed to abscond with a slight trophy, gobbling it down even as it ran. The brief commotion from the discomfiture of the meat-seller had barely subsided when a brusque clanging of termagant bells announced a procession. Large men with rounded, oleaginous faces, eunuchs in service to a foreign dignitary formed a column, piercing through the crowded market; a glimpse of a bland matron in costly robes, bored, yet with a whiff of unmistakable anxiety. Smoke rose from the glassmakers. An artisan was blowing liquid fire into a long, bulbous gourd of transparent ice. Among the on-lookers, she stood apart, her gamine eyes belied by a sad smile. No one seemed to mind her. She was there and not there, the viridian girl.

One night, Noe was listening to the men sipping on the dark, bitter coffee that was served in the cafes. They were talking of what they had seen and heard, and one of the men began to tell of a certain young woman who danced naked in the streets and amazed the onlookers by eating crickets and howling at the moon. Another told a story of a child who had been drowned by his mother to stop it bawling at all hours of the night. All manner of wickedness was discussed, particularly that of women. This was how the men blew off steam and got back at their wives for not respecting them. Noe listened and said nothing. An aged chieftain sat in the corner moving little sticks and dice marked with runes. His aged, saggy skin, exposed always to the sun and baked tough as leather, was canvas to a wild tracery of blue and black images that bled into one another, offering a constellation of incipient narratives that nonetheless withheld the key to coherent meaning. The old man possessed deep, sad eyes the color of the mud out of which artisans made carafes and pitchers with drawings of frogs and irises on them. When the men finished lamenting the times and began to descend into bawdy songs and lachrymose tales, Noe stood, paid his bill, and walked out into the chill evening.

He was briefly surrounded by a gang of androgynous youth, half fighting, half dancing and strutting. A burly youth, black as Ham, emitted a shrieking, ecstatic groan, mouthed a few barely articulate syllables, and then let forth another eroticized scream. He concluded with an irony that escaped him, "That's what I'm talking about." Noe waited for them to pass as one does a freak occurrence of the weather. He was sorry for them and also repulsed. No one loved them enough to live amongst them and show them a better way — or if they were rebuked, they were not loved. So, naturally, they did not listen. When the mad children had gone, he saw her huddled under a street lamp. The green-haired girl met his gaze with unexpected boldness. She seemed to have been waiting just for him. Look, this is what she said to him.

"They think it's just a story, and a pretty bad one at that. They think it's already happened, even though it's just a story. They don't know what it is to drown. It isn't flesh burst, it isn't bloated up and mucky, so dreadful grown men run from it, ashen faced and retching. Well, it might be that, but then again you can walk and talk in this drowning. You might be doing it yourself, this very moment."

At the end of the street, Noe saw again the chieftain. The old man was chewing on a gob of ga, his mind delirious and filled with phantoms. It was then, on the way home, that Noe felt a sudden compulsion to build a boat. He could not explain the whim, but it made him feel better, to measure and cut wood, to shape the prow, to see first the skeleton of the vessel and then the body of the boat at the end of his skill and effort. He built first a small boat for fishing. Then the news and rumors of evil, the sights that daily met his eyes grew more ominous, vulgar, almost mindless. He built a larger boat big enough for himself and his sons to sail upon a sea.

His unease grew. His sorrow began to turn into horror and a numbed feeling, the feeling of helplessness before a terrible sickness. It was then that the voice came to him. There was never any question of projection or hallucination. He had never heard another voice more objective and real. At least, this is what he told himself in the long years afterwards. The voice said, "You need a bigger boat."

He had not once, since he had begun to build, heard again the voice of the Mystery. There were times when he wished he had dreamed it all — and others when he dreaded it was all a dream. The wealth of Methuselah poured into the project.

Noe's reputation was darkened. He became the subject of confused sadness or, more frequently, open derision. His own shepherds and farmers, his blacksmith and his tanner, his carpenters and his least servant: they all laughed at him behind his back, though the men were respectful enough when Ravi showed up at the end of the week with their pay. His sons suffered mostly in silence. Priyanka, bless her, stuck by her man. Even when Iradon tried to get her to come back to the House of Auramoosh, she refused. "Live with the idiot, then," said her father, and that was the last they had spoken, some seventy years. The task became more difficult when the Syndicate put the clamp on his workers. They simply stopped showing up. So, Noe recruited his own field hands and his sons to the work. He labored himself from dawn to dusk, planing the gopher wood, notching the timbers, measuring with precision so that the beams fit snugly.

Jumbo and his men then paid friendly visits to Noe's father, told old Lamech how much they admired him and what a shame it was his son had turned out to be cuckoo and a fanatic. A nice little fatherly chat was suggested, while the well-being of Lamech's flocks was spoken of with the utmost concern. When that didn't work, they set fire to the ark, so that Noe had to post watchmen and take his strongest shepherds away from the fields to walk around at night with ready fists. Lately, unsigned letters, sometimes obscene, other times vaguely threatening or sarcastic, had begun to arrive. Ravi tried to hide them from Noe but gave away every new onslaught of the poison pen by a nervous and excessive cheerfulness.

"At least they haven't set the lawyers on us yet," Noe joked, and Ravi crimsoned, because he'd been dealing with lawyers for months.

~~~~~~~~~~~

Noe had to admit it had been a long wait. He'd expected something more. Some sign, some consolation. Neither rains, nor proclamation of clemency came with the years. Through the mute decades, he'd labored on, but he was feeling the strain. Uncle Hamish and Aunt Zelda had stopped their visits. "Too old" was their excuse, but he knew it was actually a remnant of family feeling and resentment that he had become a social pariah. "Put it on the back burner," was Zelda's advice. "Get on with life."

"Get on with life," he said out loud, in a bitter cry. Ah, he was beginning to feel old. His feet hurt; the face that reflected back from the mirror was a stranger, haggard and unattractive. Resentment began to take hold and drag him into a fragile, peevish growl of misery. Everything had changed. He paced through the streets, ignoring the children who called him "Longshanks" and "Boatbrain." What had happened to the children? There was a time they ran to him with their animals, asked for a blessing because he had a curious ability to heal the beasts. When he had begun to build the ark and its hull rose up, becoming visible in the villages and cities, they would come to him and ask if they might ride in his great machine and, of course, he had said yes, had begun to bring a long sheet with him, a ship's manifest he told them, and asked for their names, so he could sign them up.

But now those children were grown, busy people. They no longer came to Noe with their joy and their wonder. If they passed him in the street, they crossed to the other side or, worse, smiled at him that embarrassed, rueful smile, a measure of remnant affection mixed with consternation that they had ever been so naive as to take seriously a crazy old dreamer. And he wasn't that old. Not yet. Barely five centuries. Why, Methuselah lived to be nine hundred and sixty-nine. The children of those children were weaned on sour milk. They were birthed wizened. Before they had a chance to live in innocence, to entertain marvelous dreams, their pure eyes were darkened. "Education" is what the parents called it, because the world was bad, bad, and you couldn't start too soon to tell them, lest they be harmed. And the world was bad. Yet how terrible that the little children would not call him "father" or ask for a ride on his boat.

———————

Priyanka, he discovered, was in her boudoir. His mum had not had such a room. It was another innovation from Auramoosh. Priyanka had explained that it was important for a woman to have a space of her own, a place to read and write letters, to bathe and cry and think. It was especially necessary that she have a secret place where the oils and ointments that preserved and rectified the assaults on youth and beauty might be applied without male scrutiny. "Otherwise, you will discover what a sorry creature you have been tricked into marrying," she'd tease.

Noe knocked twice without answer. Concerned, he noisily opened the door to the room. His wife seemed lost in private reverie, sat staring into the mirror, her hands forming an arch upon which rested her chin. He did not like to disturb her. He had come to understand that a retreat was necessary for her. Out of her silences and mysterious ponderings came her warmth, her new words. Silently, he bent down over Priyanka, looking not at her, but at her reflection. The firmness of the jaw line, the smoothness of the brow, the brief perfection of youth had deserted her, yet her warm, dark eyes remained playful and capable of smoldering fire. She had reached a stage where maturity and the traces of youth find a delicate, ephemeral balance. In some ways, Priyanka would never be more beautiful than she was just then, the glory of the maiden princess joined to the tiny etching marks of life and struggle. A wise beauty, he thought, as he kissed her lightly on the wrist, her lips, the soft skin of the temple.

She smiled and laughed a girlish laugh.

"What are you thinking?" he asked.

"Before you came in, I was thinking about my mother, how I never saw her old or even middle-aged." Priyanka spoke in a calm, languid, almost far away voice. "It's a strange feeling, to discover that you have outlived someone you naturally accept as an elder. I tried to remember if I looked like her, if I could see in my face the face she might have had, but I can't seem to recollect her clearly."

"Oh."

Priyanka grinned, turning to him. "Come sit by me."

"That's all right, then."

"Yes, isn't it?"

"Did you see Shem?"

Noe sighed. "He was out. His latest girl . . . Shona . . . Sholon . . . something . . . answered the door in pajamas and offered to pour me a drink. Said he would be back soon if I'd care to wait."

"Is she pretty?"

"Not as pretty as you."

"Liar! But well trained," laughed Priyanka. "So, did you? Wait, I mean."

"I wouldn't know what to say to a girl like that. There were paints everywhere. The walls are papered with sketches. I felt she'd ask me what I thought of my son's work and then I should have to say 'interesting,' which Shem would hear about later and think 'interesting' is a euphemism for worthless and incomprehensible."

"Do you really think that? I like Shem's paintings."

"So do I. The irony is that my interesting would mean interesting, but I can't get Shem to believe it."

"He's a first son, Noe. Ambitious and dutiful in his way, but artistic. It's a difficult combination. My man ought to understand that."

"Is that what the ark is? A work of art? It's something else, I think."

"Sometimes, I get a feeling that I cannot put a name to. It's like a color that tastes or a smell that touches you. If I try to figure it out, it gets all hard and crusty, crumbles away before I know what it is. But if I wait, let it be, I'll think I've forgotten all about it and then, one day, I find I've put a new spice in the soup or discovered something new in a view I've been looking at for years."

"You're telling me the ark is a new flavor of pudding?"

"You are a ridiculous, impossible man."

"And all yours."

"Yes, and all mine." She tapped him gently on his chest. "Mine. Don't ever forget." Priyanka kissed him hard. "Mine."

~~~~~~~~~

The stores were utterly prodigal, stuffed with wheat and barley, pickled cucumbers, molasses, dried apricots, raisins, raspberry preserves, dark breads, light breads, spices, ginger, nutmeg, cinnamon, chives, a nice supply of coffee and green tea. There were sugars and ground flour, rhubarb, vinegar and soap. The lockers were filled with bolts of cotton, spools of flaxen thread, ropes and ladders, oil and matches, books and games — crossword puzzles and cards, colored waxes, a small music box. Japheth had even concocted a greenhouse, should there be any light to speak of. He had ready lettuce and cabbage, young tomato plants and half a dozen legumes. It was really quite impressive.

"I don't quite see the point of it," said the girl, pushing up her glasses and turning her head with an expression playful and provoking all at once.

Japheth grinned and ran his hand nervously through his hair. He did not know what to say to her. "My mother shall be sorry to hear that. She's spent a great deal of time on the candied yams in particular."

"Must you always goof?"

"It's just that, well, how am I to answer you? I know this seems like a crackpot idea. I know what everyone thinks. We're not stupid people. I can only tell you my dad isn't crazy. And as you can see — there's room for one more."

"Don't be daft," retorted the girl in a voice soft and trailing into dream.

From one of the lookout windows, he could see the small dot of his father moving slowly, pacing with a steady gate along the bottom of the long ramp. "Well?" asked Japheth, turning the conversation so that his heart might stop beating with that insistent pound that Molly always inspired.

"You've done a magnificent job. Really astounding, but I don't see how you can pull it off."

"Why not, Molly?"

She shrugged, it was an unconscious gesture. Now she would begin to speak with that voice of authority that always seemed so displaced in her coltish tomboy body. "Take the simple water shrew. Fantastic metabolisms. Of course, they have to eat every two or three hours or they will die. Miss a feeding and it's too late. You going to keep a supply of live grasshoppers and frogs to feed the little darlings?"

"Yes, I see what you mean. The insectivores and their food supply have always been a worry. You might be surprised by this, but there are lots of people who can't stand bugs."

"That's just one example, Japheth. I don't mean to sound rude, but how long do you plan on staying? I mean time is a consideration, too — hypothetically speaking."

"Hypothetically speaking, I don't know. Dad doesn't know either, I'm pretty sure."

"Isn't that something one ought to know?"

"Look, Molly. It isn't like that. There are lots of things I'd like to know. Some of them seem pretty important, too." He paused and looked at her with a sweet, sad expression. "We have to act on what we do know. But I suppose you're like everyone else."

"Am I?"

There was something in the question that made Japheth feel all fuzzy inside. A brief vertigo flashed through him. When he recovered, she had already turned from his gaze, peering with interest at the arboreal space devoted to the eventual domicile of fruit bats and flying squirrels.

~~~~~~~~

It was hard to say exactly how flour became part of the equation. Japheth had been merely remarking upon the funny little snort of Molly's laugh and then Molly had said that Japheth shouldn't talk because his ears stuck out. The mutual admiration of the evaluators next touched on various phobias, such as Japheth's unusual fear of gold fish, which, to be fair, wasn't true: he just didn't like to touch them, was all. Then Molly's habit of bossing was recalled and the time she got locked out of her apartment with nothing but a towel for modesty. Shortly thereafter, a flour bag was accidentally cut with a knife and the contents accidentally thrown back and forth until both parties were lightly caked in a fine, powdery dust. At this stage, Noe happened to show up, a wolf-like dog with pale blue eyes trailing at his heels.

"Son," said Noe.

"Father," answered Japheth, vainly attempting to brush off the flour and assume a serious pose.

"Is there something you want to tell me?"

"No. I don't think so," said Japheth in a tone that credibly conveyed absolute incomprehension.

All this time, Molly felt ridiculous. Moreover, she was fighting back the impulse to laugh which became all the more difficult because she was certain she would snort.

"Oh, this is Molly," broke in Japheth. His father evidently did not recognize her. "She is helping with the habitats — knows a terrible lot about shrews."

This last dig failed to elicit response, for Noe had come forward to exchange pleasantries, indicating the dog as he did so. "This splendid fellow is with you, I take it?"

"Yes. His name is Hontu."

"You'll have to come by the house some time."

"I'd like that."

There was more of that sort of thing, but Noe did his best to quickly extricate himself from the young people's fun. The girl, however, had evidently decided to take the opportunity to make her own get-away.

"Hontu," called Molly. The dog with ice blue eyes came faithfully to her side. "It was nice to see you, Mr. Lamechson." She held her hand out, quite the liberated girl, and shook Noe's hand. It was a firm grip.

~~~~~~~~~~

There is such a thing as a cart and such a thing as a winch and servants, yet Noe wanted to preserve the surprise. Without the servants, even with the cart and the winch, it was rather an ordeal to move the piano. Priyanka was fond of it; there were no such things in Auramoosh. She had learned in middle age and did not play well, though not badly. The instrument had belonged to Noe's mama. Senta had performed admirably before her joints ached and it was too much trouble. So, the brothers moved the thing from its cozy place in the summer house up the long ramp. They had it covered so the farmhands pressed into guard service could only guess at the ghosted entity so mysteriously shepherded to Noe's fantastic ship. It was the care that was necessary to keep it from mishap, the trip would undoubtedly bring it out of tune and then it wouldn't sound right no matter what, that put them on edge.

"You are an ox," said Shem.

"You talk too much," said Ham.

At the ark they stared daggers at Japheth: he'd been waiting there all along.

"Where's the conservatory?" asked Shem in an arch tone. He was quick to regain his temper.

"Why it's next to the billiards room, of course," answered Japheth.

"You talk too much," said Ham.

~~~~~~~~~~

"Do you remember that old fat colonel married to Mrs. Culver's sister?"

"Hmm," said Noe, fiddling with his boot, pretending that he was not deeply intent, watching her.

"He's complaining of gout."

"Very painful."

"Yes, so says Ellen. They have a new tea set. She served me with it. The most delicate designs with little ships and animals and cityscapes. It was like something from Auramoosh." Priyanka put her hat in a box and began mindlessly straightening the copious small treasures that ornamented the main parlor room.

"I'll get you one just like it," offered Noe.

"Pffft. Ours is finer, Noe. Besides, it doesn't matter. It made me think of home, that's all."

Noe ambled about the room slowly, his hands in his pockets. Even in his five hundredth year, Noe had a way about him that remained boyish, endearing. Their talk was all on the surface. They skated away whenever the dangerous roil of fear and potential conflict threatened to break through.

"Japheth had a guest this morning," he spoke impulsively, fearing a lull, then regretted it almost immediately for it touched upon the ark.

"Oh?"

How many calculations could a single syllable inspire? What was in that "oh?" Was she genuinely curious, merely polite, already giving way to resentment, ready to pounce? Noe could only catalog the possibilities before bracing himself as he was already committed.

"Yes. A girl from the city. He likes her, I think."

Priyanka smiled, flooding relief into Noe's old bones. "Of course he likes her, Noe. She's a little taller than I, wears a pony tail, and talks very bright?" Then she laughed, his befuddlement was so comical. "That's Molly Brice. He's only been in love with her since he first set eyes on her. It was the winter of the bad ice storm. We lost all those sheep. Molly pulled a lamb from the deep snow, brought it to the barn on her sled. Poor Japheth couldn't stop talking about her for weeks."

"Priyanka, that's three years ago. I think I'd know if my own boy . . . that was Molly?"

"Dear man, don't you know there are things a boy keeps secret from his father?" She chuckled then and his heart rejoiced. "I wanted to show you something." The trace of her laugh still remained, upturning the corner of her lips into a soft, enigmatic smile. Priyanka scrambled about with the contents of a large leather purse but could not discover what she wanted. "I hope I didn't leave it at the Culvers'. I'm so scattered lately. Never mind — I'll look for it later. You know that old retaining wall, the one back by the outhouse where the dairy cows are kept?"

"Of course."

"That prickly bush is back. I don't know how many times I've had it cut down, right down to a nub. You've got to respect that plant. I've told Yuri to leave it be now."

He could see the beginning of a glistening wet on her eyes.

"That's a very hardy plant," he said gruffly.

"They've got the most gorgeous maple in Ellen's garden. Its leaves are deep reddish purple. Ellen is painting it."

"Mrs. Culver is very artistic in her garden," agreed Noe helplessly.

"Did I tell you about her Rose? She's been taking dancing lessons. You should see the most darling little outfits she wears."

She could dance on the ark, thought Noe, but held his tongue.

Katya came into the room, ostensibly to polish the tables, but really to exchange a secret glance of commiseration with her mistress. Noe understood that he was held somehow responsible for all that they were undergoing. The impractical masculine intelligence, gazing at stars while weeds took over the courtyard. He clumsily changed the subject.

"I sold that timberland to Paddiger. You should have seen his face! He could barely contain himself! He drinks and carries on in that house of his, but he's no fool at business. You'd have thought I was a long-lost brother, soon as I handed over the deed. So, he thinks he swindled the crazy man." Noe whistled. The women were thoroughly uninterested in distant timberland. They had never stepped within the shadow of its pines. Noe considered that perhaps they had not even been listening to him. Priyanka had returned to foraging in her purse.

"Found it," she broke in, pulling out a faded daguerreotype, though goodness, of course it wasn't called that—Daguerre simply having rediscovered the process. "Look at this!" There was a girlish excitement in her voice now. Katya peeked over her shoulder as she displayed the photograph for Noe to see. "You know Doran passed on last summer. Well, Rudy, Ellen's son-in-law, was supposed to box up his things and he came across all these old pictures collecting dust in the attic."

"It's the anniversary party," declared Noe, feeling himself suddenly tender and sad. Senta and Lamech were seated at the center of the group; there were so many faces lost to time, hardly recalled if at all. The servants were lined up at the edges of the portrait.

"Oh, look, look," cried Katya. She had spied the youthful scamp of a porter in the picture, Jack who had captured her heart. Now the servant begins to mist, dabs at her eyes with the hem of her apron. Priyanka speaks women's words, some praise of the gallant which merely encourages Katya. Throwing her apron up over her face, the faithful retainer left the room in a fit of blubbering emotion. "*Where are my sons?*" thought Noe. He had a great desire to go outside and plane wood.

———————

"That night, the night we sought Eden, you remember?"
"Yes, dear one."
"I told a dream. Do you remember that dream?"
"The dream of the Deliverer. I've not forgotten."
"Remember the grandfather who was really a warrior?"
Noe stared into her eyes.
"I'm looking at him," she said. "I'm looking at him now, my love."

She held his hand and seemed to plead with her sweet, gentle face. "Noe, Noe. What are we doing? Why is your god so angry with them? They are not bad people. A little silly. Her husband's dull. What a dear, small girl she has . . . " Priyanka cried. It was nothing like the boohooing of the servant. Quietly her tears came.

———————

Noe decided to try a new tack. He wrote as best he could and placed an ad in the paper. He offered to readers a berth upon the ark, if only they would come while there was yet a chance. The response to the ad was various. Some wrote to say they thought Noe was such an awful man, threatening everyone and causing parents to have to explain to their children about God. Others made rather fussy inquiries, wondering as to the cost and stipulating just how the tea should be made and explaining that the sea made them sick and the last thing in the world they'd want was to be beholden to anyone and so, though the ad said "free," nothing really was and wouldn't it be better to be above board and strike a bargain? That way, everyone would have their rights and the whole thing might be done quite reasonably. However, when it came right down to it, very few seemed serious about Noe's proposal.

There *were* some visitors. One knew the reporter was a reporter because he wore a gray hat with the brim bent back and carried a small notepad with incomprehensible scratches scribbled across its surface. A group of young people from the city drove up in a row of disparate carts and coaches strung along the dirt road before the gate. They came forward in a rough, slouching line and shuffled about the vicinity of Noe's porch. They appeared restless and uncertain of themselves. They had expected Noe to be an entertaining idiot, but when he invited them into the house in a courtly, yet austere tone, he struck them as unexpectedly formidable. Soon, however, one of their numbers wakened from a private reverie and inquired as to whether there would be any beer on the ark. (The answer, of course, was yes.) The youths declared that they were students, though it was not clear where or what they studied. After some confusion, three of their party were chosen to enter into the house along with the reporter.

One of the ambassadors was a bouncy, shiny pink-skinned boy, his hair glistering black. He preened like a matinee idol. Evidently, he had been chosen merely for his glamour, for he did not say anything and the others, truth be told, ignored him. The remaining pair was somewhat slovenly and unattractive, their youth alone keeping them near the middling line for appearance. The young woman wore a drab shirt several sizes too large for her so that it engulfed her body like a tent. She evidently disapproved of the smart set. The girl's chief characteristic was the manner in which she held herself, poised and, indeed, posed, though unconsciously. This was ironic as she was keen not to be objectified. There was a stern hardness in her eyes, as if she were constantly preparing for martyrdom. In contrast, the last member of the triumvirate gave off an initial impression of sullen languor. He was one of those tall, lean young men with his hair cut very short. Every movement seemed seeped in a world-weary knowledge come too soon, suffusing his thoughts with grim rectitude made necessary by the hostile stupidity of the world. This student spoke first, his speech clipped with the accents of his era and clique, though he was utterly ignorant that he belonged to either.

"We are here," he said, "to show you that we will not be intimidated. For generations, men and women have listened to your threats, your fascist arrogance. It won't do. We see through it all."

"I compel no one," answered Noe, his unruffled, somewhat wry terseness infuriating the student so that the young man launched, in spite of his intentions, into an eclectic, disorganized babbling of current platitudes that even he felt unsatisfactory. At the end of the oration, he retreated towards a wall where he looked on with malicious pique.

The beautiful boy said nothing but sat in a posture of sensitive empathy next to the courageous girl. When Noe said something he did not like, which was practically every time he opened his mouth, the offer of sugar cookies an exception, the boy would acquire an expression of suppressed anger, acute misery, and horrified anguish. A paroxysm of flinching pain

afflicted his face as if Noe had been making obscene sugges-
tions. The young woman, however, did not seem to notice the
beautiful boy. Only after each of these performances, her own
visage would take on the righteous indignation of her silent
compatriot. Then she would grimace a hard smile, tell Noe
how refreshing his honesty was.

"Yes, it confirms, and thank you, we all like each other here.
This dialogue is so helpful; it confirms what many of us have
feared, have known all along."

"And what is that, my dear?" asked Noe kindly.

The young woman winced at the condescension of "my
dear."

"Admit you don't think women are rational."

"I think you should agree to get on the boat," said Noe.

The beautiful boy crossed his arms and sulked. The courageous girl bit her lip and tried to think of something nice to say.
You couldn't get much more patriarchal than old Noe, after all.
"We didn't come here to beg for a place on your boat," she said
at last. "We came here to try and explain to you what is wrong
with your oppressive ship. I'm sorry you can't see that." The
hard-bitten youth then raised himself straight from the wall
upon which he had been slouching. He glanced first towards
the girl and then towards the few assembled servants who had
watched the proceedings with curiosity. "I think we've done
something, Kai, today," he said. "You don't have to stay here,
you know," he declared to the servants, his voice calibrated
somewhere between pedantry and abstract compassion.

The servants returned his words of potential liberation
with blank stares. The young man was not surprised at this
but could not keep a sour note of chagrin from darkening
his features. He turned next to see if the reporter felt they

had done enough to merit a story in *The Times*. The answer was somewhat difficult to decipher, as the reporter had not stopped stuffing sugar cookies into his mouth from the first opportunity. Without a word of gratitude for Noe's hospitality, the representatives of youthful idealism rose and made their way back to their fellows. In small dribbles, they returned to their vehicles and left, though a few stayed behind, having been offered a chance at cards or dice by the local farmhands who saw a chance at snookering the city folk.

~~~~~~~~~

An aged gentleman from the city hired a cab, came with a large trunk, and sent his calling card to the maid at the door. The fellow was named Mushan, a retired professor of literature. He wore a black beret and a somewhat seedy and threadbare coat. Though his linen was clean, it was equally shiny with time's wear. The professor wrapped a topaz scarf with aquamarine polkadots about him as if it were a sign of panache and not to hide the scrawn of his turkey neck.

"I have come in answer to your ad," he said in a genial, old-style courtesy, bowing slightly.

"You are most welcome," answered Noe with a gladsome eye.

"Generally, you know, I only look at the obituaries." This was a joke, though true, and the men laughed. Then Priyanka stepped in and asked if the professor wished for tea or coffee. Such tokens of hospitality having been offered, Noe felt free to press forward.

"Is it just yourself?"

"Oh, these rags and bones are hardly worth saving. One wouldn't say they are worth saving, now would one?" Dr. Mushan said all this with the same twinkling tone with which he had introduced himself. It did, however, leave Noe briefly non-plussed.

"Professor, you said you were here because of the ad. Naturally, I understood you to mean . . . "

"Young man, don't be hasty. It isn't that dire, not yet, is it?"

Noe was of an age where being called young man is vaguely flattering or, at least, a perceptible, if illusory, feeling that one has somehow, unexpectedly, discovered a drop from the fountain of youth. Still, it was mildly dismaying that Mushan showed every sign of settling comfortably into the winged-back parlor chair. He meant to claim for the expense of his hiring out a coach a prolonged dispensation to speak, to ramble, to repeat, if necessary. "I wanted to ask you something," resumed Mushan, motioning now to a passing servant to request if he might have some warmed milk. "How does someone believe in nothing? I mean, what does it mean? Say *you* believe in nothing. I don't think it means anything at all."

"I wish my grandfather were here to speak with you. This was much more his sort of conversation."

"I remember old Methuselah. Now there was a man. Not that you're so bad yourself, Noe."

"Good of you, professor, but we both know I am a laughingstock. Not that I care for the opinions of men."

"And well you shouldn't. None of us should, but we do. You can hate the mob, think their judgment utterly worthless — I do — yet find yourself the object of the mob's disgust, there will be something visceral, perhaps it's organic, I don't know, but you'll feel it. Then your body and your will are at odds. That's how it is."

"There is some truth to what you say." Noe had decided he would not prod. The professor had something particular he wanted. He would come to it when he was ready. Mushan spoke then of his late wife and of several dons whom he had only recently read about in the paper. "It's my children, I've come to ask you about. I'd like to book passage for them, so to speak." He said this almost in an afterthought, as if he had been trying to draw Noe's attention elsewhere so that he might smuggle in the words.

"Of course, of course. But why not you yourself, as well? Your children would no doubt love for you to be with them."

Dr. Mushan shook his head. "No. No, thank you. I've had enough of them, you see. Perhaps they've had enough of me. I love them, though. Can't bear to think they shan't go on after me. It's funny. I can't remember how or when it happened, but everyone started acting as if there were nothing to believe. Gutless . . . and without charm. I retired then. It was no point exposing my children to them, when all they did was yawn or look for signs of humbug." The professor then laughed and raised himself with a grunt. He appeared mildly embarrassed and apologetic. "Forgive me. I've no one to tell these things to. I've told the man to leave them on your porch. I've selected the best of the library. They shall await your disposition as from the hand of fate. It was a dreadful thing, you see, to feel I had no one to give them to, and if you are right . . . "

———————

Ham was the first to see them, three men traveling through the northern range. These were steep and inhospitable mountains, rarely crossed and risky, even with a guide. Mountain goats often lost their step, plunged to their deaths. The little group spent the morning cutting through a path parallel to the ark, then veered sharply, turning south in a bold and difficult venture designed to take them within earshot of the keepers of the vessel. The rocky shelf ended where the ark had been built. It was the last true height for miles. As the travelers came closer, it became apparent that one man of early middle age commanded the others. He was tall, with long, dark hair tied back in a ceremonial knot. At the base of the northern side, he called up to the men of the ark. "I am Shastar," he shouted, "of Auramoosh. I am seeking the house of Noe."

Shastar was welcomed, along with his guides, strange, quiet men who spoke little, hid their faces in a wealth of turbans and scarves. They said not where they were from and seemed to communicate without words to the scion of Auramoosh. Shastar himself was wrapped in animal skins for the journey. Underneath these, he wore a simple, elegant tunic of white cambric. Ham stared at him as if he were a storybook hero come to life, for often had his mother spoken fondly of the exploits of her younger brother. A servant was dispatched to speak glad tidings to Priyanka. The son of Iradon was shown (one could not avoid it) the big boat. Three hundred cubits in length, fifty wide, thirty high, three stories — the entire hull formed of cypress and covered in pitch. Japheth wanted to conduct a thorough tour of the inside, but it was thought that could wait.

"A remarkable vessel," said Shastar, "but a little far from the sea."

⌇⌇⌇⌇⌇⌇⌇⌇⌇

The trek down the main ramp was a simple joy to Shastar after the hard path he had taken to reach them. He dismissed his guides at the base, informing Noe that they had business in the city. There were many questions. Mainly, Noe wondered why Shastar had chosen this time to announce himself and why he had chosen so dangerous a route.

Shastar laughed. "Was it dangerous? The Kai do not take notice of such things. We go where we must. It is a joy to be where we should be."

"The Kai?" Noe's brow furrowed. Where had he heard that before?

Shastar pointed to his top knot. "A symbol of my order. The Kai is both simple and difficult to explain. Where my master lives, all are Kai, but here . . . " he indicated with his arms the wide expanse of the land, "the Kai are yet few. Perhaps, even one." A mischievous smile animated his face, making him seem younger than his years.

"I would like to hear more of your master, and of the Kai," exclaimed Ham.

"If it is your path, you shall surely arrive," said Shastar, a riddle that left the son of might quiet the rest of the way, chewing on it.

At the gates, Priyanka stepped forth. It had been many years since she had last seen him. Letters few but warm had managed to keep alive their bond. When she set eyes upon Shastar, she could hardly believe it was the boy she carried in memory. So tall and changed, his very stride conveying authority. One could see that she bristled to run out like a girl, embrace her brother, but she deemed it meet to show the dignity of Noe's house by waiting.

He did not offer her a kiss of peace when they arrived but stretched out his arm and tagged her gently on the shoulder. "I've been waiting several hundred years to do that. You're it," he said.

She could see, naturally, that he was watching her the whole evening. Casually, in side-long glances that took in the whole room; surreptitiously, in quick peeks, trying to catch her off-guard, trying to discover how she really felt. In the morning, when Noe was at the build site, patrolling the decks or bent over some parchment covered with Japheth's impossible scribbles and calculations, Shastar would come by for their actual conversation. And then, what could she say? She didn't know, was afraid what might come out. How could she explain Noe's dream? It wasn't hers, after all. But now, now it was hardly worth the breath, the things they said. "This is good mead." "Yes, a fine house, where did you find that footman?" The real speech was in the clipped, stolen glances which asked, "How mad *is* your husband, spending so much wealth on a fantasia, that ship on the mountainside?" Shastar would understand about the animals. He had a strange way. Sometimes it seemed he knew what she was thinking before she knew her own mind. Very likely, he'd tell her all about it, how she felt. There was something uncanny and vaguely wicked, this peering into souls.

Noe was thinking, too. He noticed, for instance, that her brother always said, "your father" or "Iradon," never "our father," as if there were some difference in their patrimony. That was strange. It might explain why Auramoosh wanted the boy elsewhere, spoke stiffly and changed the subject, whenever Shastar was mentioned. Though, of course, it might be as simple as grief and chagrin that the boy lived while the mother did not. It was uncomfortable, too, that Iradon was not at table. They had all gotten so used to the boat, it was funny how a stranger, even if he were Priyanka's brother, made them all aware, the entire household down to the servants, how much their identity was now defined by the ark, how they were "the people of the ark." It made them considerate for each other, a vague tribalism protective against the misunderstanding of outsiders. And there was no doubt the Outsiders were hostile. They all thought Noe built on a mountain to rub their faces in it, to tell them how wicked they were, despised by God. They were wrong. It would have been easier to build in the valley. Less trouble to haul material, to gather workers, altogether easier. More practical, too, for the beasts. Noe built on the mountain because . . . because the ark was not just a floating warehouse, a cargo ship, some gigantic life raft. He could never explain it to them, when he could not explain it to himself.

It has to be high. It has to be near the stars. That's what he thought.

~~~~~~~~~

Shastar sat staring at his hands and at the curve of his tunic, noticing in a daze how the sleeve crossed high on the forearm, noting the dark line of demarcation between his skin and the snowy fabric. His head ached and a mild but increasing feeling of nausea afflicted him. His memory seemed faulty. He could not recollect the simplest things. Familiar words, the melody to a song he once knew, slipped into nothing, teasing in their elusiveness. Dotage must begin like this. Not that it mattered. Nothing mattered. Crossing the vertiginous mountains, he had not once been seized by perilous doubt, no matter the difficulty. He'd traipsed over the thin bridges of mountain arch, floated across gaps of icy void, humming. All the while, his guides made tiny grunts of pleasure and smiled at each other with winking, guilty aplomb. Their thoughts came to him like piped-in muzak. Everything they saw they turned into the banal phrasing of a mediocre travel book. Oppressive, chirpy lads, he was so glad to dismiss them.

He felt a great desire for sleep, for a long and endless sleep. Yet he also felt too tired or sick for sleep. He just wanted to be still. He imagined himself not flesh, but stone, a sinewy stone that would be still for centuries, so motionless that life would go on, flowing all about him, forgetting that he was ever anything but a peculiarly shaped rock. Moss would cling to him, birds nest in his finely carved hair. Young girls would play about him and confess the secrets of their loves into his stone-deaf ear. That was the power of Kai, the way it freed you from worry. Normally, it filled him with vivacity, giving him energy and lightness. Today, however, it was heavy. He wondered if there was any point to it and laughed a short, bitter cry.

"Shastar? You look so sad."

He glanced up into the warm, sweet eyes of Priyanka. It was consoling to see her, dear girl. She knew so little. A shame she had no daughters to echo the dance of her beauty. He patted his stomach. "Not sad, sister. A little indigestion. I have eaten too much."

At a turn in the road, across from the Inn of Five Peacocks, Ravi noticed the gathering crowd. He had with him Niri, the wife of Ham, and an old shepherd bringing a basket containing lunch for his son, who was guarding the ark. Instantly, he sensed danger in the insolent looks of the men. Ravi tried to distract Niri with a funny story. He wanted to hurry, but to do so without provoking the mob. Just a little way and they would be seen from the ark. Stout defenders would fly to them. But the garrulous old shepherd was slow and starting to feel the threat. He was coughing and holding the basket of food to his chest like a shield. This sign of fear enflamed the throng, who had plainly been waiting for them. Around a dozen men blocked the path, shuffling noisily with rough, yet still uncertain intent. Vulgar epithets and catcalls erupted from the shadows. Ravi waited, trying to calm by his impassivity the rising hysteria of his charges. A sharp little fist of a man, all hard surfaces and glaring eyes, stepped out from the crowd. "We object! The boys object!" he snarled and adjusted his hat, a worn bowler of brown felt that had acquired a green patina of powdery mold.

Ravi met the stare of the little man with a grim smile. "Why do you block our way, Jumbo?" he said. "You had a chance to be part of this. You chose to dismiss your team. Go your way then and let us go ours."

Jumbo wagged his finger at Ravi and smiled wide, revealing a mouthscape of jagged, uneven teeth. "You can't pull none of your tricks and secret handshakes on us. We know what's fair and what's not. Isn't that right, men?"

The assembled crowd gave a vigorous, if somewhat uncoordinated, shout of assent, punctuated by the sputtering enthusiasms of individuals keen to add their bit.

"That's right, Jumbo."

"You tell 'em, boss."

"What is it you want, then?"

Ravi spoke with a serenity that infuriated Jumbo. They had grievances. They felt ill-used, but it was not for them to decide properly exactly what would placate them. The men looked shyly upon one another. Some pawed the ground with a dirty boot, whilst others whistled and waited. Jumbo bit down on the stubby remains of a cheroot, rubbed his knobby hands together like a man about to throw the dice. "What do we want? What do we want?" he asked loudly, turning first to the crowd and then to Noe's man. "We want our rights, see? We're not asking for anything but what we've got coming to us."

"And what is it you have a right to?"

The skin under Jumbo's neck flushed bright red, his flesh quivered in indignation. "Why, we have a right to a decent wage, we have a right to labor in dignity, we have a right not to be mocked or told what to do when we are free men."

"Free men! Free men!" said the men. That was the sort of talk they liked.

"I'm sorry. I don't understand what it is you wish from us. No one here is denying you a fair wage or seeking to divest you of dignity."

Jumbo groaned, his wrathful face covered in blotchy purple tendrils pushing up from the scarlet of his neck. "He doesn't see. He doesn't see. He's a blind man," shouted Jumbo.

"A blind man! A blind man!" echoed like the murmur of the sea through the crowd.

"It's in the by-laws," continued Jumbo, in a markedly reasonable tone after allowing for an artful pause. "We started to work. It's our right to finish work."

"No one stopped you but yourselves," said Ravi, a note of genuine exasperation and confusion entering his voice.

"See, you hired us to work. Noe owes us the job. We got what is called a contract."

"You were hired to work on the ark. You quit. Then some of your men fired the ark. We are not going to ask you back to fix the damage you caused."

"According to the contract, you've got to take us back."

"Your covenant was broken by your acts of violence against the ark. Your men only want to destroy it."

"That's what is called 'political speech.' It's our right, because we're free men. All we want is some say in how things are. We want to say what's what, to follow out an idea, if it happens to be ours, without some mutt telling us not to."

"But the ark is not your idea."

"Who says? Maybe it is and maybe it isn't. Maybe we've got some improvements."

"You cannot improve what you do not understand."

Jumbo gawked apoplectically at Ravi. Who was this fella to tell him how power worked? Noe, give him his due, had a way with the abracadabra, but rational men knew when it was time to compromise, find consensus. The rows of men behind Jumbo meant that Jumbo had a seat at the table. Any damn fool could see that. A rumble of discontent emerged from the crowd. They sensed that the crucial moment had come. Even Jumbo was unsure how they would break, uncertain he could call them back if they decided to expel their razzled energy in sanguine mayhem. Just then, propitiously, Ham arrived, and Shastar with him. The two heroes looked with smooth coolness upon the crowd. Ham subtly flexed his arms. He was always ready to crack heads. Shastar met Jumbo's eyes. He approached him slowly, spoke softly.

"The hammer is mighty, the small brook humble, yet water wears down the mountain."

The little man shook with repressed anger. He tried to see if Shastar intended some obscure meaning or if he were trying to mock.

Priyanka's brother bent down, whispered a single word. "Wait."

Jumbo, by no means stupid, recognized an elegant courtesy in the new man. He sensed, though it made no sense, an ally. After allowing for a proper period of deliberative quiet, he rushed up to Ravi, gave him the full measure of his contemptuous gaze.

"You 'aven't heard the last of this," spat Jumbo. He turned about, moving his shoulders from side to side as proud as any cock-of-the-walk. "Let's go, boyohs. We've spit in his eye. Let the man think on that, if he will."

Obediently, they followed Jumbo, feeling content that they had expressed their cause with admirable lucidity. Congratulating themselves, they peeled off in jovial groups of twos and threes to imbibe a happy pint. There was nothing so noble as the fight for justice.

Awkwardly, Noe shipped the long bread and the bag of supplies he had brought with him to a far corner. It was the same girl who answered the door, but now her manner was completely different. She seemed timid and dismayed by his presence, while at the same time anxious that he should not feel unwanted.

"He is out, sketching," she said. "I don't know when he'll be back."

Noe stood before the paintings. Shem preferred to work slowly on canvas boards, meticulously composing, so that the majority of his work lay in a receptive, unfinished state. His lines were clear, nearly child-like. Noe meditated some quiet minutes before a painting of a night landscape. Beside it was the portrait of a wrestler marked out in bold black lines, and then fleshed in hues mainly red and brown. It reminded him of Ham.

"Everything he paints has a certain light, even in the darkness. You can't see this with the naked eye."

"No," said the girl, smiling. She seemed to warm to him then and stood at his shoulder looking at the paintings. "Why don't you tell him that?"

"I might, if I could ever find him."

"He is very busy," she answered in a soft voice, not meeting his eyes.

"You model for him?"

"Yes, sometimes. He paints mostly from memory. Would you like to see?"

Noe suddenly thought that she might innocently show him a nude of herself. He'd judged her sophisticated, but now saw that she had been pretending and was actually rather naive. In his haste to deflect her, he spoke bluntly the concern of his heart. "Why is he avoiding me? Does he think I want to take him away from all this?"

The girl just stopped as if shot through with an arrow. Her limbs fell limply at her sides and she appeared on the verge of a crying feast.

"Now, now," he said tenderly. "I'm not an ogre. I only want to understand, my dear."

And who knows what they would have said? Before she could answer, there was the crackling of parcels, the sound of fumbling at the door. The girl's face instantly paled. Shem entered, his glance taking in both his father and the girl.

"Out! Out!" he shouted in rage at Noe. "And you!" The girl flinched. "You get out, too!"

~~~~~~~~~

Ravi knocked at the door. He had gotten lost twice and had to retrace his steps through the narrowest of streets. Washing hung from every balcony. Children, old women and a seemingly infinite supply of feral cats appeared to occupy every step. Brick walls were festooned with the tattered remains of posters advertising boxing matches, a brand of green tea, and ladies' slippers claiming to be made of the Golden Fleece. He was not quite sure he had the correct house. Though Ravi was breaking no prohibition, he could not help feeling that he was somehow betraying his master by seeking this intimacy. Yet his love for Noe commanded it.

Shem answered, delighted to see him. Ravi had expected an atmosphere of anger and gloom. Instead, he found the girl happily mixing paints. Her exile had lasted at most perhaps a quarter of an hour before Shem had gone out to look for her. He'd discovered the girl hiding around the corner, sniffling like a child and trying to look brave. Ravi was non-plussed. How could Shem speak to him with such genial openness, when only the other day he had thrown his own father from the dilapidated house? Noe, of course, had told him little. Ravi guessed it all. Delicately, so as not to spoil the mood, he gently remonstrated with Shem and the boy disposed of it in the ellipsis of a breath, as if the subject were a triviality hardly recalled.

"Oh, that. It doesn't matter."

"Your father was very hurt."

"I didn't want him in the studio, that's all. I don't like anyone to see it when all my work is a mess just coming into birth. If I'd known he was coming, I'd have seen to the place properly."

Ravi looked about sceptically. Too neat — and hardly practicable. The riot of canvas and paint might be a decade in concluding and then it would be a fraction that might satisfy Shem. He'd have started countless more work in the meantime. Something else was behind it.

Shem paused, weighing in his mind, whether to share his suspicions. Then he beckoned Ravi to the window, sweeping back the thin muslin curtains.

"Do you see them, Pook?"

Ravi followed the gaze of Shem. Two young men of graceful demeanor, lithe and calm, stood as living statues, seeming to hold in their purview the entirety of Shem's street.

Ravi nodded. "I have seen them, or two very like them." He did not want to say that they were Shastar's guides.

The eldest son allowed the curtain to fall back and cleared a space on a decrepit couch for Ravi to sit upon. "I didn't understand them, those beautiful boys. I saw them first in the law courts. I go there sometimes. The other artists, they are always interested in the criminal, but I go to look at the judges." Shem pulled out a canvas from a stack of unfinished works. Three judges were depicted, bulbous nosed, the flame red of their robes sheathed in shadows that seemed to emanate from the gray and black stones of the background. The faces were at once stern, venal, arrogant, and miserable.

"I do not recognize these men," said Ravi. The picture had a strange effect on him. It seemed he was looking at a cynical, wrathful caricature, yet pity was evoked in him. "Why are they so grim? It's almost as if the judge is the criminal."

"I grant you, they are not likenesses anyone would recognize. They are more my idea of judges than a physical portrait. It seemed to me a gruesome burden to make oneself a judge of other men. Justice has a terrible grandeur about it. One can't help but seem a little pompous when one takes the scales in one's hands. These judges know that, know the depth of sickness in their own hearts, and it is that knowledge that afflicts them, though many hide from the truth."

"Is that what you think of your father? That he is judging men?"

Shem's visage was closed. He would not answer. He asked, instead, about Noe's great work, though in a voice sincere and betraying no irony. "How is the ark, Pook? Has the damage been repaired?"

~~~~~~~~~~

Ravi noticed them everywhere: in the markets, the theater, hovering unctuously nearby-standers in the park. It was remarkable that he had heeded them so little. There was something about their flesh that was not quite right. It was too pink and fresh like a doll's plastic sheen, as if their sparkling skin had just bounced off the assembly line in a sheet. They smiled, a beautiful, white smile of perfectly polished teeth, presenting a face — a little stiff, it was true, yet a face assiduous, agreeable, ready to help.

The funny thing was how Ravi could never quite determine what they were saying. He'd try carefully and unobtrusively to sneak up on their conversations. Sometimes he would be rewarded with the least snippet. Something like "We at Womble and Doubt would be pleased to represent you. You are quite within your rights." Or, "If you would look at the matter along these lines, your idea should be acceptable. Indeed, it would turn out brilliantly." Yet he was never able to parse any clear and substantial meaning from their talk. On every occasion, the speech would quickly fade into silence. The indomitable pink faces of the beautiful boys would continue to smile and the subject of their address would nod, politely or eagerly, as if the conversation had not halted in the least, but Ravi could no longer hear them. More precisely, he heard not silence, but a hushed, unpleasant buzzing noise.

Once, he tried directly to interfere. A pair of boys was subtly pushing old Mr. Baur, moving him along the boulevard towards an apothecary shop, to what end Ravi could not guess. "Hey, hey, stop!" he had commanded and Mr. Baur had looked at him with fear and confusion. The representatives of Womble and Doubt were nowhere to be seen. Ravi felt a chill run through his body, made up some excuse, any excuse — Mr. Baur would tell his wife that night that Noe's head man had taken to drink. For a brief moment afterwards, Ravi considered whether he was beginning to lose his faculties. It was unbelievable that the mysterious pair should so completely vanish. He did not panic, however. He was a sensible man. And the firm of Womble and Doubt, that was something he was familiar with. Their letterhead had been arriving for months, threatening to sue Noe, telling him to cease and desist his building project on the mountain: the ark was a defacement of public property (non-sense, as Noe held the deed to the lands), the ark was a crime of hate speech, the ark was an illicit intrusion of private morality into the public realm. The epistles always concluded with murky, vague promises of further action. Ravi had been using the letters to line the cage of his canary.

~~~~~~~~~~

Shastar was, at first, a most considerate house guest. Genial to his hosts, kind to the help, he seemed never to forget a name, not even that of the lowliest servant. Moreover, he was full of travel stories of strange sights, some too great for credulity, though possessed of the charm of the nakedly fantastic. Ham liked him best of all. They wrestled in the early mornings, conversed of throws and holds. Nothing esoteric crossed Shastar's lips when he talked with Noe's giant son. As time passed, however, Shastar's demeanor altered. He spent hours alone in his room, brooding silently at windows. Then he grew restless. Sometimes he sought uninhabited places; at other times, he would roam ceaselessly over the plains of men, racing with a pace that amazed his fellows and invited no intrusive party into the solitude of his mind. He became, not precisely rude to the servants, but flip. An irreverent gleam entered his eyes when he bantered with them. Gone was the graceful condescension that had marked his earlier, friendly relations. Instead, he seemed to look upon them as if they unknowingly sported a splash of food upon their chins. With Priyanka and the family of Noe, he was reserved, though courteous. The withdrawal of his affections stunned them all, but Priyanka most, for she felt responsible for him, loved him, and from the start, had nursed, guiltily, a secret misgiving.

One morning, he awoke to find her holding him in her eyes — not a look devoid of care, but wary, unsure of him.

"Do you always sleep on the floor?" she asked. "There's a perfectly good bed. It's a wonder Katya hasn't said anything."

Shastar smiled. "I mess the bed up before I go out. Wouldn't do to have the servants whispering." He saw the ice in her begin to melt. It was best that the mild chill between them remain. "I'm thinking of taking rooms in the town," he said.

"Why? There's no need." She was struggling to understand him. "No need," she repeated. "Stay with us. You are welcome, brother. And what would Ham do? All my sons are so different. I think you're the brother he's always wanted."

"I, too, am pleased for his friendship, Priyanka, but I cannot stay. I must keep moving."

He appeared, just then, like a hunted animal. Priyanka's heart swelled. "Is it Iradon?" she asked, her voice suddenly tipped with wrath. "Papa has no say in this house. You know that, Shastar."

"My dear big sister, do not worry on that account. I never think of him."

"What then? What is it? Is it the Kai?"

Her brother seemed surprised. "The Kai?" he asked, as if he himself had never heard the word. She followed Shastar as he slowly walked to the front of the house. He observed quietly a goose girl scolding her charges, leaned back and watched the clouds silently drift. "Some Kai is in nature," he said gently. "But the true Kai, Priyanka, is free of this world. For the Kai, everything is free and everything is permitted."

Priyanka smiled and waved her hand in the air. "It sounds very obscure," she said. Then, thinking a bit more on his words, she frowned. "That sounds . . . wrong, Shastar."

"Yes. It is not a teaching for the necrophori — the corpse-bearers, we call them."

"What a loathsome name. Who are they?"

And he almost told her, but instead he said, "I think I see Ham. I was going to show him a grappling technique I picked up in a region where it is day for half the year. The folk call it the season of the midnight sun."

———

It was decided that Noe's care for his guest should not end so easily. Shastar was offered a remote fishing cabin to stay in. Lamech had once made use of it, but now was gouty and near the end of his days. It was far from the city. They had noticed that the heir of Auramoosh had both fascination and aversion for the closely packed spaces of city dwellings. The strange combination of deteriorating amity and persistent good will precluded a festive departure. It was on a cold night in early autumn. Shastar stood on the covered porch of Noe's farm house, a good, sturdy structure. He briefly embraced Priyanka and then shook Noe's hand with a brisk, perfunctory formality, whilst a ruddy faced old man, still spry and dressed in sheepskin, stood off to the side and waited. He was an ancient retainer from Lamech's youthful days who had pledged to take the brother of young master Noe's wife to the promised retreat.

––––––––––

Ravi entered the hotel. It was fusty with old, oversized furniture, dark woods, and chandeliers that happened to have been requisitioned from a failed opera house. Shem, he surmised, was drawn to such places where no one knew or cared whose son he was. The business was run by a matron known as Mrs. Biddle, who habitually called everyone "Charlie" or "Nadab." He disregarded the breezy salutation of the proprietress and hastily approached Shem.

"Shem, a word. It might be important."

A tinny piano regaled them with undaunted, persistent gaiety. The patrons were dancing and drinking, trying to make up for lack of wit with boisterous volubility. There was a calm, unembarrassed grace to Noe's son that surprised Ravi. With mild concern, Shem directed him to an alcove.

"Peace, Pook. What is it?"

"Those Watchers — you said you did not at first understand them. Does that mean you do now?"

Shem shrugged. "I'm not sure you'd call it understanding. They're pretty, the way an advertisement is attractive, a shallow and manufactured gloss. They're happy the way the subjects of my paintings never could be."

Ravi mused that Shem had a strange kind of reverence for the revelers amongst whom he associated. Shem watched them as an artist contemplates his object, yet he listened with equal care, trying to discern a luminous spark beneath the smoke of their petty designs.

"Shem, I don't know how to say this—your paintings grip one, but they are not pleasant. Is the spiritual truth necessarily ugly?"

Shem laughed. "That's just it, Pook. I know what you mean, of course, but I don't think they *are* ugly. Or, if you prefer, I see in that ugliness a beautiful misery. My subjects are unhappy, because the soul is present, wishing and hoping for some impossible fulfillment, we cannot tell what. The glory of humanity is its unhappiness."

"But the beautiful boys . . . "

"Are not unhappy. They are serene and perfectly content. Everything they could possibly want is right here. If they can't buy it, they mine it, steal it, make it from miscellaneous parts at hand."

A fearful thought palpitated along the nerves of Ravi's arms. "You're not suggesting?" he said, preferring to leave the thought unfinished.

"Why, of course I am. It's the inaccuracy of bad art that offends." Shem gestured widely at the inebriate, dissolute guests of Mrs. Biddle. "Every last Tom and Sally crying in their cups, greedily gulping at illusions of life, every one of them carries more splendor than those cheap knock-offs."

A dawning realization, with a force and depth he had not deemed himself capable, gripped Ravi. Unconsciously, he brought his fist to his mouth, covered his lips from speaking thought into unguarded space.

~~~~~~~~

Deep lament entered into the early morning of Noe's house. The gatekeeper had espied something perplexing in the dusky light, an unnatural darkness in a nearby tree. He sent his son to look. The boy returned, his legs trembling. Noe's chief steward was hanging from the tree. The house was rustled from sleep. Noe ran, a slight robe wrapped around his bare shoulders, to the awful place. An orange stocking had been stuffed down Ravi's throat so that he gave the macabre appearance of having a large, lolling dragon tongue. There was a quality of perversity about it that unnerved Noe beyond his rage. The entire tableaux, disgusting, was oddly familiar.

Now Noe's heart was filled with vengeance. His thoughts were far from the ark. He wished only to crush the bones of his enemies. Noe gathered together his stout men, sent them questioning in the cities of the plain and throughout the countryside, to see who had killed his friend. Some said Jumbo, remembering his threats, and others named bandits or neighbors they did not like. One man, however, said another name. A mason, surly and wishing to be left alone, confessed that he had noticed Ravi in the gloaming of an evening arguing fiercely with a hulking fellow.

The scout promised the mason payment in silver coin if he would come to the house of Noe, tell what he had seen. When the amount was doubled, the mason came. He gawked at the great house, but when his turn came for speech, the mason grew voluble offering unmistakable details. The athlete, that was what he called Ravi's foe, was distinguished by a top-knot.

Noe's face grew grave. He tore his cloak, summoned his sons. Then Noe swore them to silence. Nothing was to be said to Priyanka. He took his shepherd, Yasha, and rode up into the hill country. He nearly ruined his horse, pushing towards the cabin where Lamech had fished. Yasha fell behind, dared not gallop his mount, a poor gelding so mild the children of the estate rode him on birthday celebrations. When Yasha caught up to his master, he found him sitting on the porch of the cabin, smoking his pipe. The cabin was empty. It seemed it had been for a long time.

~~~~~~~~~~

Besides Noe, three great men resided in the land. There was Auramoosh, whom Methuselah had helped, and Jared, whose men mined ore in the land of Nod, forging iron and bronze. The third was Isidore, who traced his lineage through the Nephilim. These were the princes whose wealth was outside the city. When Yasha returned the next day to Noe's house, he looked worried, stumbled over his lines. He told Japeth and Ham of the vacant cabin, said Noe had gone to speak alone with Iradon. In the afternoon, Noe came to his sons. Shem, too, had joined himself to the party, looking grim and shaken. Iradon claimed to know nothing of Shastar. Auramoosh desired ignorance to continue. Moreover, Noe was not welcome. Despite their differences, the ingratitude of the prince shocked Noe. He spoke harsh words, declared his grandfather's peace broken by Iradon's ill will.

Before Noe had time to wash the dust from his feet, Priyanka flew at him. You cannot keep such things secret for long, not when a woman's intuition and fear are involved. She felt flushed and uncomprehending. It could not be true. She asked fearfully after her brother, cried to heaven when he was accused.

"I will talk to him first, be sure of that," said Noe and his face seemed set in stone.

Then Niri comforted Priyanka as daughter to her mother. She led her wailing to her rooms. Noe rode with his sons, first to Jared. He requested men and riders to seek out the killer of his man. Jared answered that he could spare no men. Business was booming. His smithies were hard-pressed to keep up with demand. Why, just the other day, Maxwell, a grocer, had requested a dozen brass lamps for his new store. Jared offered to sell Noe a security fence of ironworks at a discount. Isidore was worse. He smirked at the house of Noe. "Let Noe search within his great boat, perhaps his quarry was hiding there."

Noe searched the ark, just in case. He asked the birds of the air to watch for his prey, the beasts to report any fugitive stranger in the woods. Everywhere in the land, Shastar was sought, but he was not to be found.

~~~~~~~~~~~

That was just the beginning. Noe discovered sheep missing from his flocks. Doves, their necks wrung, were thrown bloodied at his feet from dark windows in the city. His womenfolk were mocked in the markets. They went nowhere without an escort. The shepherds began to desert him, the hired men first, then servants whose families had been part of the clan for generations. One would look for them and simply find them gone. Cisterns were filled with muck, the irrigation canals broken with pick and axe. Only Noe's great wealth, his land, sustained them, allowed them to bear ostracism. Lamech died, went to sleep with his fathers. None of the great men came to praise him, to share sorrow. Few of the many widows, the poor to whom Lamech had been merciful, shed tears at his grave. The sons of Noe gave their handful of dust. Grimly, they marveled that life had come to seem so bleak that one might envy the dead.

Then one day, Shem arrived at the gates with Sholon. He drove a cart stacked with what they had been able to grab up from the studio — boxes of paint and brushes and all manner of painting. Shem had propped up — whether it was an accident, it was impossible to say — the portrait of a green-haired girl so that it seemed to ride behind them, a third person. The likeness was good, the face sketched in pale orchid, pearl gray, and shadows of burnt umber mixed with blue; a melancholic, mournful face, reflective and astute.

"It isn't safe. We had to come," he said.

Sholon said nothing. She clung pitifully to Shem's side, peering up at them periodically from out of shy, downcast eyes.

CHAPTER FOUR

The Animal Conclave

MIZZIKIN WAS A BARN CAT. HE had yellow eyes and a coat of brown brindle fur interspersed with patches of white. His favorite activity was sleeping. Next, he liked to chase mice and stretch in the sun. He also liked to roll and scratch and put the fright in the other toms. He was the very devil of a cat.

"But Mizzikin is a sweet cat, a misunderstood cat. Oh, poor Mizzikin, no one to rub his head and tell him sugared nothings." This was what Mizzikin said to himself when the milk maid was milking. It gave him the proper sorrowful expression, so that the girl would squirt him. He'd catch the stream of milk in his mouth, lick the warm sop from his face, think himself an amazingly handsome fellow. Next to the milk maid, Mizzikin's best friends on the farm were Hildegard the goose and Fergus, a pig of brilliance. Fergus lived in constant fear that the Two Legs would turn him into bacon before he would be able to complete his work on the therapeutic effects of mud on the skin.

"Mizzikin," said Fergus, "I am in a terrible funk."

"It's not apples again, is it?"

"Oh, sour, crab, candied, that pig thinks upon them all," observed Hildegard. "He wouldn't be happy if he wasn't stuck in a gloom." Hildegard's manner of teasing pleased the cat. Mizzikin wished his wives had half her wit.

"There is nothing duller than a stupid wife," he said.

"You greatly exaggerate the apples," answered Fergus, sounding hurt and sad. "Anyway, nobody's going to stick *you* on a spit with an apple in your mouth."

"I think, perhaps, you've lost some weight, Fergus," yawned the cat.

"You think?" Fergus brightened. "It's this black mud, shrinks pores and thins the flesh." Yet the pig immediately resumed his melancholy sighing. "There might be another reason." "Oh, for goodness sake, what is it?" erupted the goose. She was not a patient fowl.

"Have you not noticed that the Two Legs are unlike themselves? Fewer and fewer walk about, bring to us our feed. Something is amiss."

"You don't suppose the milk maid is thinking of leaving?" asked Mizzikin, for the first time concerned.

"And that's not all," continued the pig, who was so used to the cat's vanity, he passed right over Mizzikin's narrow fear. "Hasn't anyone else noticed the tolling bell?"

"Oh, one can dream or imagine nearly anything," said the goose, her disdain betrayed by a slight quiver in the voice, for it was undeniable that at least once a day, a deep, slow, ominous song, the peeling as of a bell at the center of the world echoed across the farm. Then the dogs would run in circles, birds would nervously take to the air, a general cacophony of bleats and mews and brays would witness to unease in the beasts. Yet never did the Two Legs remark the bell. They merely looked with puzzled, fearful expressions upon the restive beasts.

"What do you think it means, then, Fergus?" asked the cat, who began to rapidly lick his paw, a nervous habit.

"Perhaps it is the thing called 'tiger,'" said Hildegard. There had been stories told in the nearby farms of a big cat unlike anything that had ever been beheld, a ferocious feline striped incarnadine and sable come out of the forest, prowling.

At this, Mizzikin scoffed. "I do not believe there is such a creature. You have made it up to have a laugh on Mizzikin," said Mizzikin. *Yes, Mizzikin is an eloquent rascal. Just look at them.* Indeed, Fergus and Hildegard were suddenly staring at him so peculiarly. An electric thrill sparked through him. He arched his back and turned.

"Greetings," said Rhumirrah. "I'm awfully glad to see you."

~~~~~~~~~~

It had taken Rhumirrah much longer than she had expected to discover the lands of Noe. She had traveled far into thick woodlands in order to avoid the man-covered plains, approached carefully the country roads, the planted fields, the lonely, tin-roofed farm houses. At each new farm, she learned more of the Two Legs and the curious ways of their beasts, who neither hunted, nor sought to escape a refuge that must end in their eventual doom. The Two Legs, themselves, she did her best to avoid. What she saw of them was unlike the studied and unadorned subjects in Harold's book. The Two Legs were strange beasts, indeed — vulnerable, slow, without natural weapons or beautiful displays. They were altogether rather disappointing, truth be told. It was a most perplexing world. She believed with unswerving faith, however, that her confusions would be healed, if only she could enter into the kingdom of Noe. Thus, she was initially disconcerted when Noe's beasts were ostensibly no different from all the other beasts she had met in the places called farm. There was the usual alarm, the fluttering chickens and geese, the hysteria of the horses, dogs barking, everything. They were only too relieved to determine that the tiger had no immediate intentions of eating them.

Fergus Pig, it is true, showed an unusual valor, though somewhat fixated on mud. The hog dispensed quickly with surprise. The novelty of Rhumirrah's appearance briefly eclipsed his tragic meditations. While the rest gave her a wide birth, the pig kept asking the tiger about the kinds and quality of clays and soft wet earth available in the jungle.

"Why, I haven't thought about it," she confessed.

"But you should, you should," urged Fergus. "It is the conjoining of elements, the marriage of earth and water, the principles of foundation and motion."

Rhumirrah reflected that Harold and Fergus must be spiritually linked. She knew this because their way of talking made her feel as if she might prefer to take on a herd of charging elephants rather than continue to try and follow the thread of the argument. Perhaps they will form some sort of club, she thought. Unfortunately, the orang was in the jungle, possibly composing an ode to his red-haired girl. Unable to placate the mud enthusiast, Rhumirrah shook her head and offered a hasty suggestion. "You'd better ask the water horses," she said, but the pig was utterly ignorant of hippos.

After this, there was a certain amount of staring and some imperfect attempts at introduction. Mizzikin, struggling with his courage, asked in his deepest voice for her name. Now this was the usual thing. At last, these rustic animals had said something sensible. The tiger began in the conventional high tone, for the breed cannot escape a certain hereditary arrogance. "I am Rhumirrah, daughter of Bali and Nyssa. The sire of Bali was Dimenor, who slayed the elephant king, Bantra. Prahnhar was sire of Dimenor. Fingold, who drowned in the river Sith, was sire of Pranhar. Dandenor was sire of Fingold, and there are many more I could speak of, but that is enough for beasts such as you."

Noe's animals were abashed by this performance and Rhumirrah began to regret her pride. The tigress made an effort to speak of her mission, trying to get them to understand about Orianna. As she did not quite understand herself, the speech was vague and not to her liking. Still, she expected that here, at least, she might find a ready audience. Yet the beasts seemed confused and uncertain. Even when she asked them what they thought about the mysterious tolling of the bell, they could only yammer like frightened cubs. A beast, standing apart from the others, seemed to comprehend her, but he kept his peace. This noble creature was Manwise, a pure white bull with dark, limpid pools for eyes. Instead, the chickens began to dance about her feet and to tell her little strands of trivia about egg laying, such as the effect of the tides on brood times and how the close proximity of a silver spoon will yield a vigorous chick.

"I think," she said, "it would be best if some kind beast would show me the way that I may speak with Noe."

The suggestion seemed to calm them and galvanize the farm into action. The animals led her *en masse* to Noe's garden. They made an interesting carnival, the fowl and the horses, the dogs and the oxen, not to mention the trudging pigs and the excited cats. Already, the latter were claiming Rhumirrah for themselves. See, their high tails seemed to say, see what we are! Only Mizzikin was slightly unwilling to be relegated to a lesser role. The rough procession passed through a line of linden trees, came to a brief halt beside a bed of naked rose bushes, then stopped at the threshold of a corridor of green that led to a low stone seat set beneath a canopy of canvas and elder wood. Then there was a change, so sudden. Here was the difference in Noe's beasts. Stately they became, gentling themselves, and quiet. A hound strode forward, his head erect, his steady footfall never departing from the straight path to the stone seat. This was Kiron, a direct descendent of Bashir; he was the herald.

A little maid saw him. She went to pat his head, then her hand jumped at the sight of the sum of beasts and the tiger in their midst. She ran, frightened and crying. At the noise of her distress, a fellow with broad shoulders and a grizzled beard appeared. Kiron approached the man.

"There is someone, my lord," he said.

~~~~~~~~

Rhumirrah felt shy and fearful, even as her paws strode, apparently of their own accord, confidently towards the man who sat waiting in silence for her. She tried to look ahead, to gauge from his face what sort of Two Legs he was. Noe's visage was grave, but also benevolent. As Rhumirrah came closer to him, she saw that he was no longer young. He stood in a regal silence imbued with a veil of darkness, as if his very bones groaned. And yet, did she imagine it? Noe appeared to light up as he watched her, his countenance filling with the delight of a child enchanted by some wonderful new discovery. Closer still and the eyes of the hero conveyed sterner stuff. He measured her seemingly to the marrow, carrying in his wisdom a secret word unguessed by the tiger. She might have blushed but did not. She felt as if for the first time she had declared herself.

"Yes, yes. So, this is the tiger! I have waited for you," said Noe.

Splendorous light shone out now from his brow, a crown of light.

"Rhumirrah, your servant," she said. It was strange. She did not feel ignoble to say those words. Rather, somehow, she had been enlarged.

"Rhumirrah," said Noe, "a beautiful name."

Then he was silent and withdrew his gaze inward. When he spoke, it was as much to himself as to the tiger. "There was a time when the beasts of the forest were as known to me as these, mine own, the four-footed and the feathered of the field and farm. Even the fish of the stream would leap out from the water, have a word, mid-air, before returning to the life-giving path. But now, it is as if the beasts no longer recognize a friend in my face. They do not come, even as the bell of doom rings out from the heart of the earth."

"You hear it then? You know?"

"I hear it."

"What does it mean?"

Noe leaned upon the staff of ironwood, reserved from the days of his youth. "A year ago, I could have told you. I was sure I knew. Now I am not so sure."

Rhumirrah was astonished. "I really think you should know," she blurted. "Or shouldn't you?"

Noe shrugged. He may even have sighed. This was not what Rhumirrah expected in a hero. But when he looked into her eyes, she forgave all, there was such tenderness. "Rhumirrah, do you know what a . . . Two Legs is?"

Now this was a bit much. She was only a young tigress, after all. She hadn't expected to be quizzed. Fortunately, it was only a rhetorical question, though Rhumirrah began to think there might be another fella for Harold and Fergus's club.

"I think we are a frontier. We touch on many worlds but have forgotten all about it."

Rhumirrah growled just a little. "I'm not really a library kind of girl, you see."

Then Noe laughed and she glimpsed again the child in his eyes, but only for a moment. The dark veil returned. "I recently lost someone very dear to me, tiger. I am angry and sad most of the time, and I suspect I see and understand less because of it."

Rhumirrah thought of heroes as basically warriors, that is to say, as excellent tigers. She was confounded to discover that Noe spent a lot of time thinking and frankly admitted not knowing all the answers. "But something, surely, must be done," she cried in exasperation.

Noe wanted to tell her that stillness was the most profound and difficult action, but he knew enough about women to see that would be a wrong turn. He would have to give her something to do. "Quickly, Rhumirrah. You must go to Tâkan Mishpât, the place of meeting. One of my loyal beasts shall show you the way. Speak to the good creatures. Tell them the moment is now for them to come to the ark."

It seemed, however, that this was even worse than stillness. Rhumirrah shook her pretty head. "My lord, a tiger is for action and not for speech. Honestly, if you only knew. I'm always being crossed or laughed at, especially when it's important — which it always is — but what's a girl to do?" She gave a broad hint that Noe ought to command them himself. "Really, you better get some talky fella." It seemed clear enough, but apparently men were simply obtuse, even heroes.

"The Mystery shall guide your path. Ask, if you wish, my hound, Kiron, or some other, to share your mission."

~~~~~~~~~~

"I am to go to a place of meeting. Do you know it?"

The hound nodded quietly and matched Rhumirrah's steps.

"I am to go and ask the beasts to come to the ark. How is it they will know to be there to listen to my words?"

"The birds of the air shall precede your steps. Do not fear, they shall await you."

Rhumirrah glanced shyly at Kiron. "I am afraid I cannot speak so well. It's one thing with friends, but this is different. You do see that, don't you, or don't you?"

Kiron gave her a long-suffering look and his tail drooped. "Begging your pardon, but the wilds are full of barbarians. I fulfill my duties to the master, but his affection for savages has always seemed to me a regrettable weakness."

Rhumirrah was shocked and hurt. "You do not wish to help?"

"I will go. I have always done my duty."

Duty was a big word for tigers. Rhumirrah could not help but respect it, but she had grown to hate it and find fault with it. It was an old complaint that she had wore out poor Harold in the telling. "But what is obedience without love?" she lamented. "You cannot love us as you do not care for us in the least."

Kiron hung his head. "I am ashamed at your words. Of course, there are exceptions. You yourself . . . "

The dog was evidently ambivalent, reluctant to overcome the dilemma of his abiding distaste for the wild beasts and his grudging admiration for the tiger. "I thank you, herald of Noe," said Rhumirrah, seeking to put an end to his anguish, at which she could not help being offended. "I shall try to find a subject more willing in spirit to save his fellows from a painful end, even if they are uncivilized."

"I do not, of course, wish them harm," sniffed the hound.

"I will tell you something," said Rhumirrah, her anger flaring. "I have often heard it said, but never before now have I understood so clearly, that it is not hate, but indifference that is the opposite of love. Your concern could hardly be colder or more ineffective. Do you truly think you would be able to say anything that would matter?"

"I should tell them that Noe has never failed them; and that they are fools if they do not hearken to his generous kindness."

"Yes, you should speak honestly to them, Kiron. I see that. But they would feel your contempt and they would refuse you, if only to assuage their pride. You might be surprised to find that the wilds, too, have their own notions and that barbarians have sensibility as well. Some might even think it odd and slavish to kneel and lick the toes of men."

"Very well," said the herald, and he departed from her with a wan smile, for the tiger in dudgeon was not the pauper with words that she proclaimed.

~~~~~~~~

Rhumirrah glanced about her, pathetically searching for some beast capable of rescuing her mission from an ignominious end. She had thought Noe would solve all her problems and now it seemed he had met with her only to throw them all back. The hound had seemed the natural choice. The great hero himself had suggested his herald. Was it simply her pride that had determined her against Kiron? No, she was certain her intuition was correct, but it left her in a quandary. She had not enough acquaintance with tame creatures to discern a proper candidate and no time to remedy her ignorance. In desperation, she turned to the beasts that chance had first shown her in Noe's land. Three loping strides took her to the spot occupied by the mud specialist. She confronted Fergus the pig, requested that he join her in a quest to bring the wild ones under Noe's protection. Fergus began to shiver and his eyes narrowed so that he looked at her like a child feigning sleep.

"Ah, it is not a simple thing you ask," squealed Fergus in a high-pitched tone that barely graduated above a whisper.

"Why not? You're smart, aren't you? Everyone says you are an extraordinary pig."

At this, Fergus lifted his chin, forgetting for the moment that the tiger must have scant acquaintance, let alone possession of the hearsay of "everyone." His little corkscrew tail wagged in spite of himself.

"Well, I don't know," he said.

"I'm sure you could do it if you tried," purred Rhumirrah in her softest, sultriest voice. "The beasts would be sure to come if you explained everything to them."

Thoughts of heroic deeds briefly tantalized the pig. He was nearly overcome by the allure of the prodding Cleopatra. Quickly, however, sadness gained possession of him. He pondered the shadow of his girth, the sturdy line of his stubby legs. "No, no, it won't work," he said with certitude. "I'm portly."

"Oh, portly!" piped Mizzikin, who had been stealthily listening. The cat rolled with glee. The charm of the word tickled him to the tips of his whiskers.

"You are a very ill-mannered tom," scolded Hildegard, forgetting that she was eavesdropping too.

"You see what I mean," said Fergus. "A short, dumpy creature cannot command an audience. It's psychology. A tall beast has an undoubted advantage in the world."

"I'm sure that is not always so," commiserated Rhumirrah. "You're forgetting about charisma. A confident pig is a tall pig."

"You're a dear lass," answered Fergus, sounding ever more morose, "but no matter what they say, size matters."

"Don't waste your breath, miss," advised the goose. "Once that pig makes up his mind, a hundred elephants couldn't budge him. That's one stubborn pig, our Fergus."

"Besides," said Mizzikin, "there's only one beast here you need talk to. He's right over there, by the yew tree. Look. He even seems to be waiting for you."

Rhumirrah followed the direction of the tomcat until her eyes met the solemn gaze of Manwise, the bull, his milky skin softly luminescent, as if a lunar cast had sprinkled moon dust upon his flesh. The tiger approached him in silence and Manwise was not quick to break it. There was winsome courtesy in their mutual restraint that was neither uncomfortable, nor capable of being hurried. At length, the bull lowed at her, his breath sweet with the fragrance of clover.

"Do you like ducks?" he said.

"Ducks? Well, I can't say I've had the occasion. Now mutton I could tell you something about."

Manwise did not answer but chewed with slow patience on his cud. Rhumirrah understood then that the question had not intended cuisine. "Of course, I'm sure ducks are very companionable," she offered, blushing slightly and wondering how she might steer the conversation onto more pressing concerns.

"There's a pond on the edge of one of Noe's pastures," said Manwise. "Every spring, there are ducks and soon enough, ducklings."

"Yes, I believe . . . I like flowers," Rhumirrah suddenly offered for no clear reason.

"That is a funny thing to believe. Either one does or does not like flowers. I like ducks, for instance. The way the little ducklings line up behind their mother and how the mother grows imperious with every Two Legs and every Four Legs, commanding her troop through each impediment. I especially like the softness that strikes hard and busy men. How they stop to contemplate the mother duck and her young and a smile lost since the days of their own boyhood comes over their faces all unknowing."

"That's very cry-making, I must say," admitted the tiger. "Only, I didn't mean I believe — about the flowers, that is. I was believing about the ducks and the little peeps. There aren't many ducks where I come from. It just made me think of flowers. I can't say why."

"You are an Outlander," declared Manwise. "And I have never been further than the boundary between the south pastures and the old Lyons farm. What kinds of flowers do you prefer?"

"All sorts, really. Roses and lilies, daisies and irises. I don't know where it comes from. Tigers are not generally committed to floral interests."

"The Outlands, I suppose, have many beasts."

Manwise did not pose his statement as a question. He seemed, indeed, to be speaking more to himself than to Rhumirrah. Because of this, she found herself non-plussed, a feeling that always left her dizzy and vaguely nauseous.

"I have always considered the ivory petals of the horse chestnut a most pleasing flower," continued the bull. "The orchid and the cranesbill are also lovely, though perhaps you do not like purple."

"Purple is fine," answered Rhumirrah, feeling dizzier and faintly uneasy, because she had a sense that they would never come to the subject of urgency neatly. She was about to violently shift the conversation at the expense of nice manners, but just then, without her even broaching the matter of Tàkan Mishpât, without any change in his steady, calm diction, Manwise was speaking to her heart.

"From the time I was a little calf, I have always walked with Noe. At his hands, I have taken nourishment. His words have guided me into green pastures. To the shepherds and field hands, he speaks for me. It is right that I should speak for him."

Now Tàkan Mishpât had been the place of judgment longer than any beast could recall. Some primordial event had left it scorched and foreboding. The beasts could not say what had happened. Legend proclaimed that an invisible flame had seared the earth in the time before there were beasts. Hence, the meeting ground held a quality of dread, its dark steps, its hidden decline — it was shaped like a low cauldron surrounded by ancient, gnarled trees. A summoning was a rare occurrence. Only a high charge of treason, a deliberation of justice affecting all beasts, could ordinarily bring the creatures of the woods to its solemn precincts. So it was with misgiving that Dolmir, a young buck, was drafted to lead Rhumirrah and the bull to be heard by summoned beasts. The deer stood before Noe. "It is a three days journey," he said. "I cannot move quickly with the bull." Dolmir kept glancing back nervously at the tiger. He did not trust the carnivore but considered that the bull was slower and a greater feast. He would rely on his swift feet if the matter became chancy. The small party left in the cool of the morning. The dove-gray sky was cold and heavy with a brooding, sleepy unhappiness. Noe's animals gathered to see them off. Now that they were leaving, a collective sense of belonging had overcome the creatures and they spoke with fond anxiety to Manwise. Even Rhumirrah was politely included within their concern. Then they were off, following a steady, though obscure path. After a few perfunctory words made mainly to establish the necessary amity of travelers on a long road, they fell into the quiet of their own thoughts. Soon, every homely landmark kept under the rule of Noe was dismissed for fresh farms and wilder country. Manwise reflected upon how quickly he became one with the journey, how his familiar surroundings faded into something called "the past." The loneliness of the beginning of adventures struck him with surprise. He hung his head so that no one could see his moist eyes.

A small, cold rain began to fall. A pair of boys who had been setting traps for birds came running across a meadow, their hair streaming, eyes blurred. All at once, they stopped, skidded on the grass and blinked at the sight of the deer, the bull, and the tiger. Too stunned to move, they stood with their knees shaking, full of gaping wonder. Rhumirrah was as a fearsome jewel to their eyes. Wordless, they watched the beasts, forgetful of the rain, until the whole dreamlike tableaux had retreated into the wooded path. When they returned home, the boys babbled incoherently. No one believed them. One man beat his son for telling tales, so that the youth cried in his anguish, tasting bitterly unjust suffering. Chiefly, it was beasts, however, which Noe's party happened upon, as Dolmir led them a twisty route away from the dwellings of men.

"Where are you going?" asked a curious weasel, poking his head up along the banks of a silver stream.

"Tàkan Mishpât, gentle beast," answered the bull, and the buck shook his head at such openness. When they had gone a little further, he turned to remonstrate with Manwise. "Unless you want a train of creatures following our every step, do not tell them where we are going. Especially a weasel." The guileless bull could not understand such censure. It was always his way to answer honestly. For long minutes, he followed without seeing, for he was thinking how best to answer an inquiry without lying or portraying a rude silence. Soon, however, the tiny footfall of rabbit and mice told the bull he would not have to speak again. Dolmir might speed off quickly beyond the reach of such pursuit, yet Manwise anchored him.

Twice more did they run afoul of things having to do with Two Legs. Late in the first day, the skies had cleared. They had followed an arc of spruce and cedar trees, until they emerged at the back of the forest into a pasture rarely traveled by humans. Their luck would have it that a family of gypsies were camped out, singing and laughing at the end of day. An old grandfather sat stuffing some rag tobacco into a clay pipe, while his old woman darned a pair of socks. Younger men lay about in thin shirts playing cards, whilst a single couple danced a mazurka to a squeeze box tune. The gypsies, too, gawked at the beasts. The men put down their cards. One of them stood and ran into the tent, bringing out a girl, tousle-haired and sleepy. The old grandfather put up his hand, steadied the folk. He lit his pipe and puffed sweetly until the shadow of the animals had disappeared into the twilight.

"I have seen all this in a vision," said the old woman. "A great terror is coming."

"Hush woman," said the old man.

"It is coming, I tell you."

"Then it is coming," said the old man.

~~~~~~~~

It was the middle of the second day that Dolmir led them through a strange land. The ground was at first uneven and fetid. Rhumirrah swung her tail in disgust. Hours later, they came to a dusty plain untouched by many rains. Next, a barrow of ancient tombs lost to the memory of living men met their path. A subtle sense of profanation uneasily pervaded the place, insensible of aeons.

"Dead for a day, dead for eternity," said a voice.

Rhumirrah's ears pricked, her eyes narrowed. A kind of wispy, dry phantom like the oscillation of bent air carrying a mirage seemed to coalesce before her. The wind carried a faint odor, a breath stale and mixed equally between tin and anti-septic. The tiger froze, her attention holding her companions rooted in their tracks. As she listened closely, Rhumirrah heard two voices.

"Where are you going, Daisy?" said the first.

"Mr. Shim," said the second, "I do believe that is a bull."

"Precisely, Mr. Sham," said Mr. Shim. "I am attempting to provoke the bull which you so astutely note into revealing the nature of this unusual event."

Whether Dolmir heard them as well was unclear, but the buck spooked and ran off, leaving the tiger and the bull to their own devices.

"Now that, I say," said one of the voices (they were hardly distinguishable), "that is not quite neighborly."

"Why don't you go home?" said the other. It seemed to have creeped right up to Rhumirrah, so that she growled, fear rippling along her spine and sparking in her tail. Manwise looked neither to his right nor to his left. Steadily, he began to walk forward, following the straight path through the field of forgotten dead. Then the tiger followed, hearkening not to the voices.

"Why don't you go home, go home?" they continued to echo, until presently the haunting trailed off into nothing.

───────────

"Home office was very clear, Mr. Sham. I'm afraid our walk in the park is not to extend beyond these bounds. Our operative discourages interference. He's a solo act, you see."

"Some do put on airs."

"It's not for us to complain, Mr. Sham. So far, he's more than held up his end. Besides, I have a plan. A bit of initiative, you might say."

"Doesn't hurt to have insurance."

"Right you are," declared Mr. Shim, looking over the field of unkept graves. Their failure to turn the beasts was momentarily disconcerting. It allowed uncertainty to creep within the serene and happy satisfaction of his zealous mind. How was it that the beasts, far simpler creatures than the human flesh, should resist control? One ought to simply discover the mechanism and turn the workings whichever way one wished. A kind of unaccountable resistance had been built in, so that even when the last microscopic intelligence had been discovered, some aspect of nature stomped its foot with an unacceptable freedom, refusing to be utterly commanded. It was at such moments that Mr. Shim suspected that the game was not quite fair. Perhaps every time they reached the place of comprehension, the Enemy poured in from some hideous bag of unquenchable largesse, more freedom, more random, untidy drama, so that never should they bring the riot of gulping, breathing, sexing things into the simplicity of the void.

"Mr. Shim, this is a ripe lot. Which one do you think?"

Mr. Shim startled from his momentary lapse into the fringes of ennui. He reminded himself that he was especially special and no one in the world was more important, worshipful words that always restored his esteem to untroubled clarity. With the determined patience of a child at serious play, he puttered about the loose confederacy of tombs. As there were no stones to mark the rough, somnolent mounds, there was nothing to neatly distinguish the interred. After about ten minutes of judicious pondering, Mr. Shim lowered his bright pink face to the earth, peering deeply, as though he could see right through the ground to the desiccated parcel within.

"I would say this should do quite well, Mr. Sham. Would you like to do the honors?"

"Pleased, I'm sure," said Mr. Sham, who proceeded to lie atop the prescribed mound. Some minutes passed in silence. Then a low groan, a monotonous deep-keyed whirring began to be heard, as if a hoard of baritone locusts were droning from the pit of Mr. Sham's perfectly flat stomach. Mr. Sham's body started to shake and appeared to levitate ever so slightly above the ground. Noxious, drooling spittle ran from his mouth into the soil. Then, abruptly, the performance was over. Mr. Sham raised himself, wiping his mouth with a silk handkerchief.

"Shouldn't take long," stated Mr. Shim. "May I suggest Chalmer's toothpowder? Brighten that smile in no time."

"A white smile is the secret to winning friends and establishing financial success," added Mr. Sham.

"One day," prophesied Mr. Shim, "there shall be scientific techniques to predict those who shall have a propensity for crooked teeth. We'll save them a lot of trouble by making sure they simply aren't born."

"Progress is terrific!" enthused Mr. Shim's partner. "I think he's about ready."

The ground above the chosen grave began to spew chunks of earth, bits of rock and caked soil erupting with sporadic velocity. A hand covered in a gray, drab concoction of monstrous flesh emerged. Soon, an entire body of undead outcast stood waiting before the representatives of Womble and Doubt. The face was particularly repellent, a drawling mass of wrinkly skin that looked only too ready to drop entirely off the skull. It was blind yet held its gruesome visage pointed directly at its masters.

"I say," said Mr. Sham, "couldn't you have picked something a little less icky?"

"Ah, the necrophori. What can you do?" observed Mr. Shim. "Besides, this one is an expert archer. Just a second . . ." Mr. Shim reached into his satchel, bypassed the three-speed blender, a packet of Tuklin's hot chocolate, the brush head to Kibley's wonderbroom, and pulled out a longbow tattooed with runes. "Here we are." Lightly, he tossed the bow to the summoned undead, which caught it easily, its blindness no impediment to its actions.

"Mr. Sham, I don't suppose? I packed rather light today."

"Why of course, Mr. Shim," said Mr. Sham, who began to pick through his own satchel. "I have a monkey pox arrowhead, not very useful for other beasts, I imagine: common stone, malice, self-aggrandizement, burrowing iron, wooly fever and bronze."

"Burrowing iron will do," said Mr. Shim, "but you know that kit has been superceded. Home office issued a much more comprehensive collection."

"I'll update next time we're back." A rueful look briefly

hovered over Mr. Sham's relentlessly chipper face. "I don't suppose you've got a supply of invisa-oil? My jar is nearly spent."

Mr. Shim whistled. Mr. Sham had a discontinued kit and had failed to replenish his invisa-oil, which more than made up for his total lack of arrows. The report could safely be filed and neither party admit to mistakes. "Plenty. It won't miss, so just cover two arrowheads, why don't you?"

<hr />

Dolmir discovered them, not far off course, in ascendant waves of granite steppes. The deer did not overtly apologize for his desertion. Instead, he remarked on the dreary topography and generally became somewhat more talkative and kindly in manner. It was a country that reminded the tiger of the merciless desert she had crossed to reach the abodes of the Two Legs. The color seemed to have been blanched out of the earth. Even the extravagant Rhumirrah appeared subdued in its dreary light. Tall, narrow scrub dotted the dry land like eyes on a spud. The small beasts had stopped following them at the edge of the barrows, so that the party was again alone. Every brief sound rattled and magnified, so that the beasts became self-conscious of their vulnerability in the desolate land. Disquiet led on Dolmir's fearful tongue. He tapped the roof of his mouth and muttered desperately about the malevolence of hidden eyes. Then came the deep reverberation of the tolling bell. The dark abyss of the earth sent out its threatening dirge, met them in that inhospitable place. Wordless now, Dolmir quickened his pace. For a brief moment, Manwise felt as if they were caught in a fool's errand, running from the only source of safety in order to declare hope to beasts uninterested and unable to believe. Yet his stout heart steadied. The bull desired every little titmouse and wren to seek rescue. Almost insensibly, the ground began to change. The earth softened. They came to rough fields covered in tall, pale grass. A touch of salt met their lips. A hushed, murmuring sound filled the air with the regularity of an indifferent lullaby. Then they climbed a shaggy plain of violet heather, arriving at the top of a low cliff that looked down upon the maternal sea. Gulls soared in the horizon that seemed to reach straight down into the slate gray waters. A narrow land bridge stretched from the shore to a brooding slab of island that appeared to jut out of the churning waters like an obsidian stone. The center of the isle was a rounded bowl, suggesting the impact crater of a large meteor. All along the shore, animals of all kind stood waiting and watching. Beasts of feather and fur and scale, heavy with the onset of hibernation or scuttering with rapid energy, even in the waters, one saw the phosphorescent glow of eel worms, the plash of piscine life.

"It is Tâkan Mishpât," said the deer.

<hr>

The mood of the beasts was perplexing. The anxiety of foreboding seemed strangely muted in them. They were more interested in the fanfare of the summoning, peered at the ancient place of meeting and at each other with unabashed curiosity. Dolmir, for his part, balked at the scrutiny. He had brought Noe's beasts; his part was done. Awkwardly, with false lightness, he separated himself from Manwise and Rhumirrah with a quip about the weather. The tigress would have liked to give the buck what for, but the occasion was too grave for mere indulgence. Softly, she preceded the bull through a decline marked by whispering comments. Along the snaking path leading to the land bridge, some greeted them kindly and some turned knowingly to their friends and pronounced the entire business an extraordinary waste of time. More than one husky guffaw was directed towards the bull that bore the stigma of human association. A waggish crow pronounced the ox a natural blockhead.

At the heart of Tåkan Mishpât there was a flat space, a kind of beveled floor that led to a single standing stone. When the place was uninhabited, it presented an enigmatic koan to stray visitors, eerie in its solitude. It was here that Rhumirrah and Manwise halted. Upon the standing stone perched a hoary red-tailed hawk. Caleb had been Judge for many seasons. One claw grasped a rough rock for gavel. Perhaps ten feet to the left of the standing stone was a tall, gleaming pole of black obsidian, clearly the work of artifice. There, silently curved like a vine upon the Judgment Pole, for so it was called, a serpent watched with an expression of serene indifference. Caleb, the red-tailed hawk, pounded his gavel three times to quiet the crowd.

"Order, good beasts! Order!" he proclaimed in a sonorous cry. "Let us hear now what these ambassadors from the realm of the enslaved have to say to us."

"We are not slaves," answered Manwise in a calm voice. "We are the servants of the far-seeing by choice."

"I beg your pardon," said Caleb. "The assembly shall disregard my original designation. It is, indeed, prejudicial."

"Thank you, judge."

"As to whether the Two Legs are far-seeing, though, we shall also reserve judgment."

"Very well, judge."

The judge winked at the solemn bull. "The beast need not comment upon every pronouncement from the bench."

"I only meant to be polite," said Manwise, feeling shy and befuddled, the mild laughter of his audience abashing him.

"Indeed," answered Caleb. "And it is very fine. There are some here who could learn respect for the office and the solemnity of these proceedings." The audience hushed, if only momentarily. "Now we are all aware, most of us, I think, that there are some extraordinary happenings in the land. The creatures of the sea, too, have reported it. It is because of these concerns, the strange tolling that chills the blood, that we have deigned to come together to listen to what message may be given from the . . . from the places where Two Legs walk."

Rhumirrah stepped forward. She had a great desire to roar but did not. "I am from a distant country," she said. "I am Rhumirrah, daughter of Bali and Nyssa. The sire of Bali was Dimenor, who slayed the elephant king, Bantra. Prahnhar was sire of Dimenor. Fingold, who drowned in the river Sith, was sire of Pranhar. Dandenor was sire of Fingold. Before Dandenor, Vashnu walked the earth; he strove with many. The sire of Vashnu was Peregrin, whose consort was the renowned Lilliswan." And so on. I'm afraid the tigress went back twenty generations, feeling the weight of the occasion and wanting to establish her credentials. At last she concluded, "I do not come from the Two Legs. I come because I have spoken with Orianna in a vision and because I have seen the ancient hero, Noe. Let he who doubts my words come tell me to my face." Then she roared.

The tiger spoke her mind, sometimes invoking passionate invective, then stumbling with the perplexity of an ingénue first brought out into society. Caleb spoke gently when she faltered. It was hard not to like her. Nonetheless, while Rhumirrah did not speak badly, there was an underlying mistrust awarded her. First, as Orianna predicted, the beasts were skeptical. The witness was rather amusing, careening between angry impatience, fragile vulnerability, and jejune boldness. But visions, really? The girl had a strange dream, was all, albeit one that seemed to concur with the ominous nature of the times. Secondly, and this was more decisive, the animals remained unpersuaded that any Two Legs was worthy of trust. And, so, it came for Manwise to tell his part.

––––––––––

The bull looked neither to the right nor to the left the entire time of Rhumirrah's oration. At first, he peered down at his front hooves, apparently overcome by his place at the center of attention. He had ever been taciturn and slow of speech. Then he looked straight up at the standing stone, never taking his eyes from the majesty of the judge. Manwise scrutinized Caleb. He thought he glimpsed some humor and compassion, though the hawk became drowsy as the tigress carried on. At last, the purpose for his visit compelling him, Manwise spoke.

"The earthworm," he said, "is not a gregarious fellow."

"An honest observation," remarked Caleb. "Yet I fail to see the pertinence."

"I am sorry. I am not used to explaining. A worm can be cut in two and each part will go on, oblivious that they are separate, that a halving has occurred. It is curious. There is not much intelligence in a worm and, therefore, little remembrance or regret."

"This isn't helping, I'm afraid."

"A most learned discourse," scoffed a lean mongoose aching to make an impression.

"Surely it is true that there are degrees of knowledge," answered Manwise. "Now we are faced with trouble. What the trouble is I cannot understand, but each beast here, if he is truthful, knows it. Ask the ancients among you. Some of them will also recollect that . . . that Oglath afflicted us. Noe helped us in our need. Noe shall help us now. He has prepared a haven so that none need suffer tears, be left in darkness." The sincerity of the bull evidently reached many of the beasts. They stirred uneasily and looked about. The festive mood of easy mockery waned in them. "One thing more," added Manwise, pressing his advantage. "What will you tell your kith and kin, your little ones, when doom comes and you have done nothing? Who else among you shall devise a refuge from amidst travail?"

There was a long pause. The beasts waited for further word, but Manwise considered he had done his best. A flurry of excited conversation then erupted. Few had anticipated eloquence from a slave. Surprise leant spice to the grave words of the Two Legs' envoy. Yet before deliberation could be consummated, Caleb inclined his head towards the serpent, that the offices and procedures might be duly accomplished. The serpent twisted itself round the Judgment Pole. It raised itself above the congregated animals and expanded the fleshy scales of its back to form a cape and hood. With sharp eyes, it looked out so that each and every beast felt that it had been touched by the serpentine vision. They felt themselves lofty, serious, responsible beasts. They had never before realized the extent of their cleverness, nor the dignity of their powers. Then the serpent narrowed its gaze to Manwise, its eyes becoming soft and sorrowful, though subtly disapproving.

"You have spoken to us honestly, kind bull. We are grateful to you," said the serpent with a graciousness that warmed all who heard its words. "And as you are clearly a beast of impeccable character, blunt in speech and truthful, allow me to ask you, but one thing of consequence. It is a small thing, perhaps, but it troubles my mind."

Rhumirrah felt her breath catch. She doubted their triumph. There was something in the serpent's manner that caused her to worry.

"I have heard," said the serpent, "though being far from the Two Legs, I cannot report anything, it may only be a lie told to scare naughty children . . . " The serpent paused and the conclave collectively leaned towards the adversary, awaiting the awful truth — they didn't believe for a second that such a wise beast did not know whereof it spoke. "I have heard," resumed the serpent, "that these Two Legs practice a thing called religion. This is a difficult concept. Our most illustrious thinkers have not been able to comprehend its full meaning. It involves an action, a sort of talking at the sky or a muttering to invisible powers. The Two Legs call it prayer. Is this not so?"

Manwise bowed his head. "The man called Noe does this," he said simply. "He prays to the Origin without which all life and all that is would not be."

"And you, yourself, noble beast, do you pray to this — what did you call it, Origin?"

"I do not. Origin is a mystery I cannot understand."

The serpent smiled, ever so slightly. It rested its eyes benignly upon the assembly. "I told you this was an honest beast," it said. "Now tell us, kind bull, have you ever seen or heard anything to indicate the reality of this mystery, as you say?"

"I have seen the sun, and the stars, the seasons of the land: all these are ordered and beautiful," said Manwise, struggling for rhetoric to match the guile of the serpent. "All these are from the art of Origin. The Throne of Adam has said so."

At this last expression, the serpent noticeably blanched. Then it looked with anger on the bull. "We do not use vulgar expression in this court," it said. "The office you speak of is a foolish legend. Do not try our patience with it again."

Here, however, old Judge Caleb interposed himself. He turned to the serpent and wagged his claw. "You overstep your bounds, Adversary. You cannot speak for the court on this matter. The term is archaic, true, but in our opinion, it is not vulgar, nor contravened. The witness may speak as he chooses." There was a brief buzz amongst the animals. The serpent smiled with a cunning, genial spirit at the judge. It did not shake its head in the least. Half the Assembly felt that the serpent had been rebuked, but the other half thought the Judge old fashioned and past his time.

"I beg your pardon," said the serpent to Manwise. "I spend my time in educated circles. Doubtless, what we consider divisive and, I beg your pardon, a touch intolerant, is yet common parlance in the country. You habitually live in the rural areas, I suppose?"

"And we are all most ill-educated," said the bull. His eyes glowered with unsuspected fire at the Adversary.

"Ah," said the serpent with satisfaction. His tongue flickered like a flag in the air. The audience admired greatly the panache of the Adversary. It was indisputable that the white bull was little more than a yokel, no matter how impressive. "So, I take it," asserted the serpent (he'd slid down slightly, leaning out with an expression of affection in his buttery voice), "I surmise, that is, that you accept the reality of the so-called Origin purely on the authority of the, er, Throne of Adam?" The serpent twinkled at this last phrase.

"Ss-ss. S-ss," laughed the snakes.

"That's a good one. Hehe, that's showin' the old boy!" declared a hyena, slapping its thigh.

"Yes," answered Manwise with boldness, though his visage was now sad. "I trust the man called Noe."

A thought occurred to the serpent. He would have slid closer, come right up to the bull, but it was an unfortunate fact that he would have to slither about the ground to approach the witness and this was an action that could not carry dignity. So, instead, he raised himself to the apex of the Judgment Pole. "Tell me," he said softly, "what of the other Two Legs? Do they pray to this invisible Thing?"

"Origin is not a Thing," answered the beast.

"Indeed, I quite agree. Perhaps Origin is what we call in educated circles a sort of imaginary concept or a fictional creation?"

The bull was silent. Manwise would not answer.

"You have not answered, dear beast. You have come a long way to tell us of the Two Legs, Noe, whom you plainly call your master. Yet from your silence I suspect that the other Two Legs do not pray as your master does. Might it not be that the one called Noe is mistaken?"

"You do not know him! You do not know what you say!" shouted Manwise, tears in his eyes.

"Stop it! Stop it!" roared Rhumirrah. "Look what you are doing! He's a good beast. Anyone can see that!"

"Order. Order!" demanded Judge Caleb, hammering his gavel. "This court will not tolerate unscheduled interruptions, even from young ladies."

A titter of laughter arose. The Judge, who was not known as a wit, congratulated himself. The tiger sighed and stared into the ground.

"I have only one more question," announced the

Adversary. "I admit I do not know your master and I have no desire to unduly upset you, so I will be brief. I have heard that in pursuit of this strange activity, the one the Two Legs call religion, there is, forgive my speaking of it, something horrible that is done." Despite his desire to lessen the pain of the witness, the serpent found it necessary to prolong silence while his audience felt the strange pleasure of wondering about the unknown horror. At the precise moment when pleasure might tip into impatience, the serpent concluded. "The humans call it sacrifice."

"Sacrifice? What's that?" queried a swift cheetah.

"It means throwing a bag of rice," announced a weasel.

"It means blowing one's nose too loudly," said a mole who was sensitive to noise.

"Order. Order," bellowed the judge.

"The voice of a dear, unobtrusive citizen." The serpent indicated the mole. "He cannot imagine anything more harrowing, more odious, than a rowdy neighbor. He thinks that, just perhaps, these Two Legs bang against the walls of their houses, yell boisterously to an Unseen Force in an untimely hour. Yet it is far worse. Is it not, honest bull?"

Manwise hung his head. "I trust the Throne of Adam," he muttered.

"Is it not true that a pure and innocent beast, guilty of nothing, is taken by the Two Legs and tied to an altar? The priest of religion prays to an imaginary power and takes a real blade, cutting the neck of the beast."

Groans suffused the Assembly. She-beasts swooned.

"The Two Legs often does not even consume the beast but takes fire, burning the flesh of the innocent so that the smoke rises in a cloud of dark pitch into the air."

Rhumirrah looked, amazed, at Manwise. Still, the bull was silent.

"This is what men name Sacrifice. They claim Origin is made happy by the odor. Perhaps it dines upon the smoke of flesh."

"Indecent."

"Terrible."

"Savage superstition!"

"Order. Order," commanded the Judge, but the Assembly would not be assuaged. They spat and cried and looked with derision upon the beast that had come to speak to them from the land of men. The conclave was over.

CHAPTER FIVE

Dark Waters

THE PATH OF THE TIGER AND THE
bull was painful. They retraced their steps as best
they could. For a long while, neither spoke. The
very beasts they had come to save met their retreat
with vile names and savage mockery. The least of
it was to be called buffoon, house slave, idiot and beast-hater.
The tumult of acrimony from feather and paw and slithering
scale provoked rage in the tiger. Then Rhumirrah would fix
her eyes on prey. Those so transfixed ceased to jeer, but such
had little effect on the howling mob. Driven by a wave of
resentment, a subtle relish to torture and demean masked by
righteous indignation arose in the assembly. Manwise spoke
the obvious. What else could they do? "We must go to Noe.
Tell him. He will find an answer to all this." So, silently they
traced the road back, battling first the contempt of their fellows and then seeking to recollect the path, for as the revilers
lost interest and departed from them, their uncertainty of
the correct way back grew and Dolmir had not returned to
help them.

"He is a flighty beast and a silly fella. Half the time, he
kept looking at me like I would be so stupid as to make a
meal of him." When Manwise would not share her scorn,
Rhumirrah paced in silence, pondering. "He did not like our
mission . . . not that I can blame him for that," rued the tiger.

"I am concerned," answered the bull. "It is not like the young buck to abandon us completely."

And further they marched, guessing to the best of their ability, until they came again to the land bordering the barrows. There a new doom met them: Dolmir, shot through with an arrow. He had run his last. Already, the bright gloss had departed from his eyes. "No Two Legs would choose to venture here, not even a bandit," surmised Manwise. "And he has not been slain for sport. We must be cautious."

They could not move swiftly for any great length of time. The bull was not built for it, was cumbersome company. Rhumirrah must check herself often, growling low in poorly repressed impatience. They travelled in constant anxiety. Every small, tinkering sound intimated danger and they could not shake the persistent sensation that they were being watched. In the pastureland, while Manwise nibbled, Rhumirrah sharpened her gaze. Sometimes the shadow on the land did not look quite right. In the forest, the birds were quiet. The trees gave no warning. Every place was rife with a feeling of dread. It was the plains, however, that were most vulnerable, where each step was haunted by danger. They came, at last, to the borders of human habitude. Small white cottages with red roofs could be seen peeking from behind the brown ribbon of a hillside road. Though neither voiced it, both beasts wondered if the closeness of the Two Legs might squelch the steady terror afflicting them, offer some protection from the enigmatic menace. Indeed, the ghoulish archer had been tracking them, though to conceive the undead as possessed of intelligence would be to go too far. Yet the monstrous flesh did possess something like an instinct, a shame before living men. In this, one sees that the beasts were not false in their hope of safety, but while they were still in the region of perilous sojourn, the archer stretched forth the bow, shot a notched arrow into the innocent sky.

The missile did not err, dug with silent cruelty into the side of the tiger. Rhumirrah had detected the swift whirr of its path too late. She could not leap from harm. Crumpling in agony, the arrowhead burrowed into her with unnatural, vicious propulsion, as if it had tiny, mincing jaws. Manwise turned to her filled with shock and consternation. Stubbornly, he stood between her and the imagined path of assault. He would not leave her, dared the enemy to strike again. Fate seemed to wish them nothing but punishing violence. No other arrows came, however. The archer had been allowed two pulls at the bow, then the strange, concocted being melted, vanished unheeded into dust. Near despair, the bull bent low. He lifted the tiger as best as he could, shifted his weight so that she lay prostrate upon his back. Then began an arduous task: Manwise must walk regarding not the Two Legs and other beasts. He resolutely set his face towards Noe. They were close enough for him to find the way, if only they would be left unhindered. Soon, Rhumirrah's short breath became labored. After a while, Manwise could not tell whether the breath of life remained with her or not. Doggedly and sinking in spirit, he walked the bitter way.

~~~~~~~~~~

The aged woman Elspeth sat at her spinning wheel near the door so that she could watch the goings on of the young people. Oblivious she was to the calico kitten pawing at the spun yarn. Outside, upon the long porch, the adults sat drowsing in wicker chairs, their companionable talk undulating in frequency, rising on occasion to a chirrup of laughter or a staccato of assertion, and then quickly falling back to amiable chatter. Niri stood entertaining herself and the young children. Ham's wife had brought a bottle of soap and a magic wand upon which she was able to create translucent, brief bubbles that floated lazily upon the mild evening air. When it grew darker and these fragile ornaments no longer amused, the fireflies dotted the night. Then Sholon and Niri chased these "faeries" like little girls, laughing so hard that everyone who watched them felt their heart grow light.

Noe's shepherd man, Yasha, stayed home that evening. He played softly on a lyre. It was one of those blessed times that seem enchanted. All their worries were simply dropped. They needed the respite and felt as if they had dreamed themselves into a sacred grove where life is sweet. The stars slowly dotted the sky, appearing to burn brighter. Yet soon, in a far field, a flash of milky flesh met Noe's eyes. He peered intently and then began to stride in long, purposeful steps. Noe's concern cut short the reverie of charmed night. Young men followed, running after the patriarch. A straggle of uneven lanterns lit the way. Stumbling painfully, Manwise bore the tiger. He buckled at the approach of Noe. As Rhumirrah was taken from his wretched back, the bull fell into a dead faint.

It was thought unsafe to move them further. Noe had a tent erected. That night, he would not sleep. He stayed with the beasts and tended to them. The wounds of the wild one were pernicious — the head of the arrow did not show, had broken off from the shaft. "This is the work of dark spirits," he declared. Then Noe prayed, used all his skill. It was a near thing, but the tiger lived. The tale went abroad. The bravery of Manwise and the healing act of Noe did not go unregarded. Great was the talk among the animals and it may be that this is what countered the failure of mere speech at Tâkan Mishpât.

Lady whinnied and waved her head in acknowledgement of Priyanka. Noe carried his saddle from the tack room over to the stall where the roan mare, Fiona, waited impatiently. Her nostrils flared, anticipating the ride that was surely coming. Noe glanced at his wife with frank admiration. She was wearing a stylish felt hat with a touch of lace. The women of the day had begun to disdain such trappings, yet could they have seen Priyanka, how she glowed with the rich power of her femininity. Her gloved hand subtly brushed across his cheek. Then they smiled and readied their mounts with a poise and humor made easy through a long habit of courtesy. Once a week, they promised themselves this time. Their ardor for one another, its intense need for space, to stretch and speak and be silent, forgetful of duties and cares was made more precious by the feeling that each idyll of the horses might be their last. They rode first through the fields where peasants mowed the grasses and hayricks dotted the land like teepees. Farmers would wave and doff their caps, boys with apple cheeks hallooed and incited their dogs to briefly run alongside. Further on, they found the green, lazy pastures, loosening the reins so that Fiona and Lady galloped with gusty breaths, daring each other in speed across the easy plains. The horses did not know that never again would they meditate this land with joyful hoof and eye. The delight of the beasts invigorated the riders, they laughed and joined in the game until Lady's dappled flanks shone with a fine sheen and Noe's horse was content to parse the path with dainty steps. The riders came to the slow stream where Noe sometimes fished. A little further the mill wheel turned in rhythmic monotony, brushing the water. From here they struck out north and west, aiming for a trail that led through a thicket of pines to a meadow they treated as a secret garden. Then the horses were left to feed and wander freely while Noe and Priyanka lay upon a blanket forgetful of time. A small basket provided strawberries, cold quail, cream pastries and a fizzy drink just strong enough to take the edge off. Then there was song of songs. Afterwards, Priyanka lay flat, peering without thinking into the soft sky. Noe reclined upon his side watching the rise and fall of her bosom, breathing in the light scent of jasmine that drifted from her lambent skin.

"It's been good," he said at last, when they had been quiet and still and she had been gazing at the cloudless sky long enough for Priyanka to have begun to fall into a drowsy, waking sleep. She had not actually heard him, the words coming as a sound like a bird call, but she saw in his eyes a gentle meaning, so that she smiled, her nose crinkled with that mischievous glee that flashed when she was pleased with him. She grabbed his hand, squeezing it with unaffected warmth. Reticent they were to leave the intimate joy of that place. It was from out of that love which could never be properly told, that all that they ventured was done. But even here, the garden was not free of care. Word came to Noe: a blue jay flew into their midst, unmoved by the need for sanctuary.

"I found your foe," said the jay, in exactly the same voice he used to warn of cats.

It was not long before Noe discerned smoke in the west. Subtly, he led the horses, saying nothing yet to Priyanka. Closer still and the fires of torchlight were visible in the precarious earth that abutted marshlands.

"I will see to this," said Noe.

"I will come with you."

"Nay, Priyanka. Be guided by me in this. I will parley whilst you head home. Take the safe routes known to us. Lady, be swift."

Priyanka did not wish to argue with her husband. Her heart felt otherwise, but she submitted with good grace. She knew how to master her will.

Noe watched her, waited till she was out of his sight. Then he turned towards the fires.

———————

Shastar was living in a series of caves that overlooked the city. All manner of outcast could normally be found there. They descended like specters with the melting of the winter snow. What were they? Fringe-dwellers, nightmares, the ache of regret. They were like mad men, ghosts of ragged memory, stark men and women wearing hair shirts, full of keening and prophecy, only no one understood the language. They brought the plague. Wild dogs and creatures swift as wind, pestiferous, kicked at their heels. Boldly, Noe followed the path alone, discovered Shastar tending a small fire. He would not have been found, naturally, unless he had intended it. Shastar eyed Noe without deep concern. The mild smile on his face produced a puckish expression that briefly recalled Priyanka in a playful mood. "I heard about your man," he said, when the silence had gone on a spell. "I think I know who is responsible. It is the work of the kind who came with me."

"What are you talking about?"

"Oh, they are helpful creatures. They smooth the way. I don't know their true name. They are called differently in different places. 'The Comforters,' that's what they call themselves. Or 'the Brights.' I believe in your past they were sometimes called the nephilim. I admit, they're annoying. Had to send them away. You can't imagine, really, a long climb through the mountains with all that banal racket going on."

"You're not making any sense. Besides, the nephilim were giants."

"Am I not? Perhaps you're right. Still, your man figured them out. Came to me, I can hardly imagine why. I told him to forget about them, much the best. I knew, of course, that he would not. Once you're on to them, the whole earth smells of it." Shastar paused, his face kindly and apologetic towards Noe. "For what it's worth, I tried to stop them."

Noe was taken aback by the seeming candor of his wife's brother. Yet there was a vague coarseness in his tone that was not typical, made Noe curious and wary. "Where are they, these Comforters?"

"There's a little operation in town. A branch office. They could explain procedure better. I'd show you myself, except I'm on the outs with them. I was brought in as a recruiter, you see, but I just don't like the work."

"I think you'd better try," uttered Noe, his eyes and voice severe and commanding.

Shastar sighed and brushed the dust from his shins. He led Noe through the streets of the city. Something bland and mechanical seemed to dominate the people. In any event, they paid no heed to Noe and his guide, not even bothering to scowl and sneer. In the warehouse district, Shastar slowed his pace, refused to go further. He pointed to a jumble of dirty buildings that must have made for a wretched sight even when new. Rust and litter and blank, annihilating walls too dank to inspire the smallest protest of graffiti rose up on every side. Oily, black green moisture congregated in patches along the uneven ground.

It was an eccentric place for an office, yet a wooden sign advertising the presence of Womble and Doubt hung limply in the turbid air. A tiny, negligible foyer was followed by a long, uninhabited workspace. Noe discovered rows of desks, tidy and bare, but for an occasional typewriter. Dribbles of the mysterious dark water could be seen. Noe lifted his feet carefully, avoiding the rivulet that seemed to emanate from an interior room. Entering into the deeper regions of the building, the ground became dank and covered in rough cobblestone. Noe crossed under arches and through tunnel like halls incongruous with the shabby modern properties of the outer facade. There was no sign of an employee, no sound but the slow, steady drip of noxious liquid. A dim, flickering light led him into a chamber where at last, he was confronted by the back of a being who sat at a low table. The whole room was big with shadows, hovering purples and browns fluoresced by dim lamps that barely pierced the smoke-filled air.

"I've wanted to talk to you for a long time," said a voice neither old nor young. It was a voice urbane, with a touch of the amateur scholar, intelligent, with just a hint of the adventurer peeking out from under the robes of old money. Noe was struck by the hands of his interlocutor. The nails were finely pared. The nimble fingers were busy with some dexterous occupation. What were they doing? Noe could not be sure. As yet, he could only see the deep hood of a cassock and those hands which somehow seemed remarkable.

"I understand," continued the voice, "that you have recently had doubts about your venture. With the boat, I mean."

Noe laughed a mirthless laugh.

"After all your struggles, it would be a shame for you to give way now. It doesn't really matter if no one else gets it. It's your truth, isn't it? Isn't that what matters?"

"Crap," said Noe.

"Crap?"

"Crap."

The voice laughed, though it was not a very good one, unpracticed and savage. "The thing to remember, if we are going to be blunt — and I think it's marvelous that you don't stand for the usual pabulum — the important point to recall is that human beings, in the end, are just not very good material. They're weak and willful, industrious about money and sex, but generally lazy about truth — unless, of course, you can turn it into money and sex."

"My friend, Ravi, was an honorable man."

"Ah," said the voice.

"He was murdered by your lackeys."

The voice was eminently calm, reasonable, and smooth with feigned empathy. "My acolytes are often more eager than bright. It was not my wish and I apologize. And yet, isn't it funny? You're here. We are speaking, one rational creature to another. You are not angry with me, really, but with that other fellow."

Noe seethed with anger and despair. He began to talk, halted, could not finish.

"You expected you would be rewarded for your faithfulness? Naturally, you did. You wanted your long years of effort to result in praise, in kindness, in venerable felicity. I quite agree with you. You've every right to have expected some decent treatment. Instead, you are left to twist in the wind. I'm afraid that's what the old fellow is like. He doesn't really need you, you know, so he can't feel that anything you suffer is all that important."

"I was angry, because you could be stopped. He permits your monstrous atrocities and your petty, nasty tricks. You're mean, low, and cruel, in spite of your accent and your manicured hands, but none of it would come to a damn thing if He didn't allow it."

"Absolutely. I'm more or less just his dark side. He can't accept it, so he splits me off, pretends I'm some other being. But look here, I'm not the one encouraging you to build some big bollocks of a boat . . . in the middle of nowhere . . . on a mountain top. Damn, I bet he was just joking and couldn't believe it when you took the bait. He's like that, too."

"I didn't come here to talk theology."

"What did you come for, then?"

"I wanted to say something to your face."

Noe rounded on his host and saw that the object of those youthful hands was a dumb show made of a small puppet effigy hanging from tiny gallows, a snippet of rag sticking out from the scrawl of the puppet's mouth. For a fleeting second, Noe saw his own face staring back at him from underneath the hood. Then there was nothing. Noe stared into pure vacuity.

"Go to Hell!"

A smirking, prurient howl, stinking of death and cheap, overly sweet perfume, arose from the void. Noe turned and retraced his path through the empty offices of Womble and Doubt. When he was out again upon the street, he heard coming from the darkened and slimy windows a roar he had last heard years before in the fields of Aglore.

A few sentries could be seen poking vigilant faces from out of a screen of reeds. No one stepped forth to question Noe or impede his progress. In a patch of boggy ground just sturdy enough to sustain their camp, Noe found Shastar amidst what appeared a tribe of barbarians. A careful listening to their scattered speech, however, proved the initial impression wrong. The cadences were educated, more often than not. An engineer, two teachers, an accountant and a social worker were among their number. The acolytes that made themselves busy about Shastar were about as unlike as could be imagined from the perfect facsimiles favored by the firm of Womble and Doubt. Some primitive instinct had caused them to smear themselves entirely with the gray, murky mud easily procured in the marshland. Their clothes were made of rough hide tied with leather straps. The more exotic of their number were copiously illustrated with inky tattoos and bore long, looping rings and silver studs inserted at various eccentric points of the body. Shastar welcomed Noe as if he had been invited and shortly expected. He brought his brother-in-law into the half-shelter of a lean-to, offered him what minor hospitality he could. As to the others, they seemed either uninterested in Noe or vaguely approving of his presence.

"They judge you a slightly addled prophet," informed Shastar.

Noe could not suppress a sigh.

"Yes, I see what you mean," agreed Shastar. "They yearn for a great cataclysm. It's the after-culture they are preparing for."

A small group of tribesmen had formed a meditation circle. Some incense was burned and modest invocations to the Kai made as the members of the circle linked hands. It was not exactly prayer, more like attentive and slightly theatrical silence. The precise nature of the Kai was deliberately ambiguous so there was no distinct belief to anchor the rites of the people. After this, a fellow evidently nicknamed Shady Tom began to beat rather bombastically upon a large, bass drum. In various quarters, one discerned jugglers and sword swallowers, various crafts reminiscent of a sideshow carnival. Elsewhere, some had gathered to play cards and to talk under the auspices of the torchlight. It was unclear to Noe with how much irony, if any, Shastar viewed his adventitious tribe.

"You should tell them to enter into the ark," said Noe.

Shastar shrugged. "They do not obey me. That is not the way of the Kai. True freedom cannot be had in obedience. How can the spirit not grieve and prick against the goad?"

"Does the child attain freedom by being allowed to soil its pants and stick his hand in the fire?"

Shastar grinned at Noe. He seemed genuinely appreciative of the argument. "Well played. Easier gather the sand of the desert with a spoon than bring men to wisdom. Let them go, Noe."

"And what is *your* wisdom, Shastar? Is it not despair?"

Shastar was silent, then, so that Noe began to think he meant no other answer. At last, however, Shastar pulled out a long chain hidden in the folds of his cloak and held before Noe an iridescent crystal upon which was etched the symbol of a serpent swallowing its tail. "This is Ouroboros," he said. "What has been will be again. What is will enter into dust. Nothing is old and nothing is new. Grasp this, and you have grasped all."

Noe stared grimly at the snake. A slow anger burned in him, not directed at Shastar, but at some enemy limned in the pendant. Shastar stood, signaling that the meeting was soon to end. He grasped Noe about the shoulders as a brother and laughed. "Oh, Noe, Noe. How many times has this conversation occurred? Ten? Twenty? Ten thousand times a thousand?"

~~~~~~~~~

Noe found Fiona waiting for him at the forest's edge. He travelled back, saddened by his speech with Shastar. Yet he felt, in spite of himself, soothed by the sky of early evening which was silvered violet, a crescent moon shimmering in the waters of the stream where Noe fished. There, sitting on the edge of the water, barely visible in the gloaming light, sat a gnarled old creature. It looked like a knobby old man, his eyes squint, his shaking hands fidgeting with a clay pipe. He said nothing but winked in a knowing way at Noe's approach. He gave off an aroma of apples and spruce. Fiona's ears pricked at the presence loitering by the water. Noe remained quiet and calmed his horse. Then Noe released Fiona to graze under a nearby willow, whispering softly to her. The old fellow waited patiently, nodding as Noe hunched down low beside him.

"Ah, remember the day," he said without introduction. "When you were a lad, you'd ride out, as you went riding out today with your woman. You'd come to the green pastures careless, wanting only to breathe the air and wander, seeking nothing but the unending vistas, the stars, the trees."

Noe stared at the creature. When it moved, images of lofty, tall hardwoods seemed to dance just beyond Noe's vision. The narrow brow, the smoke green patina that streaked the gray-black hair, the eyes that glinted like darkened plums, the pupils tipped with a dab of magenta, he was known to Noe, though the actual history of their meetings eluded memory.

"We had good times, did we not?" The creature seemed to demand Noe's assent, though underneath boisterous assertion a timorous unhappiness was palpable. "The time I stole your kite, the one your uncle gave you. You ran after me for hours and hours. I'd keep you on the chase. But then you cried. You were only a child, so I had pity on you. Dropped the paper, it wasn't badly harmed, left it teetering in a field, caught by a short little dogwood easily within your reach." The creature shivered in spite of its velvet coat and hard boots. Noe gave what he hoped was a mild, consoling look. "The folk are in a bad way," continued the creature, too agitated to be helped much by Noe's sympathy. "The trouble is coming and where are we to go? We can't leave our forests. When they are gone, we shall disappear, too."

Noe sought to give reassurance. The trees and flowering plants would not vanish beyond hope. The Father of Lights would not abandon them.

"You think he recalls us, then? He has not forgotten? We think he has forgotten. He has turned his face from playthings that no longer interest."

"It is not like that," answered Noe, but the creature was hardly persuaded. It was still shaking its head when Noe retrieved Fiona, rode with some misgiving towards home.

———————

And still more was Noe tested. His words of confidence stuck in his throat, his heart froze. A servant riding a donkey met him on the way, a good old fellow. "Priyanka?" asked Noe, trembling.

"My lady sends love," answered the servant. "But the house of Noe is grievously hurt. The plague has come. Many are afflicted. The great Ham lies sweating in his bed, yet his brow is cold. We have sent for a city doctor, but my old woman thinks he will not come."

Then Noe made great speed, spurring Fiona and leaving his faithful man to catch up as he could. He stopped not for the weeping that rang out across the threshold of his manor but rode on till he had come to the house. It was worse than even the ancient retainer had said. How quickly it had come. Early in the day, all had seemed safe . . . and now. Priyanka met him without words, her eyes conveying resolve and concern. She led him first to Ham. The splendor of his flesh had retreated. Such glory is like the grass. His massive body shook. He moaned. He asked for more life like a little boy. Niri tended to her husband. She spoke tender things, but her face was ashen. So far as anyone knew, the contingent at the ark remained well. Noe called for a dove. "Take this message to my son, Japheth," he directed, tying a thin note to the leg of the bird. It told his youngest to stay where he was. Then Noe rent his robes. He prayed to the Mystery, implored in sore earnest. Beasts were sacrificed, yet the sickness did not end.

Ten days passed. The city doctor came. The physician was a young man, abrupt in speech, honest, but rather hard. He told Noe the truth. "You will lose four-fifths of the sick. Those who are not yet ill will probably not get sick. As to your son, he is a prodigious specimen, but his vulnerability is as great as any other." Then medicines were prescribed, a sop more to give the caretakers fortitude. The body would win its battle or not. Many perished in Noe's house from the sickness, just as the physician had foretold. Those servants most loyal, the oldest and the best, departed to the shadows. Priyanka lost her Katya. The old man who rode out to Noe was smote down. The blow was hard, so that there was nothing but misery to be heard there, sorrow day and night. Yet none of Noe's closest kin were taken. Slowly, Ham recovered. Niri and Priyanka took turns attending to him. When Ham began to complain of their womanly hovering, they knew that he would live. Rejoicing for his son, still Noe walked about his estate as one stricken, clutching at his beard, throwing dust upon his head.

Now the servants who were left were mainly the children of children. They saw that many had died, yet not one of Noe's heirs. They gossiped that Noe had struck some bargain with his hard, inscrutable God. Noe looked on with a somber eye as the surviving farmhands deserted the house. Even as they buried their elders, threw earth upon the graves, they shook the very dust from their feet and made haste to depart. Japheth and Shem sent word that the retainers protecting the vessel had heard rumor of general flight. The stern moralists, the prophets and preachers of the land were quick to declare Noe chastened for his pride. Then the guards left too.

"The Mystery has shorn us," said Noe. "We are cut down to the bone."

Japheth settled in the room that had been his father's study but now was a loose lumber room holding a woebegone assemblage of boxes and cluttered things destined to be left behind: dishes, some broken, ledgers bearing the accounts of decades, maps and ceramics and coin collections, a vase Aunt Zelda had given, an occasional table scarred by the temerity of a neighbor's cigar. It was sorrowful to think, but almost certain that their enemies would first pillage, then burn the estate. The storied history stretching back before Methuselah would become a pile of ashes. The hatred for Noe's house was escalating. It was only the distance from the city that so far preserved them. The neighbors, it is true, might fight to preserve the buildings if there was any chance of them falling into their hands.

Each trip to the ark had been more harrowing than the previous one. Bandits set themselves along every possible route and waited. For a fortnight, the women had stayed at the ark, whilst the boys took turns with Noe making runs to retrieve what they could, irreplaceable items that must disappear forever otherwise. Yet Noe decided that they must be satisfied with what they had been able to preserve. A gang had set upon Japheth and Ham on their last journey. The brothers had fought off their attackers, but much had been taken. Sadly, the trunk with Professor Mushan's library had been among the lost things. The pages of his books flapped in the wind, while the mob gleefully tore the gilt-edged paper, threw venerable tomes in all directions. They seemed to care nothing. Destruction was their delight.

And so, Japheth was in his father's study using the roll-top desk for the final time. He was composing a letter — or, as Noe joked, "decomposing a letter," for there was a pile of rolled up paper littering the room.

"I have to get it right," he said.

"Son, you're putting too much pressure on yourself. Just tell her you love her and want her to come. If she is worth having, she'll show."

"It isn't that simple."

Perhaps it wasn't. Nonetheless, Japheth managed two closely written pages. They were tender words full of memories and hopes. Love made him almost a poet. Then he folded the missive, dropped the hot wax and imprinted the seal of the great, much maligned house. Fortunately, the mail carrier was not yet prejudiced against them, except to charge three times the going rate to carry their packages.

———————

In early morning, the people were busy sweeping out the dark water that had seeped into their cellars overnight, the stench of it so foul that they hung little sacks around their necks filled with crushed lemons or aromatic flowers. A few boys noticed them first. Charming, the way the turtles crept along the street — like an old, married couple. A trickle of beasts soon became a veritable parade: llamas and armored rhinos, the scoop-billed pelican, the prickly porcupine, panthers and elk and burly bears. All manner of beast came forth, even the mild, comical dodo. Folk wondered at the veritable animalia. "Amazing," they thought. "Amazing, how all this comes from chance. It doesn't seem it, seems there must be more. The world is wretched for tears, *lacrimae rerum* and all that, but beauty like this — you can't deny it. It's staring you in the face; innumerable forms, and the intricate, masterful web of life. It was natural to infer a Designer; but there, you see, things weren't always what they seemed. Any young couple in love learns this lesson when they discern forever is actually six months. So, it was nothing, nothing but protein soup and, who knows, a little electricity. Given eons, chance is sure to produce a host of novelties. Then what? They replicate, that's what, repeat the pattern. Here it was, flying, crawling, and cantering into that great big box. Like a toy chest — they'd have to make a great tall room for the giraffes — and another for the elephants."

"Uggh. Imagine the smell," said a fastidious woman.

"Fur, fur, fur, fur!" shouted another, who evidently had a phobia.

"I shouldn't like to be locked in there," chortled Jumbo, who had been scanning the crowd from beneath the brim of his bowler hat. "That box is like a tomb, a prison. We want life here, not prison."

"You've mixed your metaphors," observed a timid, educated man.

"Look here. We don't go for that kind of talk here, see?"

"I, I beg your pardon. I meant no offense."

"Escapism," said a last voice, no one quite saw who said it. Ravi wasn't there to show them. Yet the word was pronounced with such finality, everyone agreed it was correct. They left the parade to itself and each went to his home.

~~~~~~~~~~

The mountain stands shrouded in mist, far from any human eye. In the lower regions of its vast body, the boldest eagles peer out from their eyries built in places inhospitable to all but the daring wing. The air is crisp and quiet. Clouds form a thick, heavy mantle about the shoulders of the purple-black rock. The stars look down impassively upon the terrible peak. The spare eagle cry echoes long amidst the lonely rocks. Time seems nearly alien here. And yet it is not. At the very roots of the mountain, the foundations of the earth quake. Suspiring like a hushed, silky chant, echoing and surging through the depths of the earth, waxing in power, growing, growing like a rush of wild creatures raging across the plain, with unimaginable strength, yet noticed only by the sharp eyes of the eagles, the thunderous waters rise.

Molly's apartment is roomy with high ceilings. Lithographs and watercolors tastefully adorn the walls which are painted mauve and olive and light buttercup. She fuddles through her magazines and journals. There is a fine article on the mating habits of the osprey. Now she cannot look at it without thinking of her boy. She tries a book of poems but keeps coming back to the letter. With a sigh, she goes to the spinet, plays a piece she learned at twelve. She's not very good. *At least they don't have a piano on the ark*, she muses. Then the floor begins to rumble. It is the marchers outside. The dog is lying on the hearth rug. He lifts his head, looks at her with melancholy eyes.

"Oh, Hontu. Don't look at me like that. What did you expect me to do, really?"

Hontu whines ever so slightly and he is not a whiny dog.

"It's a mad bunch over there. *He's* mad." The letter remains gathering dust on the desk, unanswered, though a few pages of fine stationary have been pulled out. "Yes, he's sweet, too."

Hontu perks his ears, flicks his tail in a mild wag.

She listens carefully. The floor has nestled back into restive peace. The marchers have gone by.

"I can't think in here, Hontu. Let's go for a walk."

The walk along Marquetta Street had always been one of her favorites. The old-world windows with their flower boxes, the ironwork that formed ornate lines punctuated with stylized palms and irises, the railings and fences that skirted the edges of little, immaculate lawns, each fronting the two and three-story stucco buildings painted in delicate pastels. There were always cats on the porches waiting for a saucer of milk. Rows of old elm trees were planted along the sidewalk. A little further on, one came to the boulevard, the newsstand, the cafe, the kiosk where one could purchase a vanilla ice. Usually, it filled her with delight to walk with Hontu this familiar path. Today, however, she was moved to tears. Where were the cats and the smiling faces of residents who were wont to greet her with a cheery wave? The neighborhood was mute. The single face she glanced through an open window felt embarrassed, pretended to cough, and closed the curtains. The boulevard was worse. Hardly had she set foot upon the neat cobblestones when strangers, walking in groups of two and three, pointed and whispered, as if she were a leper entered illicitly into the lands of the well. The hair on Hontu's back bristled.

"Down, Hontu, down," she mumbled, then the quick command, "C'mon."

She might have turned then, made quickly for home. She did not. She wasn't even sure who had decided. Was it her or Hontu? Now they searched each side street and alley looking for safe passage. Soon, nothing beyond the tactical demands of her present situation occupied her thoughts.

~~~~~~~~~~

Noe discovered Japheth pacing the upper decks where one could peer out the small windows. At first his son made as if he were merely inspecting from on high the various habitats he had constructed. Now that they were filled with their proper guests, the interior of the ark seemed more mysterious and wonderful. Even in the grip of the fearfulness of the moment, one could not help a sense of wonder before the sheer prodigality of creation. "You've done good work, son," said Noe. "I'm proud of you."

Yet Japheth could not leave for long the bare nerve of his anxiety. Was it his doom to lie alone at night, to be preserved from catastrophe only to live out his days without the blessings of love and heirs to honor his name? So he had risked all on her and she had not come. For however long he lived, there would be regret and the sense that he had been a perfect fool. Thus, wrapped in anguish and yet harboring a vain prayer for Molly, Japheth veiled his eyes.

Noe understood his heart. The patriarch placed a hand on his son's shoulder. His eyes glistened and Noe grinned as if he were frothing over with a great, good joke.

"Father?"

"Don't worry."

"Don't worry?"

"Don't worry." This last conveyed with a vigor of sincerity that could not but seem unaccountable. Nonetheless, Japheth watched, temporarily taken from his bitter thoughts by the strangely moving picture of his father as he danced and sang along the walkways.

Molly Brice was glad of Hontu, glad of his growl, his muscular, lupine flesh, the cool, steady look he gave that unnerved strangers. Spilling from alleys and byways, creeping from townhouses and taverns, men and women seemed to let themselves go utterly. Hysterical laughter mixed with screaming crudities. Fighting occurred next to uninhibited, lascivious acts. Young men looted the stores. Crazily, it appeared that some store owners cooperated in their own divestment. Everywhere, violence and giddy excess held the day. Molly was jostled by the human stream, but so far had been generally unmolested. She made a dart under the archway that led to the Archives, and then cut a path over a courtyard to the winding stairs that reached the terraces. These were hanging gardens where the rich lived, looking, literally, down upon the ordinary populace. Here, too, however, the oppressive malady was evident. A city magistrate stood over a group of street urchins, egging them on to stone a wounded bird to death. And this was the most innocuous thing that Molly saw.

Then the mob appeared to select her. They glared at and coveted her. In horror, she began to run. She slipped on the stones by the old gatehouse. Only Hontu's rage bought her time to scramble to her feet. Somehow, they outpaced the pursuit, though she had lost all sense of rational movement. They entered the precincts of an ancient cemetery. The dead, at least, left her in peace. For some minutes, she and Hontu rested. Then with resolution, Molly set herself towards the ark. They followed a path that she hoped would end in country roads. For a span of perhaps a half hour, the ground seemed free of other sojourners with the exception of a few stray dogs. She whistled to Hontu and they quickened the pace. At the crest of a hill, they stopped. The ordeal before her became clear. The roads were packed with a turbid flow of heretofore ordinary citizens. These joined into loose collections of tempestuous ranks that spilled over from the roads into the fields and yards of simple country homes. It was never clear whether the rural population had barricaded itself within, holding weapons at hand against the urban intruders or if the country folk themselves had joined in to the spirited mayhem. Some of them certainly did. Regardless, the windows of their homes remained dark. The old ladies shivered in their starched, high-necked dresses, praying to any number of gods. The further Molly progressed, the more packed the roads became. She found herself in the absurd position of being both carried towards the ark by the impetus of thronging people yet kept from making a decisive break for it by the same milling humanity. Moreover, thousands roiled upon the ramp, strove for every path that might allow them to shout enmity at the house of Noe. The struggle to get this far had been at the limits of her strength. She had lost Hontu in the crowd, his bark calling to her, full of anxious fury. The darkening gloom over the sky was increasingly threatening. Never had she seen such portents. At midday the air was thick with smoke, green-black like the color of poisoned water in the desert. Trapped amidst the mob, Molly sensed the inevitability of her doom. She was surrounded by strangers. She could not even face her troubles with Hontu by her side. She took all this in, accepted it in horror, though shock still managed to grip her.

"This is the end," she thought. Her eyes searched for Hontu. She could no longer hear him. "Japheth," she cried. "I'm sorry."

Shastar tread a path along the mountain trails adjacent to the great height where Noe had built the ark. These were some of the footpaths he had tried when he first came to the land. From this distance, he could minutely survey the advancing of the hoards. He thought, for a moment, of Iradon. Iradon yet breathed somewhere. The rift between them had long since become unbridgeable by the onset of his old father's dotage. The thought seemed to bring a few beautiful boys out from similar perches. With amiable, confident steps, they huddled next to Shastar, beaming at him with pink, content faces.

"Lovely weather," tittered one.

"It's all come off rather nicely," said another.

"Go rot!" barked Shastar, so that the nephilim moved off, looking hurt.

~~~~~~~

Molly was never as alone as she imagined. Noe had sent two eagles to spy her out. They had soared high overhead, buffeted by the noxious winds that imperiled the sky. The birds-of-prey had been told to seek a girl and a dog with ice blue eyes. Noe gambled that Molly would not go far without her canine friend. The eagles had spotted Molly struggling; while one stayed and circled, the other returned to the ark. Noe had prayed heartily. He had placed wolves, lions, and elephants near the threshold of the vessel's open door. They were there to protect from evil, to admit only those who wished mercy, but none of these could have rescued the girl. Astonished, the crowd stood gaping, but only those near Molly. The others did not see the unicorn and might have denied it even if they did. The chivalric beast that honors the pure came right for Molly. Then somehow, she could never tell how, she found herself upon the strong back of the angelic steed. Her tears of sorrow became tears of wondrous joy. A silver nimbus of light emanated from the unicorn, most brilliantly at its horn, allowing her to see quite through the ominous veil that had descended upon the horizon.

"Oh, but Hontu! Hontu!" she gasped in renewed anguish. But this, too, had been provided, the Mystery hearing Noe's prayer. By some elevation of his nature, Hontu was running swift as the unicorn beside his mistress' mount. Those who looked up did not know them. They saw instead a bright comet splitting the sky.

~~~~~~~

A flash as bright and quick as lightning struck before the ark. While beasts and humans were yet blinking, Molly and Hontu stood before them. Japheth was the first to move. He had been waiting in anguish at the open door, so that now he ran to the girl, joyous and utterly surprised. He could make little sense of her words. "I came with the unicorn," she seemed to babble. "Yes, yes. You're here!" he babbled back in a delirium of delight. Then the guardians crossed the threshold. Noe had ordered them back into the vessel. When all were safely in, the giant door of the ark glided shut. With a clear, smooth thud, it closed, untouched by beast and human hand. At this, some of those outside the ark began to blanch. A tremor of real fear ran through their bodies. The shock was largely absorbed by the on-coming masses, but the urge to flee created a counter-current that soon formed its own eddies.

Shastar remained, standing alone on a ledge. He seemed destined to be forever apart from his fellows. The heavens grew dark and heavy, full of dark dreams, yet he seemed barely able to maintain interest, stifling a yawn even as the throngs ran helter skelter, some to their homes, and others to their barges, their canoes, their colorful hot air balloons. Priyanka spied him with the glass, cried to him, knowing he could not hear. And yet he seemed to mark her. His face turned, in the glass, displaying a droll smile.

"Not worth it. None of us is," he seemed to say.

~~~~~~~~~~

From the top most windows of the ark, Noe and his sons peered down upon the gathering mob. As far as the eye could see, they filled the land. More chilling than anything else was the remarkable order that had suddenly descended upon them. Gone were the signs of orgiastic abandon and mindless violence. The horizon itself seemed low and dotted with the innumerable ranks of the Kai marching, marching towards the ark. Already they were filling the lower portions of the main ramp. On every side, they came.

Each Kai thought that rights must be respected, that freedom and self-determination were the essence of morality. They were passionate. Each felt strongly the righteousness of their cause. Yet from the ark, the countenance of the throng exhibited a character morbid and sinister. As they came closer, with their torches and their song — yes, they sang, a hideous, slow, strident noise like insects murmuring — one could see their faces. Every trace of individuality and nobility had been drained from their visages. Even the children came, forming chains of protesting infants, mouthing the words of their elders in precocious, high pitched emulation.

"It is as if the dead walked," observed Shem, shaking.

"They are coming," said Priyanka, not because it was not obvious, but to put a name to their common dread. The beasts, too, trembled. Ham wanted to say that he would fight them, fight them all with his magnificent strength and undaunted courage, but no courage could meet such a challenge. He stared, flummoxed by the sheer numbers of the massing army.

"There are a hundred thousand within a quarter hour of the hull," said Japheth.

"Be not afraid," shouted Noe, so that the beasts could hear as well. "The Kai shall not touch the vessel."

Shortly after this, a rumble could be heard in the earth. The sky darkened directly overhead, obscuring the far rows of the enemies of the ark. The fires of the Kai dimmed in the gathering gloom. For half a minute, the stamina of the marchers wavered. Their infernal song began to wilt. Yet they rallied. The song resumed, the march quickened. Now the lead ranks were at the top of the ramp. Up close, their faces were blankly uniform, yet glowing with an odd semblance of beneficence. "For the people," thought one. "For my kind," another. No one rushed to throw flame upon the ark in order to support crime and infamy. Each Kai was filled with joyous hope of a better world. No matter what they thought, the same cry of "Kai, Kai, Kai" thrilled their lungs.

Niri and Sholon began to weep. There was nothing to do. They bowed their heads, tried to pray. Suddenly, the entire world seemed to hold its breath. One could see the Kai shouting, but no sound came from their mouths. It was not silence, however, but the might of a great wind that seemed to overpower them. A towering wave of water built, rising higher and higher, barely visible in the darkness. And then the waters fell, dousing the torches of the Kai, smashing them like flies so that their song and all their hopes came to nothing. A strange, sorrowful wailing emerged from the depths of the hold, as if the beasts, too, mourned the loss of their dear ones. And the ark shifted ever so slightly, like a sleeper pushed by the gentle, ineffective pat of a solicitous lover.

CHAPTER SIX

Absinthe

I T WAS NOT LONG BEFORE THEY DISCOV-
ered the ark was more than they had counted on, possessed,
perhaps, a mind of its own. Ham was on patrol with Niri
when he noticed a small gray marsupial, about two feet
long with tufted ears, shambling softly through one of the
ship's many passageways.

"Hey, I don't remember this little fellow coming on board,"
he said, pointing at the koala.

"Most likely the sweet thing came in with one of the rushes.
We just missed it, is all," guessed Niri. "I do wonder where it's
supposed to be, though."

"Fancy being called it," said Ham.

"Well, go ask it if it's a Mr. or a Miss, why don't you?"

"I'm not my father," grumbled Ham, who was miffed that
his small attempt at wit had provoked his woman.

Niri was not really put out, however. She had intended her
own response as a sort of joke. Ham was always misreading.
It was no good explaining, so Niri moved towards the koala
making tender little clucking noises and coos.

"It's not a baby, Niri," observed Ham, but the koala obliged
her all the same, stretching up its little arms and hugging the
girl so that she carried it quite like a small child.

"Don't baby listen to big, nasty man," advised Niri.

Ham at last understood that he was being joked, but his

smile was so much like a scowl it was difficult to tell.

Niri wondered aloud where "the baby" wished to be when another koala peered down at them from the rafters of a nearby alcove. "Oh, look, look," cried Ham's wife, pointing with her free hand. She was considerably more excited than the first koala, which appeared content enough to be on the edge of sleep. Following stairs and walkways, the couple eventually came to the alcove which turned out to be a spacious chamber with a tall, aromatic tree rooted in a substantial vat of earth. It seemed nearly certain that neither Japheth, nor anyone else had planted it there.

"Best get father," said Ham. "He can ask the little buggers how they got here."

~~~~~~~~~~

It soon became apparent that everyone had a mystery to share. Some reported hearing odd creaks and rattles in the ship's bones. Others claimed to hear whispers in shadows. When one approached in order to investigate hushed conversation, the ghostly chatter would stop and the walkways would be empty. No one recollected the koalas and Japheth confirmed that he had nothing to do with this particular habitat. "The question," pondered Noe, "is whether there is any connection between our noises and these koalas."

"I prefer 'tree babies,'" interrupted Niri (this is what she called the koalas).

"Well, what do they say? About how they got here, I mean," asked Molly, in spite of everything rather incredulous that Noe could actually communicate with the beasts.

"They can offer no illumination. Karkar and Miranda were simply feeding as they usually do when they suddenly found themselves here."

"This means that we cannot take the ark for granted," declared Shem sensibly. "We've been on board for weeks and had no idea about these, er?"

"Tree babies!"

"Yes, well, there might be any number of other things it seems."

"You speak true," agreed Noe, but his manner was distant and distracted. He was thinking a strange thought, for it appeared now that as large as the ark was, the Mystery was not shy to make it even larger, to add into it depths and riches they had not prepared for. Conversely, the ship was haunted by the unnerving rattle. "Let's do a search," commanded Noe, recovering himself. "But go in pairs for today—just in case." He did not say just in case what.

There were golden lions and harmless milk snakes, but cobras, too. There was the great and lesser auk, the industrious beaver, the harlequin okapi, shorter cousin to the giraffe that looks like a child's paint box creation. Amidst the transplanted trees, arboreal martens chattered and peeked from behind green foliage. Elsewhere, slow-moving manatees sweetly floated in one of Japheth's tanks. Not since the first days had the Two Legs come so close to the intimacy of the garden. A truce held a brief fragrance of Eden. So, the house of Noe sported with the wildebeest, the walrus, and the graylag goose. Rhumirrah, it is true, paced a great deal. She wished to run in wild places with the mate chosen for her by destiny. The horses yearned as well for the open meadows, but, generally, harmony was given to the creatures of the ark. And this was not all. Proud Mizzikin strutted because his favorite wife, Solitaire, had brought forth five kittens. It was an event for praise. That evening, Noe and his family held a feast in honor of young, fragile life.

Several uneventful weeks passed before the mongooses were upset. They scurried about making angry chirping noises. A single sentinel would pop its head out from hiding in the mounds and look about vigilantly as if it expected a falcon to swoop down any moment. When Noe appeared, the sentinel barked loudly at him.

"We don't likes this," said the earnest fellow.

Then another popped its head up. "It isn't ours," it informed rather timidly.

A third mongoose jumped up on the mound, began to furiously dig, before Noe realized the purpose.

"Stop!" he commanded. "You must allow us to try this matter."

A scribble of dots and swirls had been left in the sandy mound. Noe studied the marks. They were patterned in such a fashion that they appeared to be information, but the writing was in a tongue even Noe could not decipher. Naturally, the Latin script had not yet been invented, so he could not discern the meaning of "Absinthe is here."

The ark would not let them rest content. It kept presenting puzzles, a gathering of mysteries. Soon after the incident at the mongoose mound, Noe was cleaning out the muck from a paddock where zebra and antelope watched him with curious, innocent expressions. For a glimmer of a second, he thought he heard, incongruous, the sound of children's laughter. "Who's there?" More laughter, this time louder, slightly embarrassed, slightly caught. "Who's there?" he called out. After a few moments, a young female antelope stepped forward shyly.

"We are all here," she said, blushing (if an antelope can blush).

"Ah, ah yes," answered Noe. "I thought I heard children. Did you hear anything?"

"It is hard to say," said the doe. "We have never heard children before."

———∼∼∼∼∼∼∼———

"Why did I never go to see Maaren when she wanted me to see her blue dahlias or learn to make those little strawberry croissants with the feathery crusts, to dance the way that woman with the sinuous limbs danced, the way she stole all the men's eyes? But I do not want their eyes. I only liked the way she moved, for its own sake, but I could not make him understand.

"He was sketching then, too, always sketching, and I loved him. I love him now. See the way his lip trembles? When he is painting he tries to see into you with his impudent eye, but his mouth shakes, just ever so slightly, as if he were afraid. What is he afraid of?

"He took me to a lecture once, wanted to improve my mind. Because I'm shy and quiet, he sometimes forgets and thinks I'm simple. Why doesn't this make me angry?

"Because his mistake is so naive, I forgive him and even rather like it.

"In all the hurry, I forgot my favorite sundress. It seemed so frivolous to ask them to look for it. And now the sun seems so far away.

"He thinks I do not know about the sketches that he is hiding in those notebooks. What woman does not pry? What a burden he must feel, but I won't say anything. I'll wait. *So many, so many of them. Won't they let him alone?*

"It's silly, but I can't help thinking of the sundress. The white fabric with the pale lilac design. My purse goes perfectly with it and now it shall never seem complete.

"He spent a whole day once trying for a certain shade of blue. They were probably Maaren's flowers, poor things."

~~~~~~~~~~

The rain is pounding as it has for months upon the solid roof of the ark. "No leaks, no leaks," they laughed at first. Something else, Ham hears. A child's tune tapping on the piano, only shifted creepily into minor keys. It's a wonder that no one else hears it. "Niri? Niri!" he cries. Niri sleeps through anything. *Crap. Have to do everything myself. What a life! Damn rain. Wonder if it will ever stop.* Groggily, he stumbles forth to investigate. The ring-tailed marmoset has gotten out of its cage again. With a sigh, he lets it go. *One crap thing at a time. Doesn't anyone else hear the infernal stupidity of that racket? What the — ?!?*

A monstrous being stood over the piano, rapping the ivories with perverse insistence. Its upright frame was balanced by a long, lizard's tail. From behind, its head was round and squat, the size of a cannonball. Yet most repugnant to reason were the arrogant eyes, the scornful mouth embedded in the small of the creature's back. When Ham appeared, a tongue razzed him from this dorsal orifice. It turned then, placed its primary face before the son of Noe. This was almost lacking in expression, more simian than might be expected, though the complexion mixed drab olive with a sheen of gray and pale gold.

"I am the Argak," it hissed in a rough, throaty voice that sent a thrill along Ham's nerves. "I have heard and I have answered."

Ham stared with consternation. Never had he understood the speech of a beast. Was he becoming like his father at this late date? "What do you want?" he shouted in a kind of desperate yell.

"What do you want?" mimicked the creature.

"Who has summoned you?" asked Ham, retreating as the monster advanced.

Before there could be an answer, Shem came to the threshold of the room, cried out, stunned by the hideous thing menacing his brother.

"Two against one," announced the Argak. "Unfair."

"No stowaways," barked Ham, approaching the intruder with a terrible look.

The strange creature leapt at Ham, then pivoted, and made a run at Shem who tumbled onto the floor, surprised by the agile, unpredictable angles taken by his monstrous opponent. But the Argak did not take advantage of its foe. Its head did not glance down, but glided laterally, maintaining an odd stillness as women do in certain Asiatic dances. Ignoring Shem, the lizard reached with its tail, snatched Ham by the ankle, brought him down to the floor. Then Shem charged with a battle cry, threw his shoulder into the ribs of the creature, yet this barely shook the Argak. With a short punch, it sent Shem reeling. Gripping Ham about the shoulders, the Argak pulled the warrior close, whispered into his ear.

"I know your secrets," it said.

Ham struggled to reduce his enemy's hold. "I have no secrets, stowaway," he puffed. Turning and twisting to the limits of his great strength, he was just able to find some space, thrust a sharp palm upward into the chest of the Argak. It was a shattering blow that would have rendered any human combatant dead or unconscious, but the Argak only laughed.

"Who sayss I am a stowaway?"

Ham grimaced at the demon, thinking of the koalas he had discovered with Niri. "You are ugly," he said at last, unhappy with his answer.

The Argak appeared to rejoice in Ham's disgust. Locked in a violent, mutual clench, the lizard demon breathed softly, gave to its foe an ardent look. "I was born in your heart, sire."

Ham's body shook. A chill ran through him and he felt a sickness that caused him to sprawl on all fours, retching.

Thwack. The alarum had been given. Noe and Japheth came. Noe's ironwood staff hit its mark, a greasy gray-green blood dripped from the Argak. Even this seemed not to dismay it. The creature dismissed the others, renewed its struggle with Ham. "Your deep thoughts strengthen me," it whispered.

"You are . . . nothing of mine," declared Ham doubtfully. Panic raced through him. He was less afraid of the monster than of what it might say in the presence of his family. Then Ham went at the Argak in fury. He minded not the blows of the opponent, gripped him close so that when the creature tried again to throw him to the ground, the pair fell as one. Painfully, they battled, oblivious to the shouts of the others. When both had rolled, then pulled themselves up into standing position, Ham saw his chance. Hurling himself into the air, he fell upon the Argak from above. With a sharp crack, Ham delivered the death blow, breaking the vertebrae high, where the neck met the strange, amphibious head. Then Ham roared as the creature shuddered and fell backwards, its predatory limbs flopping like useless noodles.

Shem helped his brother up. They peered in uneasy fascination at the taut, golden skin sculpted like a cobra distended over a supine wrestler. The dorsal face frowned at them.

"That's not very nice," it said, then fell mute.

Niri was still sleeping when he returned to their bed. Ham debated waking her — to complain she had not come with the others, to tell her of his victory, but in the end, the rush of adrenalin and joy in victory deserted him. He let her sleep, looked on with admiration at her quiet, innocent slumber, at the lovely curves of her recumbent form. Then exhaustion swiftly felled him. Later, he was less tolerant. No one spoke of his battle with the monster. When he mentioned the creature, they appeared half perplexed, half suspicious, as if he were pranking them. Full of a new fear, Ham went to the room they had playfully dubbed the conservatory, looked all around for the Argak. Nothing. The space was empty of any sign of the conflict. It would not be easy to dispose of so large a carcass. Perhaps Shem had wanted to draw it, dragged it to his studio. The elder brother was in a foul mood. He could draw nothing and thought Ham ridiculous.

The middle son was left befuddled. Had he dreamed it? It must be so. Yet his side ached, was bruised where the enemy had struck.

~~~~~~~~~~

More scribbles of cryptic symbols began to show up on the ark. The mice discovered strange figures etched into a bit of sawdust where they had been gnawing. A gyrfalcon showed them tarrish ooze that had been swathed in rough patterns on the tall rafters. No one claimed responsibility. No one knew what it meant. Noe paged through the scattered notes upon which Japheth had attempted to discern the meaning. He had small, discrete units that might have been the beginning of something . . . if his cipher were correct. Inevitably, the lucidity would prove illusory, the code broke down. Perhaps the code changed, perhaps there was no code.

Life is like this. Ham is in the shower, thinking of a dozen things he must do. First, he must repair the bulkhead where the rhinoceros was overly rambunctious and then there are mama's flowerbeds that the goose keeps messing up. What else? Ham's breath catches sharp. Under his arm, there is a something. He stops, stands frozen as the water pours over him. Perhaps he is mistaken. That's possible, isn't it? Rapidly, his nerves shocking, Ham looks again beneath the fold of his arm. It's there! A patch of discolored skin, leathery and green-gold. Horror and anguish join with sheer panic. Ham lathers and scrubs until he nearly bleeds. There is no mistaking it. Already, this new thing, which five minutes before was less than nothing in his thoughts, has become the center of everything. His mind starts making practical arrangements. He'd have to wear a shirt to bed, for instance. Think up some excuse for Niri. Noe is the closest thing to a physician. Never. He'd go to Priyanka first. But he is not ready for that. And now he is toweling off, dressing with unsteady, fumbling fingers. Next, he is rummaging through the stores, lots of herbs and roots that Noe would understand, but Ham has never had much use for. In a small supply closet, he finds a canister marked balm. He will try rubbing with this. It may help. It's good balm; says so on the label.

All day he is distracted and short with others. "What a grumpy fellow he is," they mumble.

———————

The face came to Shem unbidden with a tenacious hold. He tried to put it out of his mind — it was inconvenient, after all, but it would not leave. Why was it that it should pester his consciousness, drag itself into the seat of imagination when he wanted other things? There was nothing even remarkable about the man: a blocky, square head with a rather pronounced frontal bone, the lips bowed with a slightly truculent turn of expression. It was mid-afternoon before he recollected the foreman of the machine works. Shem had spoken to him once about the art of clock-making, a hobby of the fellow. Yet, remembrance did not exorcise the image of the face. In exasperation, Shem grabbed a sketchbook, dawdled with a piece of graphite until the clock-making enthusiast stared back at him, true to life. And then another visage came to mind: a thin, febrile image of a great-aunt who habitually dipped her madeleine in weak lime-blossom tea. Shem added the likeness of his half-forgotten relative to the pages of his memory book. A half dozen others followed in rapid succession — and at the end of it, with a knowing, bemused smile and those sharp eyes that always hid something from him, the green-haired girl, Absinthe.

———————

Solitaire was in a panic. Her kittens were missing. Mizzikin had yawned, said that kittens always turn up, but all Solitaire could think was hawks and coyotes and terrible falls. There were plenty of fears upon the ark. In the end, to placate her,

Mizzikin went looking. When the tom could not find the mischiefs, he was unwilling to admit any real anxiety. Why, there must be dozens of interesting places he had not had time to discover just yet. His kittens were naturally adventurous, taking after their papa. It wasn't good to hover. How could a cat learn the necessities of being intrepid and dashing, acquire that manner of being so resplendent and so forth? Still, he went to see Noe, rubbed himself ingratiatingly around the patriarch's shins, just to remind him the honor of Mizzikin allowing him to share space on Mizzikin's boat.

"It's nothing, really. The feline, you know. She worries. The kittens are missing. I'm sure they'll turn up. If you see them, you might put in a word. They shouldn't worry Solitaire. Tell them from me."

Noe said he would keep an eye out for the new young. What he did not tell the tom was why the hairs on his arms had stood at his news, and why the beat of his heart had caught in his chest, for this was not the first report he had heard that day. The tiny rabbits, their eyes barely opened, and the baby black goat, docile and affectionate, had all gone missing.

~~~~~~~~~

Shem cannot tell you, because he does not know why he is sixty feet up measuring out line to cross the width of the ark when there are walkways to keep one safe, why he is pulling the line tight and making sure it is secure, then doffing his shoes, taking a thin stick of willow wood, and then launching himself so that he is soon tiptoeing with his twitchy balancing pole over an abyss, traipsing dangerously across the collective heads of Noe's menagerie.

Ham sits alone in the corner of the room he has taken over. He has moved out. Niri cries and cries outside the door. His mother brings his favorite dishes. He will not unseal the door. What if they should see him?

Scraping and scraping, he takes the broken pot, strikes against the Argak.

Japheth does not sleep. His desk is covered with papers. He cannot leave his calculations.

~~~~~~~~~~~~

"What is wrong with Ham?"

"I don't know, Mother. He doesn't talk to me. You know how he is."

"He ought to talk to you."

Niri was silent then, folded the wash and waited to see if Priyanka would say something to break the awkwardness. When she did not, the girl felt her hands begin to tremble, her face grows hot. "How can she blame me?" she thought.

"*She doesn't look after him,*" thought Priyanka.

~~~~~~~~~~~~

"You must see to your sons!" shouts Priyanka, angry and bewildered. "None of this should have happened! None of this!"

She does not say it, but the stress of condemnation is clear. But what would she have had him do? Would they have been better off drowned?

Later, he goes to Ham. "There is no one else here. Open the door to me."

For a long time, there is no sound and then the sliding sound of a lock undone. Swiftly, Noe rushes to his son. What is there to see? A creature half human, half demon? Ham's body is scraped and bleeding, his pure skin mutilated by the boy's own hand. Noe watches in agony as his bold young man breaks down into tears.

"Now you know! Now you know!" cries Ham.

~~~~~~~~~~

If things had been ordinary, if it made sense to speak any more of ordinary, he would have summoned the house of Noe which was now simply the house of Man. He would have told them the trouble, asked them to search with him for the young ones. But he knew he could not add new troubles, so he searched by himself with anxious step. Somehow, this new life was especially precious. He walked for hours. Deck by deck, room by room, he investigated with waning expectations. When he saw one of his children, he fibbed, told them he was on other errands or just checking the ship. All too easily they were ready to believe him. They were each heavy with their own concerns. And the hours brought no relief, no happy discovery. Downtrodden, Noe thought of checking in with the mothers to see if any young had returned when he was distracted by the gentle strumming of a mandolin. He followed the winsome tune, half expecting the music to die out into enigmatic, unoccupied space. So, it was a surprise when he rounded a turn and came upon the green-haired girl sitting content at the foot of a silver birch.

"That's a nice melody," he said.

"Yes, the jongleurs made it up. Isn't it clever?"

Noe remembered the painting Shem had brought with him. "I think you know my son."

"I know all my children," said Absinthe.

"My wife will be surprised to hear that."

The girl laughed a guileless laugh. "You are thinking like a dusty head."

"Well, I've been told that quite often now that you mention it."

"What happens when I stop playing?"

"The music stops."

"And what do you hear then?"

"Silence, of course."

"Where does the music come from?"

Noe was baffled by this catechism but answered as best he could. "The music is the joining of the craft that made the instrument and the art that knows how to play it."

Absinthe waved her hand as if to shoo away an irritating fly. "Yes, yes, but where does the music come from?"

"I don't understand."

"Ah, wisdom," said the girl, clapping.

"You'll have to explain."

"It cannot be explained."

Noe dropped his head in bemused resignation. "Do you know anything about the missing babies?"

"No one is missing. The lost are found. You are never alone."

"It doesn't feel like it."

Absinthe looked tenderly at him with real sorrow. "No, it doesn't."

"You're trying to tell me something with the music thing, but I can't get it."

"The dust thinks how and with what. It never thinks the gift. It thinks the music, but not the silence."

Noe smiled ruefully. Was it his imagination or had the mandolin changed color? "No, I'm still not getting it."

"You might try walking that way," she said, pointing to a black asphalt road bathed in moonlight.

"What is this road?" he asked.

"The long way home," she said.

~~~~~~~~~~~~

For what seemed a number of miles, the road was empty. Then Noe came to a slow stream that widened out into a river that was spanned by a bridge made up of stone arches. At the end of the bridge was a stout, square building of ancient brick. It was the color of the bridge and not the color of the gray buildings that stood in somnolent grandeur behind the gate-house. He had to knock three times at the shuttered window before the keeper grudgingly responded. The gate-keeper was old even by the standards of old men. Some people, when they get old, expand into a sort of shapeless jelly-fish, with just enough skeleton to quiver in unsteady steps. And others shrink into themselves, neatly and compactly, into a kind of brittle stick. The gate-keeper was a stick.

"The boys are mostly out," said the old man, shaking his head. "I hope nothing terrible happens to them. Last Michelmas — or was it Candelmas? — well, it was sometime most likely, we had a young Edmund, Skipper or Kipper or something like that, he fell into a canal and was drownded. His father came all down-hearted and his mother crying like April showers and the boys all read poems about how terrible a loss it was."

"That is very tragic," answered Noe politely.

"But then, even in term, there was the young fella who jumped from the bell tower." The old man hushed his voice and winked at Noe. "They do say it was a prank, see, and somebody got out of hand and maybe pushed . . . "

Noe cleared his throat and informed the gate-keeper he did not wish to see a student, but someone in authority, perhaps one of the masters.

"Alright, alright," answered the old man. "But none of them die during break," he added with a curious chagrin. The porter led down a path filled with ivied walls and arched walkways. He grumbled the whole way, but it was impossible to decipher more than an odd word or two. Some fellow named Kotko was compared to a chamber pot, but nothing of any real significance was conveyed. At last, they arrived at a Commons Room gloomy with dark woods and plush worn chairs where a number of dons lounged, blithely oblivious that they were enveloped in clouds of ill vapor. A picture of indescribable ugliness and banality resembling a squashed fly pressed against a background of volcanic flame stood hanging above their heads. They looked with incredulity upon Noe. When he began to speak, they frowned. A brief quorum resulted in one of them taking him down a corridor and then through an open arcade to another building. The professor was only too glad to usher Noe into a small office and be rid of him.

———————

"You are not from here, I think," said the expert at the desk who was named Dr. Thorenson. From the upturn of the scrawl of his mouth, it was evident this was meant as a wry bit of humor.

"I am looking for the babies. Do you know where they are?"

"Have you been here long?" continued the man, his sterile coat pressed and gleaming. What was it about his movements, the pauses and the manner of speech? He is one of their priests, concluded Noe. As Noe continued to stare silently, Dr. Thorenson shrugged his shoulders. "Let's just have a little chat. Dialogue is the first step towards understanding." Noe would have liked to say that the expert was at this very moment emitting a repugnant syrup of ashy drool from his nostrils and from the corners of his thin, colorless lips, but he decided such candor unwise under the circumstances. Instead, he observed how tidy the room was.

"Yes." Dr. Thorenson made a note to himself that the new pea green coat of paint was soothing to schizophrenics. "Now let me ask you," he continued in his mild, professional, confidential voice, "what brought you to our fair city?"

"A friend in the country suggested I look up one of her pals."

"Ah. I have friends in the country," prodded the doctor. "Might I possibly know her?"

"I doubt it."

"What's her name?"

"She might know you, of course," asserted Noe.

"I can respect that. Let's move on. Why did you come to the university? Several dons expressed concern."

"How is that?"

Dr. Thorenson gave Noe an apologetic look. "In the past, you see, people did not understand about germs and electricity and plate tectonics and all manner of things. When bad things happened, they tended to connect it with some moral failing or scapegoated some vulnerable outsider."

"There is no sin?"

"Why, there is error. There is crime, I admit. Sin is another matter. Sin is all tied up with guilt and projection. It's a terribly inefficient concept." Noe possessed some quality, in spite of his obvious deviancy, that Thorenson subconsciously admired, though he could not identify precisely what it was. "Our ancestors," he continued, "were sadly trapped in mythic ways of thinking. They tended to project, to take feelings and responses constructed by their environments and to proclaim them the voice of some god, for instance. I'm sure you are familiar with all this."

"It happens, no doubt."

The doctor was agreeably surprised by the open-mindedness of his patient. "Then you will also be aware of certain cognitive dissonances that occur. Sorry, I don't mean to be technical. The person who projects can become alienated from themselves. They suffer a radical breech between their ordinary, decent selves and the authority figure in the imagination."

Noe did not seem to appreciate the knowledge the doctor had condescended to share with him. Thorenson was frequently frustrated by the dullness of his listeners. With renewed effort, he made a stab at clarification. "The important thing is to gain objectivity. One has to grasp fundamental reality. We know how to do that. We have spent centuries developing a proper method." The black smog was now so thick it veiled the features of the doctor.

"If you cannot tell me about the children, I'll be going," answered Noe.

"Ah, yes. Thank you. I see that theory does not interest you." He wrote down magic words in a crabbed scribble: "monomania, possibly psychotic break. Interesting case."

~~~~~~~~~~

"This is the children's ward," declared Dr. Thorenson as he opened a heavy door that led into a large dormitory. "Come, have a look. You might find it instructive."

Rows and rows of iron beds with sterile, starched sheets filled the room. The fluorescent lamps built into the ceiling cast a depressing light that seemed to make everything they touched somehow stark and uglier than they would have been under the ordinary sun. Noe was immediately struck by a wave of sadness. A smell of antiseptic pervaded, its pungent opposition to malodorous interference bespoke not cleanliness, but a kind of desperate camouflage. The faces of the nurses were masks professionally neutral or tinged with ennui. All the children suffered from some form of severe malady. There were babies confined to cribs, their heads swollen to the size of large watermelons. "Hydroencephalitis," informed the doctor in a cool, clinical tone. The nurses had most of the children strapped down in beds or in strollers where their heads lolled to one side like abject ragdolls.

"Nature is profligate, but she makes mistakes," said Dr. Thorenson, stopping before a girl with a cleft palate. "Think of all the unmerited pain," he uttered almost in a moan of anguish. "With genetic screening and therapeutic selectivity, none of these children need ever have suffered." Noe's eyes suddenly left the physician. In a distant corner of the dormitory, an exile from the geriatric floor appeared to have been left to babble mindlessly amongst the children. "That is Father Peguy," sighed Dr. Thorenson. "We used to keep him out, but he kept wandering in." A closed, pinched expression settled onto the doctor's features. "I must admit, he does have a calming effect on some of them. Like calls unto like, I imagine."

The intercom buzzed, taking Noe's guide away from further comment. The patriarch was left to absorb the lesson. Should these children never have been born, then?

"You are a child waiting for the snow," said Father Peguy. The little boy was wearing a leather helmet because he was subject to seizures. The boy laughed with a giddy joy and clapped his hands at Father Peguy's pronouncement. A flustered, impatient voice rang out from the middle of the great room, its echo resounding with brief anger. "Agnes! Agnes!" it yelled. "Put down those blocks before you hurt yourself." The nurse to whom the voice belonged sighed, her short, rounded legs carrying her first to the disobedient child, then towards Noe. She evidently mistook Noe for an important visitor because of the way Dr. Thorenson had been speaking to him. She grabbed the boy with the helmet roughly by the hand. "Stephen, can't you see that Father has a visitor?"

She dragged the boy off, who was mute before her chiding. When they were gone, the priest turned to Noe a tolerant smile, his gray-blue eyes displaying no discernable signs of dementia. "The people of the city brought them to me," he said without introduction. "Afraid the Mercy Laws would find them out. They would come, shame-faced or desperate, pleading that one more space be made. And always, somehow, the space was made. Dr. Thorenson is thankfully one of those illogical men who is better than his education. He is ashamed of his love for the children, but he helps me to protect them."

Noe understood then that Father Peguy was under the delusion that *he* ran the asylum. Unconsciously, he backed away slightly.

"Ah, you find it unbelievable? A pious tale, grotesque even?" As Noe did not answer, the priest drifted. "Stephen. Stephen is a special one," he announced, a smile of whimsy etched into his craggy face. There was something otherworldly about the priest.

He seemed to exude a permanent sense of mild playfulness, as if some invisible companion were forever at his side whispering an array of gently amusing jokes. "I saw him once, scrambling about in a mad rush. He is hyperkinetic. And I called to him. Emily, Nurse MacReady, thinks he is a devil because of all he gets into. And she's a simple woman. Stephen's not pretty, so in her mind he is already half evil. But I know." The priest held up his hand as if to take an oath of veracity. "He is exceptionally obedient and he tries all the time. You just can't see it for all the mad gyrations his body makes. So, I called to him and when he came, I saw such brightness in his eyes."

Nurse MacReady returned with two cups of tea. Evidently she felt some kindness towards the man. Father Peguy sipped silently on his tea. For a long time, he was taken with his own thoughts and Noe considered leaving him to his reflections, but when he made to rise from his chair, Peguy checked him.

"I was telling you about Stephen."

"Yes," answered Noe.

"They let me have my books, you know." The priest volunteered this with pathetic happiness. "Catherine of Siena had been given the stigmata and a wedding ring of flowers." Again, the priest fell silent with his head bent in an attitude of attentive listening. Noe could make nothing of this gratuitous information and sipped nervously at his tea. The sepia liquid was more hospitable than good. Shortly, the priest resumed his narrative. "Catherine asked the Lord to keep them invisible because she was a great woman and did not wish to provoke others or magnify herself, but I was thinking how many to-day" — his voice emphasized that "today," making of it two stressed syllables — "would hear of it and prefer to think that she wished them invisible because they were not there." For a moment, the quiet smile disappeared from the priest's face. Noe desired to query him about the identity of this lord he spoke of, but Peguy was evidently wrestling with great emotion. "You know what has happened?" His eyes seemed to stare right through Noe. The patriarch was quite sure he had nearly been forgotten. "We have stopped loving life. We no longer believe it is a good thing. That is why the men in the city scold their loins and mothers apologize to their children for having borne them into such a place. And *my* children! We have no use for them. What a word — 'use' — as if a man's worth was in what he can do and not in the great and mighty mystery that he exists at all."

Father Peguy rose from his seat. When he did so, Noe saw that a toy had been left at the feet of the cleric; a miniature boat with little plastic animals and a plastic figure that looked like a shepherd. Noe's head began to swim while the nerves in his limbs tingled with an electric thrill — but the priest was distracted, warily peering about at the nurses and doctors. "We have grown monstrously tired. Even our children are born old and leering, enticed by the serpent . . . " Then the cleric fixed Noe with a sharp look. When he spoke, his voice trembled. Noe had the odd sensation that the old priest had been waiting for someone he could tell his secret to. "Into each one of us, there is spoken a name. I don't mean the name your parents gave you!" He paused for a moment and tilted his head as if he were listening to a voice hidden in silence. "Of course, sometimes it is apt — a kind of promise to the future. The name I intend is buried deep in our hearts."

"When you hear the name given from eternity it does not come to you with the clarity of speech, but as a mysterious call of love. This is what Teresa calls the interior castle. We all have this, but we are apt to confuse it with our individuality. This fraudulent imposter is what we love and when we protect it, we think we are protecting the secret name, but it is not the same. It is a mesh of various factors, our temperament, our education, our ancestry, and the accidents of life. We are all of us wounded. No one hears the name without help. Every man lies to himself. You have to cut away the fake, but to do that you must desire joy — and we are too weak for that. We confuse the gift with our chosen pleasures." The priest's rambling words somehow reminded Noe of something Absinthe had said about silence. He nodded gravely. Father Peguy had a fit of coughing. Noe's discomfort rose, even as he tried to make sense of the eccentric oration. It was hard to understand, but the priest was by no means a fool. Abruptly, the cleric finished his thought. "They are eventually not even pleasures, but urges to vanity, lust, gluttony — tiresome pests we must bear with as much equanimity as we can muster." The nurses were milling. Soon they would come to break up the meeting. Noe actually breathed a sigh of relief, but the priest had one last word to divulge. He tapped Noe fraternally on the shoulder, one father to another.

"I called to Stephen and the child came," he said with tears in his eyes. "'Aren't you longing for your Lord?' I asked and he shook his head as if he really understood. There was such a look of excitement in his eyes and I said to him, 'You are a child waiting for the snow.' It came to me like a glimpse of his true name." The priest lowered his voice as the nurses descended upon them with industrious vigor and little nothings of "that's enough, dear" and "time for a rest, Father."

"So, I brought him the Sacrament." Father Peguy smiled. "And I have gone on doing so. All the children, I have been feeding."

"Hey, see what I can do. Look here," said a small voice.

"Pet me next, me next."

"Me, too," said another.

Noe followed the voices, his heart renewed with hope. The kittens and the rabbits and the kid goat and more besides gamboled and pranced about. Even some older beasts had joined them. Why, there was Fergus wiggling his tail like a happy piglet and a mouse brown wren preening like a peacock. Every young thing had slipped away, made a careful path to this common destination, a bay stacked with feed. In the foreground, where there was room to move about, Absinthe stood at the center of the babies, a gentle smile of warm regard on her face.

"The dams need not fear," she said to Noe, who was too astounded to say a thing. "The children are safe with me. But go now, little dears. We will play again." The babies complied, not without small lament and some tarrying. Then the girl gave to Noe a glance of power and mysterious beauty, a radiance for which he was unprepared. There was something in her expression he could not take in: it seemed to contain contraries, though in a pleasing manner that promised rest that was also adventure, plenitude rich in desire without the anguish of lack. His mind clouded with an excess of light that was hard to distinguish from darkness.

When the First Mother had first discovered herself ripening with the first child ever to be born, she hearkened back to a word the Mystery had given. Origin had promised enmity between her seed and that of the serpent. It was a male child that was spoken of. The serpent would bruise his heel. He would bruise the serpent's head, all very misty. Then when Eve bore her son, she said that she had "gotten a man with the help of the Mystery." She thought perhaps of that slim hope that seemed to be hinted at; that her progeny would undo the harm of their sin . . . but then that son was Cain. The vision of Absinthe filled Noe with hope. He would return to it at all hours, trying to discover its meaning. Yet, even so, tedium beset them and anxiety of life went on. At times, he felt as if these were a surface of weather; that he, himself, was a mountain, deep and silent, majestically serene. Mostly, however, he felt that this must be an illusion, for the weather was his feelings and thoughts. Then the ecstasy of vision that sometimes warmed his heart was like a flash of brilliant light in a misery of darkness. It might be consolation, but it wasn't enough. One thing did change. He found that his hearing was improved. The haunting voices that arose by caprice or some unfathomable law became more distinct and he could often discern long stretches of conversation though almost all were smatterings of private thoughts or intimate conversation too opaque for a stranger to understand. Once, he hesitantly broached the subject of Absinthe with Shem.

"So you've seen her?" he said.

"Recently," he answered.

Then Shem laughed. "I knew it."

"What do you know?"

But Shem could not tell his father. He shrugged. "Woman is a puzzle. Sometimes I think even to the God."

~~~~~~~~~

Someone was shrieking inside. He was praying for death. The ivy had taken over the back of the yard, draped over the side of the shed like a robe half flung over a naked shoulder. On the weathered door of the garden shed was the empty carapace of a caramel colored beetle, a beautiful shroud.

She remembered going across the street to Mike's. It was just a house in the neighborhood where they fried fresh fish and wrapped them in newspaper. Mike's old woman fixed the pike or haddock right in front of you while you waited. Everyone sat on the porch and ate, watched the twilight dim into sleep.

In exile, far from home, he loved the little maple tree and the tiny bridge over the koi pond. The moment lost to his dull eye leapt radiant in memory.

Pathetic the body. Ripeness of youth squandered complacently in a rush of years, then losing hair, except for in the ears and the nostrils, how quaint. Ugly tags and dark spots begin to mottle the skin. The shoulders slump, the knees ache, one carries it about with awkward, humiliated patience. Longing to be rid of this rotting box, some danger comes and the familiar stranger appears, reverence for the flesh.

Those who did not court silence spoke no words. They could only babble the garish tongue.

The property was out in the sticks. His feet trudged unevenly upon the dirt. At the fence, the old horse waited. He approached hesitantly for the creature was unfamiliar. Then in a startle, the stallion's head lurched forward, nuzzling the stranger with the gift of kindness.

Some of the women were quiet and composed. Others

cried softly, while still more wailed. Behind each with shadow feet were the silent men that marched them in rows to the prearranged site. Kneeling, their necks bowed, they never saw the knives that rendered them pilgrims to join the emperor to whom they had been so foolish not to bear an heir.

"I am only here to say one true thing. Do not mutter and do not squint and skeptic. I am not here to care whether you believe or understand, though perhaps if none discern, the truth will be barren and then I do not know if it is truth or a possibility lost." They had not, really, expected the girl to speak like that. They were, what you call, taken aback. The emissary in her dark blue velour, and the headdress the color of sky, looked out from bronze skin and viridian eyes.

A number of crows had been following her around. They would not actually attack her, but swooped low in a menacing way. When she had come to the edge of a garden wall, the crows flew into a linden tree and stared down at her. As she watched them, they transformed into old women with faces like gnarled apples. Veils of black cloth swathed bodies shrunken, nearly fleshless. The women cackled amongst themselves, until one of them looked directly at her.

Dundeedle eggs. Very rare. Priced two hundred pounds. Available by special delivery.

He'd done his graduate project on the color yellow, videotaping yellow objects and people wearing yellow. There was no attempt to explain, though Max had asked a physicist to speak about wavelengths and color. This was the only credible expression of fact. Yet it had been a great hit. De Witt had taken his degree "with honors" and his professors wrote him glowing recommendations.

There were worlds where the torture was clear, where soldiers raped the women and then tied their limbs to vehicles that moved in opposite directions. And there were quiet places where no one is appalled while the sweet eye of the soul is plucked and pickled in brine.

"I can't find Matilda, Sebastian? I've looked everywhere."

"You haven't looked everywhere, Winnie."

"I have."

"How about the Pacific Ocean?"

"Sebastian! Stop teasing Winnie."

"Uncle Robin was talking to Mama and Papa. I heard him say coyotes were seen about. Suppose they got Matilda, Etty?"

"Pffft. Uncle Robin. Coyotes are nowhere near here, Winnie. Put that out of your mind. Besides, our dogs would keep them off."

"They can't keep them off if they aren't around."

"Sebastian, now look. You've made Winnie cry. You're a regular rotter. Matilda . . . Matilda . . . Where are you, Matilda?"

"Don't cry, Winnie. I'll go look in the loft. I bet that's where she is. Matilda likes it up there almost better than anywhere else."

"Then why doesn't she come and answer, Sebastian? She always answers."

Scotty dog magnets. Sweater girls. Saddle shoes. Root beer floats.

"Anyone who is honest will have to admit that most of the time, one simply can't stand people."

"You are a perfectly dreadful man!" declared Elspeth.

"But honest," laughed Eric.

"I suppose just this minute?"

"Indeed, I despise you all."

"Then why do you stay? I dare say you haven't the money for a taxi. Here, let me get it for you."

Guts and feathers and bone, skin speckled, peeled back, the flesh of fowl pared by the cook's knife, the smoke of the fire tapering its soft silent dance, stretched thin until its darkness reaches up to the roof tree and through the chimney, joins the sleep mask of the earth, star sprinkled. Dog lay drowsing under the table, lost to dream.

Karanda, advisor to Ibn Shadad, claimed to be a genie, though no one ever saw him disappear into a bottle or otherwise behave in a ghostly manner. When Mia, the most beautiful and favorite wife to Ibn Shadad, was discovered to have taken a lover from amongst the white devils, Karanda was blamed, for it was suspected that it was through him that the affair had been allowed to take place. He had a weakness for very small things, intricately made. It is said that one of the white devils was carrying back miniature furniture he had acquired for his daughter. When he showed them to Karanda, the advisor offered him tea with a flower in exchange for a Queen Anne love seat the size of a thimble. And so, it began. The match could only have lasted a matter of weeks. The embassy left and all would have been well, but for a certain swelling of belly and talk from the rival women. If you are queen, do not slip. Mia fled, along with Karanda. The white devil had long since disappeared. Pursuit was given to the four corners. A horn was sounded and the great man sent for. Ibn Shadad, in black wrath, came upon Karanda leading a quaking figure hidden in veils. He cut down Karanda with a swift blow from his scimitar, cleaving him in half. It is claimed that when he went to garrote the veiled one, the cloth instantly sank into an empty heap and that the slain Karanda spoke one last time to his master. "I am definitely not going to serve you any-more," he said.

"I have never in my life been so cold. It isn't cold. I mean, I can see the sun, today gold and benign. Little girls are playing beside me. Skip ropes, obedient snakes twisting, loop, loop, and loop. A few of them nudge and stare. I, with my round, swelling, melon belly, with my shawl and my shifty-eyed, hunted look. See, I give them a quick, ironic, loving smile. I am you. Oh, I am you, little ones. Not so long ago. And now off for the shadows, though I am cold and the young men won't look at me."

"I feel as if I am a peach," said Featherhawk.

Adam glowered for a full ten breaths, wondering what to do with this being that had so abused her intelligence. "You look quite a bit like a young woman," he said at last, doing his best to reign in his irritation.

"Yes, I look like a woman," answered Featherhawk brightly. "Society has seen to it that I appear to be a woman, but in reality, I am a peach."

At midday, along a dark path, narrow and fading in from dust and rocks, it could not possibly be considered a path, this path, came a boy. A boy sun brown with glittery eyes and a fine white cloak and he led a man old, withered, blind, dirted with muck, his beard full of twigs and small mice, smelling like rock that is buried deep within the earth.

The boy said nothing, but the old man said, "Beg, beg."

Sister Agnes had, from the time of their decision to take a detour, grabbed Bridget's hand and was now unconsciously squeezing it with a vice-like grip as she led her with increased haste to the hall devoted to natural history. Once there, Agnes pulled her past exhibits of mounted bears and lions, glass cases filled with insects in amber and the eggs of obscure birds. She carefully maneuvered Bridget to what she thought the most advantageous view of an almost complete skeleton of a stegosaurus.

"Isn't it marvelous?" she exclaimed, at last releasing her cohort from painful bondage.

"What is it?" asked Bridget, trying to take in the immensity of such a being.

"They say it is a large, armored dinosaur from the Upper Jurassic strata of geologic rock, but I have often wondered if this is not what is meant by a dragon."

"Where did they find it?"

Agnes did not hear Bridget. She was caught in her own excitement. "It couldn't be a dragon, though, because the stegosaurus is supposed to be from millions and millions of years ago and there were dragons when men lived in mead halls and castles, when heroes traversed the earth." Sister Agnes was a terrible romantic.

Then she turned to Bridget and whispered in a soft, almost frightened whisper. "But tell me, have you heard of Darwin?"

"No, Sister," answered Bridget, feeling herself entirely overmatched.

"Mr. Darwin was an atheist and had no use for God at all."

"I suppose he feels differently now," said Bridget, not knowing what to say.

"Oh, yes," giggled Sister Agnes. "Quite roasted."

In the quad, two men were discussing Bell's Theorem. The quantum world exhibited enigmatic affinities, the entanglement of electrons separated by vastness beyond any conceivable pull of gravity. The stable atomic billiard balls of the nineteenth century were dinosaurs unaware of their extinction. Matter was less and less a thing. It was a kind of unknown receptivity that revealed its presence when energy congregated into a pattern registered by mind. The discarded metaphysical concept of form had returned unrecognized as the flash of intelligibility.

Napoleon's sister had very fine feet and liked to show them off. Pushkin seems to have swooned rather badly over a petite foot. There was no mistaking these feet for those belonging to any fine lady. They were dusty, thick and leathery, with bunions and profuse hair on the joints of the big toes. The feet themselves were plainly embarrassed, as anyone could see from the way they shuffled and squirmed, afraid of the light. Then there was a fine, firm hand, its very motion full of noble authority, an artisan's hand commanding an obedient stillness. Worst of all, the pure, sweet water was poured into a bowl and then dispersed onto the humble, stinking trudgers.

"You were always the most gullible, dreaming dunce of a boy." She bit down on that last word, spitting out her contempt with relish. "Did you think I wanted to spend my life surrounded by country oafs, opening windows to the smell of animal dung and hearkening to the pleasantries of dandies talking endlessly of their hunting adventures and the speed of their horses? Narrow little provincial idiots — and what conceited moralists, too! And now I suppose you think I'm just going to pack up and come off with you, a fool and a boy!"

Three women, darkly shrouded and of uncertain age, were busy, but to what extraordinary purpose she could not fathom. One sat slightly apart from the others and spun a fine thread. Another stood and gathered the line, stretching it out and peering closely, as if eager to discern its quality. The third, perhaps strangest of all, seemed to measure out uneven lengths, cutting them, and tossing the bits into a basket at her feet.

"Aren't you afraid of cats?" she began in order to have something to say. It was a fine red thread they spun and cats like a scarlet toy. "Shhaa," said the one spinning and she looked at her as if she had suddenly and obscenely sprouted a second and grotesque head from the area of her right shoulder.

"You are an impertinent girl," said the woman examining for quality.

The black-skinned tents crouched low outside the walls of the City. It was a gypsy Sabbath. Some spent the holiday in a survey of booty. Others recalled the ghostly presence of lost family, so that the dead may rejoice, too, in the general prosperity. The men and women smoked or drank wine, played cards, music, and danced. Dogs and children raced about noisily without censure. Their stay within the City had been profitable and now, outside its walls, they looked forward to the resumption of the journey. In one tent, a gypsy mother called in her children to see a new addition. "This one has been given into our care. Look at her, a child of the fairies." Her children peered over in wonder and agreed it was no ordinary baby. "See how little, how precious she is," and they marveled at the fineness of the babe, its thick dark hair, its bronze skin, its shiny, emerald eyes.

The great fear of death is known to all men. What is less known, except to the mystics, is that the fear of death is nothing but a prelude, miniscule in comparison to the fear the spirit feels when it begins to rise into angelic precincts. We know little of this; quite rightly, or we should spend our entire lives in trepidation. Besides, it is the human way to encounter the eternal in the prosaic and particular details of our earthly lives. It pleases God to coax us, however unwilling, from our many hiding places.

God of horrors, rich in grief.

~~~~~~~~

When the voices had subsided Noe closed his eyes and breathed in slowly. Hontu, who had joined him on his rounds, came to heel. Breathing out, he opened his eyes to discover Father Peguy standing before him with a small round wafer in his hand. "Don't you want the little ticket?" he said in a soft voice. "Here it is — the lightning seed."

Instinctively, Noe glanced down to see if Hontu were also aware of the priest. The dog appeared to be vigilantly looking upwards, but in that brief flicker of inattention, Father Peguy had disappeared and the wafer had grown into a glowing orb slightly larger than a tennis ball. The orb hovered above them.

Then it began to trace a path forward into a region of the ark unknown to Noe. When the man and the dog appeared reluctant to follow, the orb returned and floated gently before them. After a while, it resumed its slow passage into an unmapped interior softly illuminating a mild ascent. At the point where the height of the trail hid any inkling of the silent land, the orb waited as if beckoning them.

"What do you say, dog? Up for an adventure?"

"Maybe there will be rabbits," said Hontu.

———————

For a long while, the orb led them. Then, it seemed to perch companionably at Noe's shoulder. When it dropped down and floated before his bosom, he took it in his hands. The orb settled against him like a warm dove. Then the wind kicked up and brought a nervy, gelid touch that made them both afraid. Noe did not think the orb capable of fighting it, so they sought temporary refuge in a cave. Though apparently large with a high ceiling, they were instantly aware of a feeling of cramped, suffocating clutter combined with musty air, damp and sour. Molten rock suffused by glittering shards of glass spilled over into nearly every available space. By crawling between and over these twisted mounds and bridges of magma, they were able to survey the depressing reality. The whole chamber was stuffed with igneous formations. A strange gelatinous growth in the rock turned out to be a liquid, ebony eye that stared unblinkingly back at them. Hontu began to howl a bitter lament. Noe lifted the light orb high above his shoulder. He had seen that eye before.

"You are here," said a silky, calm voice. "And soon you will not be," it continued without any harshness of threat. There was an interminable, slow shifting of massive weight. The dragon turned its head full upon them, lifted itself far enough for them to discover a dark, graduated path located between the front limbs now discernable in the darkness. "Go or stay. It matters not," said the voice wearily. The last image they had before they entered the dark was the ambiguous curve of the dragon's smile. "One word of advice," said the dragon. "You must do nothing kind for them."

All the time they were in that place, the light never changed. Neither day, nor night, the sky retained the sickly pallor of murky dishwater. A district of grand townhouses and elegant shops lined themselves right up against the system of canals that connected every part of that realm. There were flowers in window boxes and store fronts exhibiting jewelry, the latest milliners' art, pastries and sausages, whatever fit the custom of the house. It was very nearly charming. Of course, the skeletons punting the gondolas were rather morbid. After a while, eyes became attuned to the flocking spirits. They moved with a restless earnestness, but it was clear that nothing was bringing them relief from a sense of dissatisfaction that endlessly spurred their efforts. Noe saw that one of the chief modes of frustration afflicting the shadow people was their inability to grasp any solid thing. For instance, he noticed that a single flower had risen in the crack of a sidewalk. It was an ordinary dandelion, yet somehow it drew a number of passing shades who tried to take hold of it. This was not all. Noe discovered that if he concentrated upon a single shade, not an easy task, he could almost hear an interior thought escape from it. As the shadows reached their flimsy hands about the stem, immense sorrow and, what was it, respect? — for such a simple thing came washing over him.

His heart went out to a sad, old woman who cried like a child when she could not grab hold of the flower. His compassion forgot the shrewd words of the dragon. He reached out his own hand and plucked the dandelion, hoping to free it for the wretched shade. Yet, in doing so, a radical change occurred. Heretofore Noe and Hontu were outside the consciousness of the shades. By uprooting the flower, however, they became objects of vivid interest to them. All the shades near him circled about sending forth waves of incomprehensible thoughts. The magnitude of mental anxiety and need was overwhelming. Noe and the dog fled, racing up and down streets until they reached a bridge that seemed to present an insuperable barrier, for no souls followed them.

They stood at the bridge looking out at the phantasmagoric traffic of the shadow kingdom. The longer they stayed, the more their eyes adjusted, so that the activities of the shades became easier to discern. There was a great deal of bustling about, a jostling in the mob that shifted from one house to the next. It became apparent that the terminal restlessness that agitated the citizens of that realm was somehow a factor in the actions of the gondoliers. Every so often, a shade would weary of the game. It would peel off to the periphery of the crowd, and then slip away. The dissenters came and stood at the edge of the canal, waiting with resigned patience. The gondoliers would stop to take on a passenger or two, then push off swiftly, move steadily down the length of the canals. There was a singular detail that could be observed: the gondoliers worked both sides of the canal, but once they had acquired a fare, they traveled in one direction only. "I think I see now," said Noe. "This city is not a place for living. They are brought here in order to learn the lesson. When they have learned it, they drop away, seek out the gondoliers."

It was strange. The effort of concentration required to ascertain the shades with any acuity was such that the simple act of walking caused the mob to virtually disappear. When Noe and Hontu left the bridge, they might have been passing through dozens of spirits as they made their way to the edge of the canal. Noe had some question as to whether the skeleton pilots would even acknowledge their presence. There was also the matter of the weight of flesh. A single water-taxi came directly to where they waited. On a guess, Noe deposited the plucked flower in the bony hand of the gondolier, an offering which seemed to satisfy the requirements of the fare. The pilot waited indifferently as the two stepped onto the gondola. The craft may have sat lower in the water, but the alteration of ballast was negligible. Silently, they glided past rows of majestic houses. They came to a district of warehouses, buildings where phantom laborers loaded and unloaded equally insubstantial goods. Further on, the canal brought them through increasingly deserted areas. At first, the roof of a cottage, invariably fallen into ruin, would occasionally peek out from the trees. Then even these rare signs of human habitation gave way to an expanse of dull, gray-brown reeds that offered no respite for the tired eye. Noe's head was nodding when they came to the end of the waterway. Hontu barked to rouse his attention. The gondola was no longer moving. The skeleton pilot stood impassive. It was not in its power to speak. No sea beckoned the constrained water with unbounded freedom. Not a single building was erected at the terminal point. Before them was a vista of dark shaped stones so expertly laid upon the earth that they fit with a precision that allowed for not even the space of a penny between them.

They were beyond counting, certainly billions, every one of them exactly the same. He had walked the plain of stone for many minutes when he realized the truth. *They are tombs.* He glanced over at the faithful dog. The stones stretched on and on for as far as eye could see, nameless, without fear or hope. The Nazi torturer and the kind saint, the child whose brains were dashed against the wall by barbaric soldiers, the drunkard, the prostitute, the gatherer of taxes, poet, mother, athlete, all here, all the same. No more conversations. No more complaints. No more joy. The patriarch felt an urgent, desperate need to look on life, any life. Even a dung beetle, a wretched, vile maggot would be beautiful against the bleakness. He instinctively sought Hontu. The dog seemed not at all worried. "Someone should remember," he said. The light orb dropped from his bosom, rolled off into the bone yard. Then the dragon rose like a dark, murky fog, stretched itself, and writhed in long, twisting turns until it was quite near Noe. It did not blink. It did not exactly greet the son of dust, but the smile was there. And the great beast unleashed its word hoard. The hero raised not his staff to ward off the onslaught — and Truthteller? Truthteller was safe in a velvet lined box, stored with other relics on the ark.

~~~~~~~~~~~

"What do the gods know of risk, of suffering? What could they possibly know? Oh, perhaps they sometimes feel distress. Let us grant that. Zeus may suffer a pang for a mortal child, the fruit of one of his philandering conquests. Most likely he took some poor, fearful girl, rode off into the waves with her in the form of a bull . . . then, of course, vain Hera will take it out on the woman hardly more than a child, because she can't stand up to that old rapist. And then we are supposed to share a tear when a favorite son, a mere demi-god, is carried off into the shadows? It isn't like the human race hasn't been there, done that a thousand times over. But here's the difference. Do you think Zeus mourns forever-and-a-day over the passing of some brief beauty, feels a moment of pathos on the odd day when an accidental memory recalls a face, a voice lost for eternity? Don't bet on it. He's off playing cards with Poseidon that very night. That's just how the gods are — you can't value loss when everything is given to you."

"But wait! Wait! I know. You do not subscribe to the petty gods that cannot see into the secrets of mortal men. Your god does not run from the pale last breath of his dying ones. You think he is different? Tell me this? Why, if your Ancient of Days is so all-powerful, so benevolent, why did this superior being choose to make just *this* world? Couldn't he have thought up a better one? Oh, and don't trot out that tired old saw about wanting to share his love with his creatures. I mean, really! Don't you know what a god must be? Do you want a serious and satisfying relationship with a slug? And you are much, much closer to a slug, old boy. Well, let us grant all that. Did he or did he not have to create? If he did, then something must be compelling him and that doesn't sound very god-like, does it? And if he didn't, perhaps, when he saw all that was going to happen — and he must, mustn't he, being all omniscient and everything, then why, pray tell, didn't he have the decency to just say 'no'?"

"I once listened to the death agonies of some beast. It was a cold winter night. What happened to it, I cannot say, but it yowled and yowled for what must have been hours."

"And consider the dullness of his folk. The prudery, the smarmy morality, the humorless, shouting killjoys — florid, pious old women mumbling at their beads, droning on and on. The blind sadism that happily contemplates the eternal misery of those who don't agree, those who hurt their feelings, those who damn well deserve it! Not to mention the hysterical sensitivity, just try to say something to make the little dimwits think, shake them out of their soporific torpor. Though there's plenty of rank hypocrisy, but then they make a show of that, bawling about how sinful they are, making a greedy little spectacle of themselves so they can go lick-spittle on their knees and kiss the ring of their jealous, jealous god."

"I feel less like killing them when they show a bit of old-fashioned lust. At least they're alive. But this heavy, dull fairy tale, a children's story that they insist on treating like a serious proposition — who are they kidding? Not that they've any notion about saying something interesting with even a trace of irony and nuance. Not their style. It's Sunday school and piously scare them all with hell. Later, it's yawn a lovely little monogamous marriage and baby-popping by-the-book. Do as you're told. Do your duty. Then, la-di-da, here's your harp-playing reward in the sky, though as you see it never gets to that. Good thing, too, because the squalid little apes wouldn't have the slightest idea what to do with eternity. Dear me, even you must see it. Any god who could possibly put up with such ignorant dopes, let alone love the snotty-nosed, craven louts — " But here the serpent stopped, either because he felt enough had been said or perhaps because the air had grown so thick with dragon's breath, he could no longer see Noe. Besides, it was pretty much the usual speech. In truth, he gave it for the sheer pleasure of it, so it didn't matter if Noe was there to hear it or not.

~~~~~~~~~~

Hontu was the first to detect it, cocking his head towards a liquid music subtly impressed upon the air. A brisk walk revealed a rather plaintive fountain in the forecourt to an

abandoned temple. Noe listens carefully to the tranquil sounds
it makes. Does he or does he not hear the faint echo of tap, tap,
gurgle, tappety tap tap? If the rattle *were* there, it was a trace so
delicate it was easily passed over. The temple itself had entered
into desuetude, taken over by lizards, mice, and encroaching
scrub plants. The inner sanctum was large and bare. The back
wall alone was marked by a stone clock face without hands.
"Let's go," said Hontu. "I don't like this place."

"Just a bit more," said Noe, opening a door that led into a
tiny chamber that might once have offered domicile to a servant
or a humble priest. Sky light entered in from missing slats in the
roof. In the center of the room, a motionless lump covered in
the tattered remains of a silk garment met their gaze. Noe was
about to hastily take Hontu's advice, when a sallow whisper
emerged from the forgotten closet.

"Guess. You must guess where he is."

The man and the dog approached warily. Noe had the distinct impression that the rough shape they had initially observed
had taken on a more specific shape once they had entered the
room. A slouching body tilted over a series of half shells which
it continuously shifted upon the wooden floor. The silken
garment resembled a smoking jacket with long, loose sleeves.
Ostensibly, the creature was human, though there was something unnatural, almost mummified about its skin and features
that appalled and fascinated. Not once did it look up at them.

"You must guess," said the creature without explanation,
shifting the shells with rapid assurance. "Guess right and clemency may be granted. Guess wrong and the soul eaters shall
come and consume you." Up close, its eyes appeared to have
been sewn shut, but they could not be sure. It was certainly
blind to them.

Noe glared at the weird creature. "We shall not guess," he said through grim teeth.

"You must guess. You must guess where he is," said the creature with the mechanical monotony of a trained parrot. Noe turned away. The bile rose high in his throat. Nausea, revulsion, and a slow boil terror urged his feet. Hontu had felt it early on. Swiftly, they crossed the barren sanctuary and moved through the other rooms. Yet when they came to the doors of the anteroom that surely must reveal the lonely fountain, they found yet another vacant chamber. They discovered that they could return to the empty clock face easily enough, but each attempt to exit the temple was met with baffling failure. It was as if the configuration of the various rooms was continuously altered. Their energy flagging and now hopelessly confused, Noe and Hontu returned to the threshold of the priestly chamber. The creature remained busily shifting shells about.

"You must guess," it said.

"Who are the soul eaters?" asked Noe.

"Guess," said the creature. "Guess right is for answers. Guess wrong is for doom."

Slowly, the creature turned over a shell with a yellowed hand. A small rounded ivory sculpted into the form of a skull lay motionless on the floor. Calmly, the solitary custodian lowered the covering shell. With dexterous and clever vitality, the shells moved until the blur of shifting hands defied the sharpest powers of observation. When the machinations of the game had ended, Noe quickly selected a shell at the far end of the line. The creature did not hesitate. The shell was turned over to reveal the tiny skull. It might have been a lucky guess, but Noe carried it off with the panache of one accustomed to winning.

"Now, good creature, tell us," he said with swaggering bravado he did not feel, "who are the soul-eaters and who is it we
are supposed to find?"

"One right guess, one answer," responded the creature.
"The soul-eaters are everywhere. There are two right here."

"I'm not sure," said Noe, "but I think we've been insulted.
Well, now. Shall we try again?"

"I don't like this," answered Hontu.

The custodian paid no heed to the dog's words. The hands
moved again, this time, if possible, faster than before. When
at last he stopped, Noe felt bereft of intuition. Hontu could
not help. The bone token had no smell. The middle shell was
upturned. A loser. The skull was under the same shell as the
first game.

"Your doom comes! Your doom comes!" chortled the odious custodian, its eyeless face and rubbery lips curled into a
grimace of cruel delight.

"Not before yours!" shouted Noe in rage. With crushing
blows, he lowered his staff upon the creature. The weapon
landed with a soft thud. The custodian emitted not a single
yelp of pain. It collapsed on its side like a half-filled sack. A
fine dust like flour or powdery sand leaked out from the gashes
where the sickly skin had broken. Then they left the useless
sanctuary. The shifting rooms were returned to the original
order. With a sigh, they observed the court and the forlorn
fountain. They walked quickly and with no evident design but
to get far from that place. The orb had returned, but it offered
no guidance. It held back, softly pulled in the wake of their
aimless wandering. The ground melted into sand. Everywhere
they looked was desert.

~~~~~~~~~

"You see, dog?" exclaimed Noe. "You've cast your fate with a fool."

Hontu remained untroubled and serene. The light orb nestled in his paws like a play ball.

"Well, then. Perhaps we can walk for a while. Pick a direction, dog. See if some mercy shall be shown us by the Mystery."

Still, Hontu did not move, but looked peacefully at Noe. His ice blue eyes began to sparkle and blaze especially bright. As Noe watched, astonished, Hontu grew before him, first to the size of a draft horse, then to as large as a small barn. Finally, the dog was massive, the size of a mountain. Yet as he grew, his body faded, so that in the end all one could see was the light orb and Hontu's shining eyes — and one was the moon, the other, a morning star. For some minutes, Noe stood with his face to the stars. He mumbled, walked in a circle, sat down and then he threw pebbles aimlessly. "What? What does it mean?" he yelled to the Father of Lights. Then he curled up where he was and fell into a moody, sorrowful sleep.

After this, Noe studied the horizon. He must have slept for a very short time for the sky had not changed. The strange morning star was still visible in the sky. Dusty sand crackled beneath Noe's feet in the cool desert morning. The noise of men and beasts led Noe across a path of dunes until he looked down upon an impressive camp comprised of men who might have been princes or merchants. There were numerous riders among the cohorts, some armed, and many tents. Swift desert horses and camels loitered or stood at their feed, yet none of the usual hangers on were evident. No women, no hard luck men with a story and guile to spare. A watchman kindly asked the patriarch his business. There was a quality unusual and

difficult to name going on with these people. They seemed
expectant, almost joyful; vigilant, too. "I would parley with
your leaders," said Noe.

The watchman conferred briefly with his peers, then
chose one among their number as guide. The guide followed
a path that revealed care had been taken to order the tents.
Attackers would not easily harm them. Noe was brought to
a large tent that recalled the splendor of Iradon. A dozen
men, young and old, with a small group of servants at hand,
kept counsel among themselves. Yet three were paramount,
gave each other consideration. It was to these that the guide
spoke quietly, then left with swiftness to return to his post.
The princes gazed upon Noe. Though they had been busy
preparing to break camp, none hurried or showed irritation.
The first to speak was the noblest to look upon. Dressed in
raiment of golden silk with pearl drops of ruby and an orange
sash about his waist, he offered Noe great courtesy, taking
him for a shepherd king as the assurance of command was
evident in the old man.

"Good father," said Melchior, "we are pleased you have
come among us. Now say freely, for you have honor here, what
is it you seek?"

"I seek the Deliverer," spoke Noe in candor.

Then Melchior turned to his comrades. They looked with
gladsome eye upon the desert chieftain. "We, too, seek a king
foretold. It may be the one we search for and your Deliverer is
one and the same. There can be little doubt about the portents.
Jupiter has risen in Aries. The Ram signifies Judea. There have
been two lunar eclipses of the regal star. The secrecy of the
moon foretells the birth of divine splendor. Moreover, look
yourself." The Persian prince pointed at the bright star that had

risen from Hontu's eye. "Jupiter is stationary for the second time in the year. Saturn and Jupiter are attendant on the rising sun. The signs together are unmistakable. A king shall be born in Judea." The fervor had risen in Melchior's voice. It was clear that he exulted in the prospect of such a ruler. "Indeed, look at the gift we have brought for the majestic child." Then he drew open a small chest filled with gold.

Next spoke Gaspar, a dark-skinned prince of Abyssinia. He wore a garment of emerald and azure. His face seemed more guarded and perplexed than his peer. His voice was both warm and solemn. He placed questions where Melchior put exclamations. "Old father, I too bid you welcome. Know that my people have long studied the sacred Scriptures that come from our ancestor, Abraham. Centuries ago, our great queen of Sheba made loving friendship with wise King Solomon. She asked him many questions and found his answers a delight."

"You speak of things unknown to my people," said Noe.

Gaspar could not hide suspicion. He was incredulous that the things he spoke should be lost to the people of the desert. Noe then bowed to the magi. "Great princes," he said, "understand that I have come from a place unimaginably distant." The Abyssinian rejoiced, felt in his heart that Noe spoke true. "Listen, then, man of distant land and arduous search. I, too, have questions." Then Gaspar clapped his hands and several scrolls were placed before him. "Hear first the word of Balaam, who prophesied in spite of his dark heart: 'a star shall come forth out of Jacob, and a scepter shall rise out of Israel.' The prophet Isaiah has also said that 'a maiden would conceive as a sign, that her son would be called Immanuel, that is, God is with us.' So, too, he sang 'a child is born to us and that the child should be called Wonderful Counselor, Mighty God, Everlasting Father, Prince of Peace.'"

Melchior held up a hand. "You see that we agree in principle."

"Indeed," replied Gaspar, "but there is more. Isaiah also speaks of one who shall be greatly afflicted." The Abyssinian rapidly turned his scroll, discovered what he wanted. "'He was wounded for our transgressions, he was bruised for our iniquities; upon him was the chastisement that made us whole and by his stripes we are healed.' The great king David, singer of psalms, appears to foresee the same person: 'I am poured out like water, and all my bones are out of joint; my heart is like wax, it is melted within my breast . . .'" Gaspar sang the psalm from memory, drifted into sudden sadness. A young man in the Persian party broke the silence that descended upon Gaspar. "These cannot be the same, Prince Gaspar."

"I do not know," answered the African sage, "but I sense there is some connection we do not yet see. So, it is that my people have brought a gift for a priest, an intercessor." Then Gaspar opened a bronze casket containing amber chips of aromatic frankincense.

The Scythian was the youngest of the three. Nonetheless, he had roamed far and fought many battles. He underwent the tutelage of a shaman. Balthasar wore a royal purple kaftan and an indigo cape trimmed with ermine. He sat awkwardly on silk cushions as if he could only be comfortable on the back of a horse. His dark mustache curled thickly downward, giving his young face a fierce look. The horseman appeared sobered by Gaspar's words. His deep-set eyes stared at the gleam of his curved sword. Then he turned to Noe and roared. "I was married once," he announced. "She was a fine warrior, Vasha, only a terrific temper." Balthasar rolled back the sleeve of his tunic, exposing a thin white scar like a highway along his forearm. "That was not in battle," he explained. "Well, maybe it was. She thought I looked too long at a slave girl. And maybe I did."

Noe smiled slightly. Then the Scythian continued, telling his story with the gesture and intonation of a born actor. "One day I wanted to go fishing with my friend." The young man gave a short cough of a laugh at the memory. "Vasha doesn't like Marek," he said. "She says he is — how do you say?" The horseman surveyed his peers, but as they did not know what he was striving for, they could only shrug. Then Balthasar slapped his thigh and said something incomprehensible in Scythian, laughing again at his own memory. "She says he is searching for brains in pants. So, I went fishing anyway, because you cannot let a woman rule you everywhere."

The old men in the tent nodded gravely. There weren't any old women.

"I fished extra-long to make my point. Then I bid Marek the night well and started to ride for home. I saw a rogue, a Laplander, wandering crazy, trying to avert my gaze. I asked him, 'Laplander, what are you hiding?' but he would not say. Then, I don't know, something went cold in my heart. I hastened my horse, rode storm-strong for Vasha. Three of them had come in my absence while I was fishing. I rushed to the door and opened it. My woman was sitting against the wall. Two men lay bloody, mortally wounded. She'd fought them off, my Vasha. Do you know what she said to me when I came in?"

Noe shook his head.

"She said, 'Gone all day and I bet you didn't catch so much as a cold.'" Balthasar paused here to appreciate the delicious-ness of the joke, of his woman's brave wit. Then he stood and stretched, walked closer to Noe. "Never did she say a word of scorn, because in her heart she agreed that I ought to have stood up to her. She didn't die that day and I thanked the gods. It was when the child came that they plotted their cruel, double blow. The little girl was born all wrong. The wee child hardly had a face. It was so misshapen; the midwife did not wish to show her to Vasha. She would have placed it on a cliff for the night creatures. Vasha said to love the baby, it was only right." Balthasar glanced about. The old men looked down or stared blankly. There was nothing to say. "The girl did not live through the day," concluded Balthasar. "Vasha did not want to let her go. She went chasing after her within two suns and a moon. Tell me, old father, is there an answer to that?" Balthasar did not expect Noe to speak. He drew forth an alabaster jar. "It would take an ordinary man a year's wages to buy a tenth of what is here. If this child is to satisfy me, he shall have to have an answer. And so, I bring him myrrh, the death spice."

~~~~~~~~~~

It was only later on the path lit by the star that it came to Noe. Somehow, the three princes reminded him of his sons. He was nearing a small town. There should not have been snow, but there was. A field was sprinkled in powdery down. Further on, boys pelted each other with snowballs from behind fortifications built up around a wall. The crunch of soft snow and the play of the children lightened Noe's heart. He began to resume his pace — and he couldn't help but realize the vanity of it, but the knowledge that the children were watching him caused the old fellow to want to make a show of his strength. Soon, the muscles in his calves began to burn. Noe laughed at himself, stopped near the wall. A single boy was near, his mischievous dark eyes sparkling in his handsome face. "*Yes, I see that snowball you are hiding. I was a boy once, too,*" thought Noe. There was something familiar about the boy, but Noe could not place him. He was like, yet unlike — "Stephen?"

The boy smiled. "Father Noe!" he cried, tossing the snow harmlessly into the air and running up to the wall.

"It's you! But how?"

Stephen seemed ready to break with joy. "She's waiting," he said breathlessly. "Keep going, Father Noe. It's that way." The boy pointed to a humble little path that led to a small cavern at the edge of a small town. The cave was used as a stable. Noe did not stand out. He appeared a simple shepherd as he entered the threshold of the cave. Cows and donkeys and goats rested in their beds amidst a scattering of dry hay. A place had been made for a young woman holding to her breast a newborn babe. A middle-aged man with a dark beard hovered protectively over her. At Noe's approach, he turned an anxious face upon the newcomer, but the lady touched her betrothed softly on the arm. When she turned towards the patriarch, there could be no question. Her dark hair was covered in a soft blue fabric, yet surely it was the girl he knew as Absinthe. She waited for him with that regal, whimsical expression she had shown before.

"Who are you?" he cried, his voice whispery and full of wonder. Then the stable, while it remained a humble shelter for the beasts, seemed to take on extra dimensions. The cows lowed and the sheep lay bleating, while children peeked out from every nook and corner. The young of every creature filled the hollows of the spaces, invested with innocence and a lush and elemental joy that seemed to flourish just here, in her presence. The tapestry of the cosmos sang from nebulae to impala, dwarf stars to briar roses, the whole place teemed with faces, playful and kind, as if they, too, were waiting for Noe. Among them were Methuselah and Lamech, Senta and Ravi, even Shastar. Strangest of all, Noe seemed to see himself and Priyanka as they had been in the dawn of their love. His eyes returned, met those of the young woman. She sang out to him, rejoicing. "I am; I am the ark that carries the life of the New World!"

CHAPTER SEVEN

Rainbow

"I HAD BEEN KING FOR MANY YEARS. A long time had passed since we left the ark. He was a rough fellow, this wandering chieftain, but there was something in him that reminded me of father. At first, everything was very formal. He was a wary one, this Abram. It was clear he didn't trust Sodom. Most kings are nothing more than trumped-up warlords. I explained that I was not of that sort. Such violence is too weak to build an abiding kingdom. Then I was invited under the pavilion, the tent of amity. We talked for nearly an hour, exchanging stories. He was reluctant to say too much—as was I. They know me here by a different name, this name I took when I came to the land called Salem. Of course, we are still a long way from peace, but it was a way of planting a seed. He must have relaxed, because he began to tell of the beginnings of his journey: of how he left the comfort of a known and protected home to embrace a wandering life. The Mystery had whispered to him and desire had welled up like a song in his heart. That was it, I suppose. He and my father were both daring, willing to endure risk and ridicule for the sake of a hidden Good. I might have told him something of our adventures. There are already numerous versions of the tale, none of them particularly accurate. In the end, I remained silent on that account—mainly because it is difficult to tell and hard to explain the disappointment, really. The legend is simplified into a common coin. It's told as a triumph, but we were there. Evil was not simply outside of us. We carried it in ourselves. Later, the mischief and heartache of history returned. The deluge had excised precisely nothing.

"My father felt great anguish over the struggles that dragged us down. He tried to reconcile his vision of the cosmos made new with our failure. I often think about the stories he told me. 'This city is not a place for living.' And then I hear a voice say 'Let the dead bury the dead.' What I think is that life is a gift and that we do not understand the gift or what we are or who we are meant to be. One day, I had been sketching a fella in his cups, broken down and permanently miserable. And Absinthe came and stood at my side. What she said was, 'Do you think his torment is for him alone? Is your joy or insight for you alone?' After that, whenever I drew, I did so without the safety net of censure. I knew that we were all connected so that we who lived inside the ark did so on behalf of the drowned. The rest of this I do not understand myself, so I shall have to babble like a child. Joy is the ecstasy of life. Life and Love are perfectly identical. Of course, none of us has known time without sorrow and mortality. The bell of doom that Rhumirrah heard was the cry of the flesh in all its spontaneous vitality already sick with death. Yet that is not all. Sometimes, you will see a child dancing amidst indescribable poverty. Sometimes, in a little broken down rural shanty, there will be a radiance of existence denied to the pleasure palaces of the rich. Here is a secret if you can grasp it. The eternal is not lots of time, nor is it outside time. The transcendence of the God is the mystery of divine nearness. Some people say the God cannot be moved and isn't this monstrous of him? They do not reckon the astonishing innocence of the God that endures every betrayal, for love that alters in the heart is not love.

"People forget that the covenant with Noe was also a covenant with the creatures of the earth. When they forget this they also forget that the flesh of nature is the robe of the spirit. The child who cherishes the love of an animal is already weaving a thread in the wedding garment. No love is barren, even if the joy of it is profoundly hidden. Sacrifice was a form of bargaining with our fragility and our fear of death. We will destroy the once and never more if only the rest would be left alone, at least for a time. But life does not bargain with death. On a hill outside the city, a fella was made to die in a gruesome way. Thousands had been killed in a similar manner. Folks thought he might have been a prophet or perhaps even more. Those who loved him were sad or frightened out of their skulls that the authorities would next come looking for his pals. It was a Friday and the bell of doom was ringing. Nature, as everyone knows, is a treacherous economy. The living survive at the cost of the dead. But this fella who was dying shamefully like so many others had told his friends that there was a baptism he longed for. They didn't understand. Why would they? They had misunderstood everything else. What he did was to invite them to a feast, but it was unlike any other. Here, the eaters did not consume dead flesh. They did not gain a precious time by annulling the life of another. The exchange was quite different. The eaters were transformed into the eaten. Deathward life was ushered towards the kingdom of joy. Yes, yes, the ark—but the Spirit brooded over the waters, concocting some crazy plan to heal and resurrect the drowned. This was too much to try and explain to Abram. I had tried and failed with my father. In the end, Noe returned to the pious ways he had known in his youth. I know it troubled him, though. There was a cost, but he refused to speak of it with me. And so, as best I could, I tried to suggest. The sacrifice I brought was bread and wine."

——————

Noe was troubled. He could not see into the heart of the beast. Manwise looked upon the Throne of Adam with trust, even as he was bound, but at the glint of metal, fear arose in the great bull's eyes. Noe prayed to the Mystery and gave thanks for the well being of Priyanka and his sons, for the safety of their wives, for the children that must come. He thanked the Wisdom for preserving the beasts and replenishing the earth.

And Manwise took the knife, his blood splattering upon the high ground.

"War," growled Rhumirrah, and her feet sought the green jungle. No longer would she desire the habitude of men. Long, long would be the journey to peace.